Breach of Crust

Ellery Adams

BERKLEY PRIME CRIME, NEW YORK

BERKLEY PRIME CRIME

An imprint of Penguin Random House LLC
375 Hudson Street, New York, New York 10014

BREACH OF CRUST

A Berkley Prime Crime Book / published by arrangement with the author

Copyright © 2016 by Ellery Adams.
Excerpt from *Murder in the Secret Garden* by Ellery Adams
copyright © 2016 by Ellery Adams.
Penguin supports copyright. Copyright fuels creativity, encourages diverse voices,
promotes free speech, and creates a vibrant culture. Thank you for buying an authorized
edition of this book and for complying with copyright laws by not reproducing, scanning, or
distributing any part of it in any form without permission. You are supporting writers and
allowing Penguin to continue to publish books for every reader.

BERKLEY® PRIME CRIME and the PRIME CRIME design are trademarks of
Penguin Random House LLC.
For more information, visit penguin.com.

ISBN: 978-0-425-27603-7

PUBLISHING HISTORY
Berkley Prime Crime mass-market edition / April 2016

PRINTED IN THE UNITED STATES OF AMERICA

10 9 8 7 6 5 4 3 2 1

Cover illustration by © Julie Green.
Cover design by Diana Kolsky.
Interior text design by Laura K. Corless.

This is a work of fiction. Names, characters, places, and incidents either are the product of
the author's imagination or are used fictitiously, and any resemblance to actual persons,
living or dead, business establishments, events, or locales is entirely coincidental.

PUBLISHER'S NOTE: The recipes contained in this book are to be followed exactly as
written. The publisher is not responsible for your specific health or allergy needs
that may require medical supervision. The publisher is not responsible for
any adverse reactions to the recipes contained in this book.

If you purchased this book without a cover, you should be aware that this book is stolen
property. It was reported as "unsold and destroyed" to the publisher, and neither the author
nor the publisher has received any payment for this "stripped book."

Penguin
Random
House

Praise for the *New York Times* Bestselling
Charmed Pie Shoppe Mysteries

"Delicious, delightful, and deadly! Full of enchanting characters in a small-town setting, this Charmed Pie Shoppe mystery will leave readers longing for seconds."
—Jenn McKinlay, *New York Times* bestselling author of the Cupcake Bakery Mysteries

"Enchanting! The Charmed Pie Shoppe has cast its spell on me! Ellery Adams brings the South to life with the LeFaye women of Havenwood."
—Krista Davis, *New York Times* bestselling author of the Domestic Diva Mysteries

"[A] savory blend of suspense, pies, and engaging characters. Foodie mystery fans will enjoy this." —*Booklist*

"A sensory delight for those who like a little magic with their culinary cozies." —*Library Journal*

"An original, intriguing story line that celebrates women, family, friendship, and loyalty within an enchanted world, with a hint of romance, an engaging cast of characters, and the promise of a continued saga of magical good confronting evil."
—*Kirkus Reviews*

"Adams permeates this unusual novel—and Ella [Mae's] pies—with a generous helping of appeal."
—*Richmond Times-Dispatch*

"Charming characters and a cozy setting make this mystery . . . warm and inviting, like a slice of Ella Mae's pie fresh from the oven." —The Mystery Reader

Berkley Prime Crime titles by Ellery Adams

Charmed Pie Shoppe Mysteries

PIES AND PREJUDICE
PEACH PIES AND ALIBIS
PECAN PIES AND HOMICIDES
LEMON PIES AND LITTLE WHITE LIES
BREACH OF CRUST

Books by the Bay Mysteries

A KILLER PLOT
A DEADLY CLICHÉ
THE LAST WORD
WRITTEN IN STONE
POISONED PROSE
LETHAL LETTERS
WRITING ALL WRONGS

Book Retreat Mysteries

MURDER IN THE MYSTERY SUITE
MURDER IN THE PAPERBACK PARLOR

This book is for all those
who have lost a loved one to cancer.
It's also for all those who are fighting it
and for all those who have won the fight.

"Hope" is the thing with feathers—
That perches in the soul—
And sings the tune without the words—

—Emily Dickinson

Chapter 1

Ella Mae cut a wedge of black bottom peanut butter pie and slid it onto a plate. Wiping away an errant crumb with the edge of a paper towel, she garnished the surface of the peanut butter mousse filling with a drizzle of melted chocolate and then piped three neat polka dots of chocolate directly onto the white plate. Setting the pastry bag of chocolate aside, she reached for a bag filled with whipped cream and piped two peaks in between the chocolate dots. She'd just put the plate on a server tray when Reba pushed through the swing doors leading from The Charmed Pie Shoppe's dining room into its kitchen.

"You won't believe this," she said, pulling a red licorice twist from her apron pocket and dropping on the stool next to the worktable.

Ella Mae shot her a wry grin. "We live in a world where people have magical powers. My aunt Verena knows when people are lying. Aunt Dee can infuse her metal animal sculptures with sparks of life. Aunt Sissy can influence people with her music. My mother can make plants grow by humming to them. And what about you? How many fiftysomething women could win a mixed martial arts championship with one arm tied behind their back? I can believe in all sorts of things."

Reba's expression turned wistful. "I've always wanted to try cage fightin'. It looks like so much fun."

"You know it wouldn't be a fair fight," Ella Mae scolded the woman she'd known all her life, the woman who'd been a second mother to her. "It'd be like watching a cat toy with a bird that has a broken wing."

"I guess so. But what about among our kind? It could be a whole new source of entertainment. Just imagine! Saturday night fights in groves across the world. You could watch me . . ." She trailed off, looking horrified. "I'm sorry, hon. I don't know why I keep forgettin' that you can't enter a grove anymore. I still can't wrap my head around that."

Ella Mae pointed at the wedge of pie. "Why don't you tell me what you came in here to tell me so you can deliver this to our customer? It's almost closing time."

Reba searched Ella Mae's face as though expecting to find signs of regret or pain etched into her smooth skin, but Ella Mae had learned to accept what had happened to her earlier that spring. She only wished her friends and family would make their peace with the fact that Ella Mae was no longer magical. Their constant scrutiny and deliberate avoidance of certain subjects were driving her crazy.

Brandishing the pastry bag of whipped cream, Ella Mae narrowed her eyes and said, "Spit it out, Reba, or I'm going to pipe a Santa Claus beard on your face."

"Whipped cream and red licorice do not mix." Reba held

up her hands in surrender. "Well, here's somethin' you don't often hear, but the lady who ordered this piece of pie will only taste one bite of it. After that, she'll put her fork down and push her plate away."

Ella Mae, who was headed to the sink with a mixing bowl and several utensils, abruptly froze. "How do you know?"

"Because I've watched her do the same thing for the past hour and a half. She orders a piece of pie, takes a bite, lays down her fork, and then has a few sips of water. She dabs her lips with her napkin, as prim as the Queen of England, and raises her index finger to signal me—like I'm supposed to come runnin'. When I get to her table, she orders another slice." Reba looked thoroughly put out. "Ella Mae, after I deliver this pie, she'll have ordered every pie on today's menu."

"She's probably a food critic." Ella Mae shifted the bowl to one hand and used her free hand to push a strand of whiskey-colored hair from her brow. "I hope you've been patient with her, Reba."

Reba made a dismissive sound. "She could trash us on the front page of *The Atlanta Journal* and it wouldn't matter. The Charmed Pie Shoppe will have a loyal customer base for as long as you live and breathe, Ella Mae. Not only did you save the people of Havenwood, Georgia, but you saved plenty of other folks as well. Why do you think we have lines out the door every day? And our catering side has taken off, too. Every bride within a hundred miles wants a pie bar at her wedding."

"Our popularity isn't what defines us," Ella Mae said, depositing the bowl in the sink basin. "We must treat every customer as though they were our very first. Bring that lady her pie with service and a smile. If she only eats one bite, that's her choice."

Scowling, Reba grabbed the serving tray. "It's a damned

waste. Just because you don't enchant your food anymore doesn't mean that it isn't incredible. No one should be samplin' the whole menu like this without even takin' notes. My inner alarm is goin' off."

Ella Mae had learned to pay close attention to Reba's instincts. "Is she the last customer in the dining room?"

Reba nodded.

"Send the rest of the waitstaff home," Ella Mae said. "If this lady has an ulterior motive, she can make it clear to us privately."

Reba's eyes gleamed, and Ella Mae knew her friend was probably envisioning smashing chairs over the customer's head or body slamming her into a café table.

"Just let her enjoy her pie first!" Ella Mae called after Reba, but the only reply she received was the swinging doors flapping in Reba's wake.

Shaking her head in resignation, Ella Mae loaded mixing bowls, pots, pans, and plates into the dishwasher. After cleaning the cooktop and prep area, she took a moment to stand and gaze out the window above the sink. It had been a frenzied week, and she was looking forward to having both Sunday and Monday, which was also Memorial Day, off.

Tomorrow, she and Hugh Dylan planned to take their dogs on a hike in the mountains. They were also going to swim in one of rivers that fed into Lake Havenwood. It was only May, but the Georgia summer heat was in full swing and Ella Mae couldn't wait to submerge in the cool water. After spending a day in the wilderness, she and Hugh would attend the Memorial Day cookout and concert at Lake Havenwood Resort. There would be food, fireworks, and live music. And maybe, just maybe, Ella Mae and Hugh could stretch out on a blanket under the stars and hold hands like they used to. Back before they'd been forced to keep secrets from each other. Before another woman had come between them.

That's in the past now, Ella Mae thought firmly. *We're starting over. He and I are a fresh piece of dough rolled out on the worktable. We're not the lovers we once were. Nor can we settle for being the friends we've been since childhood. We have to create something new.*

Ella Mae ran the dishrag over the spot on her palm where there was once a burn scar shaped like a clover. The scar was gone now. It had disappeared at the same time Ella Mae had poured out all of her magic to defeat a powerful enemy and save her town. She had lost the symbol that marked her as the Clover Queen, but she'd never wanted to rule over anyone. All she'd ever wanted was to prepare delicious food for people. To bake pies in a brightly lit kitchen, filling the warm space with the aroma of melted butter, cinnamon, roasted nuts, sugared berries, and so much more.

"Are you reading your own palm, Ms. LeFaye?" asked one of the college students Ella Mae had hired for the summer.

Ella Mae smiled at the pretty blonde and the two other servers standing behind her. "You caught me gathering wool, Maddie. Enjoy your time off, everyone. You all worked really hard this week and you deserve a break."

"So do you, ma'am," said Royce, the young man in charge of deliveries. "I hope you have good weather for your picnic tomorrow."

"Me too," Ella Mae said and bade good-bye to her employees.

Reba reentered the kitchen with her serving tray and the remains of the black bottom peanut butter pie. One bite had been taken from the slice. Two at the most.

"The lady customer would like to speak with you," Reba said. "Here's her card."

Ella Mae read the white lettering on a field of black, "'Beatrice Burbank, Camellia Club president.'" The card was thick, elegant, and expensive. Other than the design of a camellia flower in one corner, it was unadorned. "What's the Camellia Club?"

"No clue," Reba said. "But this woman is a cool cucumber. When I told her we were closin' and asked her to settle up, she said she'd make it worth our while to stay open a few more minutes. When I told her we weren't interested, she got up, walked up to the counter, and put a hundred-dollar bill in the tip jar."

Ella Mae sighed. "I've had my fill of pushy women, Reba. I don't care if her wallet is stuffed with hundred-dollar bills. I'm ready to call it a day, and I'm going to march into the dining room and tell President Beatrice Burbank as much."

When Beatrice saw Ella Mae, she got up, smiled graciously, and extended her hand, as though she were welcoming Ella Mae to her establishment and not the other way around. "Ms. LeFaye, it is a pleasure to meet you. I haven't tasted such a wonderfully fresh tomato tart since my grandmother was alive. I had to pay my compliments to the chef in person."

Despite her determination to dislike the stranger, Ella Mae felt herself softening toward Beatrice Burbank. "That's very kind of you, Mrs. Burbank, but—"

"Please call me Bea. I know I'm old enough to be your mother, but 'Mrs. Burbank' is so terribly formal, and I'm hoping that by the end of our conversation, you and I will be on our way toward becoming friends." She indicated the chair opposite hers. "Would you sit with me for a moment? I have a proposition for you."

Ella Mae knew she should be wary. Beatrice was much like her business card: rich, elegant, and understated. She wore a blush-colored skirt suit with a gold camellia stickpin on the coat lapel over an ivory silk camisole. Her silvery blond hair was gathered into a low chignon and her nails were polished a subtle pinkish-beige hue. Her voluminous handbag, in contrast, was a vibrant turquoise, as though she wanted to convey that she had a playful side to her as well.

"I'd be glad to sit for a spell," Ella Mae said politely. She'd been raised in the South and it wouldn't do to be discourteous.

Bea seemed unsurprised by her response. "I tried every pie on your menu. The tomato bacon tartlets in the cheddar cheese crust, the ham and grilled corn, and the chicken potpie. I particularly liked the herb crust on that savory delight." She put her hand over her heart. "But your desserts. Oh my, Ms. LeFaye. You have a gift. I promised myself one bite of each pie. One bite of strawberry rhubarb crisp. One bite of lemon mascarpone icebox tart, brown butter raspberry pie, and black bottom peanut butter pie. But I took two of the last one. I just couldn't stop myself."

Ella Mae was about to thank the older woman again when Bea held up a finger to forestall her. "I'm not here merely to praise you. In fact, I'd like to hire you. I came to Havenwood to finalize the details of the Camellia Club's annual retreat. This year, we'll be renting a block of rooms at Lake Havenwood Resort. But we'll also be renting kitchen space there."

This caught Ella Mae's attention. "Oh?"

Bea nodded enthusiastically. "Every decade, the Camellia Club publishes a cookbook of dessert recipes. This year, because we're celebrating our centennial, we've decided to go all out. We're hiring three of the best chefs in the South. Actually, 'best' isn't the right word. We've sought out the most innovative, creative, and hip pastry chefs to teach us what makes an unforgettable dessert." She paused for effect. "Maxine Jordan, the founder of From Scratch, an organic bakery in Charlottesville, Virginia, came aboard in March, and we secured Caroline James from Carolina's Cakes of Raleigh last month. All that remained was to find a champion pie baker. I've traveled from Texas to Maryland tasting pies, tarts, crisps, and cobblers. I had no idea that I'd find a pie virtuoso practically in my own backyard!" She laughed merrily. "I'm from Sweet Briar, as are all of the members of the Camellia Club."

Ella Mae had heard of the town. Not far from Savannah, the scenic riverfront community was filled with historic homes, gorgeous gardens, and quaint shops. Sweet Briar was larger than Havenwood and had more restaurants, movie theaters, and nightclubs. It also boasted a thriving art scene and real estate prices that would intimidate anyone without a trust fund.

"And you'd like me to give you and your club members a crash course in pie making during your annual retreat?" Ella Mae asked. "When is it?"

"The first week in August," Bea said, pulling an envelope out of her handbag. "I realize that I'm asking you to step away from your business for several days in order to instruct a group of women you've never met before, but I can assure you that every penny of profit that the Camellia Club makes from our cookbook sales goes toward a worthy cause. Not only do we contribute to several scholarship funds, but this year, we're also raising money for a young lady who was badly burned at the Georgia State Fair. The dear girl was making funnel cakes when a vat of hot oil overturned, splattering her arms, chest, and face. Her family can't afford her medical care, and we've offered to help."

Ella Mae's hand flew to her mouth as she tried to stifle a gasp. Her aunt Dee had suffered terrible burns that spring, and the memories of the fire came rushing back to her now.

During that horrible night, her aunt was admitted to Atlanta's Grady Burn Center, where she'd undergone multiple surgeries, and many weeks later she'd returned home to her animals and sculptures. Had it not been for the intervention of several brave and selfless people, she could have died in her burning barn, but she would never again be the same person.

Bea touched Ella Mae lightly on the arm. "Are you all right, my dear?"

"My aunt was the victim of a terrible fire not too long ago. She survived, but she will always bear the scars." Ella Mae pointed at the envelope. "Is that a contract?"

"Yes. I thought I'd leave it with you," Bea said. "If it's to your liking, you can sign it and drop it off at the resort. I'm staying through Monday." She gathered her handbag and stood to leave. "I think you'll find the remuneration acceptable, and I know all of the Camellias would be thrilled to have you as a mentor. You, Maxine, and Caroline would truly be our Dessert Dream Team."

After promising to examine the contract and respond to Bea's proposal before she left town, Ella Mae walked her guest to the door.

"I don't know what it is about this place," Bea said as she stepped out onto the front porch. "Every detail of this pie shop—from the fragrance of the flowers in the garden to the fresh herbs in the garnishes and the ripeness of the fruits in the dessert tarts—is magical. No wonder it's called The Charmed Pie Shoppe."

With a smile and a wave, Bea walked down the flagstone path, crossed the street, and got into a gleaming white Cadillac. As the sedan eased away from the curb, Ella Mae noticed a glittery camellia decal affixed to the rear windshield.

"All she needs is a wand to complete the fairy godmother look," Reba said from behind Ella Mae. As usual, she'd appeared without a sound. "I heard what she said about the cookbook profits, but is her bibbidi-bobbidi-boo act genuine?"

"I'm not going into this blindly." Ella Mae held out the contract. "I'll review this very carefully."

"Why bother?" Reba asked, putting her hand on her hip. "I can see she's already won you over."

Ella Mae shrugged. "What if she has? I love the idea of working with Maxine and Caroline. They're serious up-and-comers, and both of them have been experimenting with dessert recipes for people with food allergies. That's something I've wanted to explore as well. Also, Caroline just started shipping her cupcakes nationally. I'd love to talk to her about how she handled that kind of expansion. Her shop isn't any bigger than ours."

Together, the two women reentered the café. Reba closed and locked the front door and then turned to Ella Mae. "What about these Camellia Club gals? Do you really think it'll be a barrel of laughs teachin' a bunch of debutantes and their mamas? What if one of them breaks a nail? You'll have to call the National Guard."

Ella Mae gave her friend an imploring look. "I need this, Reba. I need to grow as a chef. Without magic, I have to keep honing my skills. There are no shortcuts for me anymore." She glanced at the framed four-leaf clover hanging over the cash register. "I don't want people to come here because of what I used to be. I want them to come because of what I am. A top-notch pastry chef. The best pie maker in the South."

Reba nodded in understanding. "Okay, then. But I'm comin' with you. Someone will have to keep these high-society sugar queens in line."

She hit a switch on the wall, killing the lights and inviting the late afternoon shadows to crawl across the dining room.

* * *

Ella Mae watched Hugh Dylan leap from a rock into the middle of the river with a jubilant holler. His dog, a Harlequin Great Dane named Dante, jumped in after him. Chewy, Ella Mae's Jack Russell terrier, raced along the bank, barking wildly.

"You can go in, boy." Ella Mae made shooing motions with her hands.

"Why don't you both join us?" Hugh asked, floating on his back and staring up at the cloudless blue sky. "After that long hike, the water feels amazing."

Ella Mae couldn't help wondering if Hugh missed being able to hold his breath for twenty minutes. Like her, he'd once possessed special abilities. He could see underwater and swim like a dolphin. And like her, he'd lost his magic and didn't seem to regret the loss.

Pulling off her sweat-soaked Dr Pepper T-shirt and cut-offs, Ella Mae tossed her socks and tennis shoes aside and waded into the water. Hugh was right. The river, fed by the mountain's underground spring, was refreshingly chilly. Ella Mae's skin immediately broke out in gooseflesh.

"You can't stand there like that!" Hugh chided her playfully. "Take the plunge!"

Smiling, Ella Mae dove into the water. She surfaced, momentarily shuddering over the cold, and then swam over to where Hugh was treading water. "Chewy! Come on!" Ella Mae called to her dog.

When her terrier continued to bark in agitation, Hugh paddled to the nearest rock and slapped it with his palm. "Here, Charleston Chew! Here, boy!"

With a joyous yip, Chewy bounded over the rocks until

he reached Hugh. After licking him on the cheek, Chewy barked once at Dante and hopped into the water.

"I guess he needed a formal invitation," Ella Mae said and laughed.

She and Hugh rested on the largest rock while their dogs splashed about in the shallows. When she wasn't watching them, Ella Mae followed the path of water droplets trailing from Hugh's dark hair to his cheek and jawline. When one gathered at the base of his chin, she raised her finger and caught it. At her touch, he looked at her, a question in his lagoon-blue eyes.

In answer, she moved closer to him and slid her arms around his wide, muscular back. His kiss was both familiar and strange.

"I feel like I'm cheating on my longtime girlfriend with an exciting and exotic creature," Hugh said when they broke apart.

"That woman is gone," Ella Mae said. "You're left with the girl next door."

Hugh arched his brows. "No one would call you that." He took hold of the hand that had once been marked by the clover-shaped burn scar and ran his fingertips across her water-puckered skin. "You might not bear the mark of a queen, but you're still undeniably regal, Ella Mae. When you enter a room, everyone turns and stares. It's impossible not to. It would be like shutting your eyes just as a shooting star blazes across the sky."

Embarrassed by the compliment, Ella Mae flicked water at him. "They're really looking at you. The big, tall fireman with the beautiful blue eyes."

"Right," Hugh scoffed. "I smell like a kennel and have a farmer's tan because I've been spending too much time doing paperwork at Canine to Five." He twisted one of Ella Mae's damp curls around his finger. "Let's escape whenever we can—try hard to be alone together—just like this. Tonight will be fun, but it won't be the same. When we're with other people, I feel them watching us. I can sense them wondering about us."

Ella Mae nodded. She'd experienced the same sensation. "That's because we don't belong among the magical and we'll never fit in among regular people. Not after what we've seen and done. We still have scars, Hugh. They're just on the inside now."

Hugh kissed her palm. "I don't care about being outsiders. As long as we have each other. I don't need anything but you."

"And some sunscreen," Ella Mae said with a smile. "Your nose is turning red."

That night, Ella Mae left Chewy with her mother, who promised to take the little terrier inside the main house before the fireworks began. Chewy wasn't afraid of much, but he didn't care for the loud bangs and explosions that accompanied pyrotechnics displays.

"Until the show starts, I'm going to let him have the run of the garden," Adelaide LeFaye said. "The first of the lightning bugs have arrived, and Chewy loves to chase them. It's my hope that he'll be so tired by the time the first rocket whistles into the sky that he won't even notice."

"I might be half-asleep myself," Ella Mae said. "After a crazy week at the pie shop and a day of hiking and swimming, I'm beat. Still, I wouldn't miss this evening with Hugh for anything. I also have a contract to deliver to a special guest at the resort."

Her mother listened as Ella Mae told her about Beatrice

Burbank's proposal. "It sounds fun," she said when Ella Mae was done. "But maybe you should have Reba research this Camellia Club before you sign anything."

Ella Mae held up the sealed envelope. "I did the research myself. The Camellias are a philanthropic organization—a group of mothers and daughters who get together to discuss books and attend garden parties, cooking classes, and art exhibits. They raise money for college scholarships and other charities. They're good people. Besides, I don't have to be on the lookout for enemies anymore. That part of my life is over."

Ella Mae's mother shook her head. "Your childhood nemesis is still at large, and Loralyn Gaynor is bound to seek revenge against you. You were instrumental in her father's arrest, and because of your influence, her mother made peace with our family. Loralyn is undoubtedly holed up in some luxurious locale, plotting. She's dangerous, Ella Mae, and you have no idea how, or when, she'll come after you." Cupping a clematis bud in her hand, Ella Mae's mother said, "Things are not always as they appear on the outside. What color do you think this flower will be?"

Peering more closely at the bud, Ella Mae answered, "Pink."

Closing her hand gently around the bud, her mother hummed very softly. She then withdrew her hand and Ella Mae watched as the bud slowly unfolded, revealing purple petals edged with pink. The purple hue was so dark that it was nearly black.

"People are not always what they seem at first glance," Adelaide said softly. "You should know that by now."

"Point taken," Ella Mae said and gave her mother a kiss on the cheek. "I'll be careful. But not tonight. Tonight, I just want to eat, dance, and watch the sky fill with rainbows of light."

After asking the front desk clerk at Lake Havenwood Resort to deliver the envelope to Beatrice Burbank by the end of the evening, Ella Mae walked through the lobby and out into the carnival atmosphere on the back lawn. She spotted Hugh speaking with another volunteer fireman at the cotton candy booth and waved. Hugh said good-bye to his friend, grabbed Ella Mae by the hand, and pulled her toward the food tent.

"I was worried that I might not have enough energy to be the man you deserve tonight, but then I saw you and all the cells in my body came alive," he said, smiling at her. "I plan to dance to every song the band plays tonight, so you'd better fuel up."

Ella Mae did. She and Hugh loaded their plates with pulled pork, smoked brisket, cheese biscuits, grilled corn, and pickled tomato salad. After a dessert of banana pudding and s'more cheesecake bars, they danced on the terrace overlooking the lake.

During one of the band's short breaks, Ella Mae glanced around in search of Bea but she didn't see her anywhere. As the sky darkened and the master of ceremonies announced that it was almost time for the fireworks show to begin, Ella Mae gave up on finding her.

"I can't believe we never ran into Bea," she told Hugh.

"Maybe bouncy houses and barbecues aren't her style. You described her as being elegant and polished, so she probably ate in the dining room and will watch the fireworks display from her balcony while sipping a glass of sparkling wine."

Ella Mae laughed. "I bet you're right. And where's our special spot?"

"It's a bit apart from everyone else," Hugh said with an impish glimmer in his eye.

Sliding her arm around his waist, Ella Mae grinned up at him. "It sounds like the perfect place."

* * *

It was very late when Ella Mae returned to her little guest cottage behind her mother's house. She hadn't felt so happy or optimistic in months, and though she was physically exhausted, she was too wired to sleep.

Chewy must have been woken up by the sound of Ella Mae's car, for she could hear his muted barking coming from Partridge Hill's kitchen the moment she turned off the ignition. Ella Mae rushed to let him out before he could wake her mother. Together, Ella Mae and her terrier wandered through the fragrant garden, across the dew-covered lawn and down to the dock stretching like a finger into the lake.

When they reached the end of the dock, Ella Mae sat cross-legged on the rough planks and listened to the water lap quietly against the wood. Chewy nestled beside her and put his head in her lap. Ella Mae stroked the soft fur on the top of his head and gazed across the lake at the resort.

She smiled, recalling how Hugh's face had lit up with wonder during the fireworks show. And of how he'd kissed her during the finale. At that moment, she'd sensed the brilliance of the lights in the sky overhead, but it was nothing compared to the sparks of heat she felt between herself and Hugh. They were forging their new beginning. Tonight marked the first of many memories they would make together.

After a time, Ella Mae whispered to Chewy, "All right, boy. Time to go."

As she stood, she saw something floating in the water. It was hard to see clearly because the moon had ducked behind a cloud, but when it shone unobstructed again, Ella Mae cried out in fear.

The thing floating in the water was a body.

A woman's body.

Ella Mae reacted quickly. She pushed the small rowboat kept on the dock into the water and leapt into the craft. Using the oar to push herself away from the dock, she paddled toward the body.

It only took a second for Ella Mae to know that the woman was beyond saving. Her upturned face was just below the surface, and her pale hair looked like a tangle of watergrass. Her dress, the shade of a water hyacinth, billowed around her legs and bare feet.

She wore a single piece of jewelry. A gold camellia stickpin was fastened to the upper-left breast of her dress, just above her heart.

Chapter 2

Ella Mae grabbed hold of Bea's arm and tried to pull her into the boat, but her efforts almost capsized the shallow craft.

Refusing to leave Bea in the water, Ella Mae paddled with her right hand and held on to Bea's bloated wrist with her left. It was a nearly impossible undertaking as the boat's bow continuously swung off course, veering back toward the center of the lake, and Ella Mae quickly felt her arm tiring as she fought to reach the dock.

When the bow finally bumped against the side of the dock, Ella Mae dragged the dead woman's body as close to the dock as she could before awkwardly lunging onto the rough wood. The boat shot out from under her feet and though she landed hard on her right shoulder, she didn't let go of Bea's wrist. Chewy barked in alarm and then began sniffing near her hand.

"No," Ella Mae commanded with unusual harshness.

She tried not to look at Bea's bloated, jellyfish-pale face, but she knew those unblinking eyes would haunt her sleep for many nights to come.

"I'm sorry," Ella Mae murmured to the dead woman as she laboriously crawled over the dock toward the shore. She could feel splinters piercing the skin of her palms and knees, but there was no other way for her to proceed without releasing her hold of Bea's wrist.

At the end of the dock, she finally had to let go. She hurriedly kicked off her sandals, waded into the water, and dragged Bea's body onto the sand. Bea felt heavy. Weighed down with water and with death, she was far heavier than Ella Mae had expected. She dropped on the sand and tried to catch her breath. Chewy sniffed the dead woman once, and then he bared his teeth as a growl rose from deep in his throat.

"No, boy. Hush." Ella Mae scooped up her terrier and carried him back home. Once inside her house, she released Chewy and dialed 911.

It didn't take long for the police to respond.

Ella Mae only had time to change into dry clothes and extract the worst of the splinters before she heard a series of authoritative raps on her front door.

"You and I keep meeting over dead bodies, Ms. LeFaye," said Officer Jon Hardy. "I wish that weren't the case."

"Me too," Ella Mae said. "Though I'm glad you responded to the call and not someone else. You'll look after Mrs. Burbank."

Officer Hardy was instantly contrite. "Forgive me. I didn't realize you knew the deceased."

"I just met her yesterday, but she seemed like a lovely person. To find her floating in the lake . . ." Ella Mae trailed off.

Officer Hardy gave her a paternal pat on the shoulder. "It took courage to pull her out of the water. That was well done. Can you take me to Mrs. Burbank now?"

Ella Mae managed a smile. "Yes, but as soon as I'm done, I need to tell my mother what's going on. I don't want her to wake up to find cop cars and a coroner's van parked in her driveway."

"Of course," Hardy said. After issuing commands to his team, he signaled for Ella Mae to lead the way. As they walked, he pointed at her bloodied knees. "Those are some nasty-looking scrapes."

"Splinters from the dock. There was no graceful way for me to get Mrs. Burbank ashore. I wasn't able to pull her into the boat with me."

Hardy studied her with admiration. "Did you notice any objects floating in the water near Mrs. Burbank?"

"No. Nothing." Ella Mae thought of Bea's bare feet. "She wasn't even wearing shoes. She had on a pretty dress. There was a gold camellia stickpin affixed right here." Ella Mae touched her fingers to her chest. "She wore that pin yesterday too."

"And her purpose for being in Havenwood?" Hardy asked.

By the time Ella Mae filled Hardy in on the Camellia Club's annual retreat, they'd reached the lake's edge.

Hardy held up a hand and the other policemen came to a halt. Distancing himself from both Ella Mae and his team, Hardy walked up to Bea's body. For a full minute, he peered down at her, his expression somber. He then squatted even closer, staring fixedly at her face.

"What's he doing?" one of the cops murmured.

"It's like he's paying his respects," another whispered. "I've seen him do this before. Don't go thinking Hardy's soft because he sees victims as people, not just cases. He's a damned good investigator. He closes cases."

Returning to the group, Hardy addressed Ella Mae. "Your formal statement can wait until the morning, Ms. LeFaye, but we'll need it first thing. Until then, take care of those splinters."

And with that, Ella Mae was dismissed. Hardy, whose attention was now fixed on his team, began assigning tasks.

Ella Mae trudged over the lawn and through the garden. When she reached Partridge Hill's back entrance, she found her mother standing in the doorway.

Seeing Ella Mae, Adelaide LeFaye rushed forward and enfolded her daughter in her arms.

"I saw the flashing lights and I didn't know what to think," she whispered in a thin, shaky voice.

"I'm okay," Ella Mae assured her. "I found Mrs. Burbank in the lake. She's dead, Mom."

Adelaide glanced up at the moon. Its light fell on her long, silver hair and her ageless face. To Ella Mae, her mother could have been a fairy queen from one of her childhood storybooks. All four of the LeFaye sisters were beautiful, but Adelaide possessed an otherworldly beauty that continued to ripen as the years passed. One only had to look at her to believe in magic.

"Did you see Mrs. Burbank at the resort?" she asked, looking at Ella Mae again.

"No. I assumed the festivities were too boisterous for her, but now I'm wondering where she was while they were taking place." Ella Mae tried to shut out the image of Bea's bloated face. "Officer Hardy will undoubtedly head to the resort when he's finished here. He'll find out what happened to her."

Adelaide pointed at the second-story windows. "Should we wake Jenny and Calvin?"

The Upton siblings had been living at Partridge Hill since

they had moved to Havenwood from Tennessee. For a while, both Jenny and Calvin had worked at The Charmed Pie Shoppe. Jenny had been a server and Calvin had handled the deliveries. Since then, Jenny had become Ella Mae's partner, and Calvin, who'd been an electrician in Tennessee, had gone to work for his friend, Finn Mercer. Finn designed furniture while Calvin made innovative light fixtures. Their business was really taking off and Calvin had been so busy that Ella Mae hadn't seen him for days.

"Let them sleep," she said. "They have a double date tomorrow. Though I don't think Jenny realizes that it's a date. Actually, I doubt Finn does either."

"But Finn has feelings for you." Her mother was clearly surprised. "He can't just turn those off. Jenny could be headed for a miserable evening."

"Finn barely knows me," Ella Mae protested softly. "When we met, he'd just lost his mother and I became his first friend in Havenwood. He'll always have a place in my heart because he helped rescue Aunt Dee from that burning barn, and I want him to find someone who will give him the love he deserves. I think Jenny is that person. Calvin does too."

Adelaide smiled. "I hope you're right. I'd like Jenny to experience a little happiness. She's had more than her fair share of suffering, and yet she never lets anything get her down. Whoever wins her heart will be a lucky man."

"Yes," Ella Mae agreed through a yawn. "We should try to get some sleep now."

"Not until I remove those splinters. I'm going to make an Epsom salt poultice for the deeper splinters. You won't be able to cook on Tuesday if your hands hurt."

By the time Adelaide put aside her tweezers and applied bandages to Ella Mae's knees and palms, it was well after midnight. Ella Mae didn't even hear the sound of police car tires crunching over the gravel driveway on their way out. With Chewy curled up by her feet, she slumbered without dreaming for hours.

However, when the sun began to rise and light snuck in through the gap in her bedroom curtains, images began to fracture Ella Mae's sleep.

She was in the rowboat again, but this time, the dock was gone. The lake water was ink-black and Bea's body bobbed in the current like a white buoy. She was beyond reach, so Ella Mae stretched her arm out, straining to grab Bea's wrist. Suddenly, Bea's dead, glassy stare shifted. She blinked and her mouth curled into an ugly snarl. Seizing Ella Mae's forearm, she yanked hard, pulling Ella Mae overboard. Immediately, unseen hands yanked her under the surface. Ella Mae tried to wriggle free, but the hands wouldn't let go. She could feel cold fingers digging into the skin of her calves as she was dragged deeper into the gloom. She tried to scream, but her lungs filled with lake water.

Ella Mae woke with a jolt. Her hair was plastered to her cheeks and her mouth was full of grit. She'd just finished wiping her face with a cool washcloth when the phone rang. It was the Havenwood Police Department. She was being summoned.

"I'll be right there," she told the officer and ended the call. To Chewy, who was dancing around her legs in anticipation of his breakfast, she added, "I smell like lake water and look like a zombie, so I'm not going anywhere until I feed you, make coffee, and take a shower. They'll just have to arrest me if they have a problem with that."

As Ella Mae drove into town, she considered the fact that most of the officers had probably been up for the better part of the night. After securing the scene at her house, they'd have gone on to Lake Havenwood Resort to conduct interviews and search Bea's room.

With this in mind, she stopped by the pie shop to collect four pies from the freezer. She didn't have time to cook them, but she knew there was an oven in the police department's break room and hoped to use it to make the cops a late breakfast.

Luckily, the young officer tasked with taking her statement was amenable to her idea. After Ella Mae repeated the same story she'd told Hardy the night before, the officer switched off the recording device and escorted her to the break room.

Left to her own devices, Ella Mae squeezed the pies into the preheated oven, brewed a pot of coffee, and then tidied up while the pies were baking. She was just cutting the first pie into slices when Hardy entered the room.

"Has The Charmed Pie Shoppe relocated?" he asked, sweeping his arm around the room.

Hardy's attempt at levity was undermined by both his haggard appearance and the hint of irritation in his voice. Ella Mae didn't think it was directed at her. Handing him a mug of fresh coffee, she said, "It must have been a very long night."

Lowering himself into the nearest chair, Hardy nodded. "Yes, and to top it all off, Mrs. Burbank's daughter will be here any minute. This is the part of my job I hate the most. Not only will Mrs. Fisher have to identify her mother's body, but I'll also have to ask her questions no child should have to answer about her parent."

Ella Mae wondered what secrets Beatrice Burbank might have been hiding. How had she ended up in the lake? Had she consumed too much alcohol and somehow lost her footing, fallen into the water, and accidentally drowned?

Using two forks to slide a wedge of pie onto a plate, Ella Mae served Hardy his breakfast. "In other words, you'll have to ask Mrs. Burbank's daughter if her mother had a drinking problem. Or some other addiction. You'll have to make a painful situation more painful."

"Exactly." Hardy sipped his coffee. "I hope Mrs. Fisher brought someone to lean on today. Even the strongest of us aren't prepared to lose our mothers. Especially like this."

Hardy had eaten half of his pie by the time the front desk clerk poked her head into the room. She opened her mouth to speak, and then closed it again, sniffing the air instead.

"Come in, Officer Thaler," Hardy beckoned. "Ms. LeFaye brought breakfast."

"That's mighty kind of you." Officer Thaler flashed Ella Mae a brief smile and turned back to Hardy. "I'd better wait, sir. Mrs. Fisher is here. I put her in your office. She came alone. Said her husband had to stay with their kids."

Hardy sighed. "That's not good. Do you mind sitting in for the interview?"

"Of course not," she replied. "I already asked Hughes to cover the desk. I'll find out if Mrs. Fisher would like some coffee."

"Thank you." Hardy got to his feet. "And thanks to you as well, Ms. LeFaye."

Ella Mae nodded. "I'm glad you were able to get in a few bites of comfort food. If you need more, you know where to find me."

As she walked back to her pink truck, which had once been used to deliver mail, Ella Mae heard the haunting strains of "Taps" drifting through the air and knew that the Memorial Day ceremony honoring Havenwood's veterans was under way.

Ella Mae changed course. As though hypnotized by the bugle call, she headed toward the sound of the music. It was very faint at first, but the lone bugler was soon joined by other instruments, and by the time Ella Mae reached the war memorial statue—a marble column with a bronze eagle at its summit—three stooped and grizzled veterans had just finished conducting the laying of the wreath ceremony.

The music ended and the crowd began to disperse. Ella Mae noticed the bright, orange-red hue of the artificial poppy flowers affixed to the men's shirt collars and to the ladies' blouses or purse straps and remembered that Hugh and some of the other firemen had volunteered to help a group of veterans distribute poppies at the community center.

She found Hugh standing beside an elderly man in a wheelchair. The man, a Korean War veteran, held a straw basket filled with the artificial flowers in his lap and was laughing heartily over something Hugh had said. As for Hugh, he appeared to be in charge of the donation can.

"All proceeds provide assistance to the veterans of foreign wars, ma'am," he explained to a woman who'd paused by his companion's wheelchair. "And partially to the Veterans of Foreign Wars National Home for Children as well. Because every child deserves a happy family. That's the organization's motto."

The woman glanced over her shoulder to where three children were sitting at a picnic bench, enjoying ice cream cones with a middle-aged man who was undoubtedly their father. After thanking the man in the wheelchair for his service, the woman removed several bills from her wallet and pushed them into Hugh's can.

"I told you that mentioning kids will fill up the can faster than talking about crusty old men like me," the vet grumbled.

Seeing Ella Mae, Hugh gave her a conspiratorial wink.

"I bet this lady is different. I bet she has a thing for guys in uniform."

Though Ella Mae wasn't in a lighthearted mood, she couldn't disappoint the aged veteran. After all, he'd risked his life to defend her freedom. The least she could do was smile at him and show her gratitude.

"Would you like a poppy, miss?" he asked.

"I would, sir," she said, stepping up to his wheelchair. "However, this shirt doesn't have any buttonholes. Would you mind putting one in my hair?"

The old man was delighted to oblige. "Such pretty hair too. Smells like vanilla and oranges."

Ella Mae caught his hand and held it. Looking into his eyes, she thanked him for his service.

Grinning, Hugh rattled his can. "You can assist veterans like my friend here to receive rehabilitation services and other necessary programs."

"It would be my honor." Ella Mae slid a twenty into the can. Lowering her voice to a whisper, she jerked her head in the direction of the community center entrance. "Can we talk inside?"

"I'm going to grab some water for us, Bert. Be back in five," Hugh said and put the donation can inside Bert's basket.

Bert arched his bushy brows. "If she was my girl, I wouldn't come back at all."

Laughing, Hugh accompanied Ella Mae into the building.

"I keep thinking about last night." Hugh took Ella Mae's hand. "About all of yesterday, in fact. Poor Bert. He must be wondering how he got stuck with the fireman with half a brain."

As they walked, Hugh and Ella Mae waved at friends and neighbors. It was only after Hugh purchased the bottled water that Ella Mae led him to an alcove near the restrooms and showed him her bandaged palms.

"What happened?" he asked, his blue eyes darkening in concern.

Ella Mae told him as succinctly as possible.

When she was done, Hugh leaned against the wall and exhaled. "Maybe you didn't see her during the festivities because she was out on a boat."

"How would she have fallen overboard? The water was totally calm. And why would she have gone out alone?" Ella Mae argued. "I have a bad feeling about this."

Hugh put his arms around her. "It was an accident, Ella Mae. It must have been. She didn't know anyone in Haven-wood, right?"

"I don't think so, no."

"Then there's no reason to believe someone meant her harm," Hugh said reasonably. "I'm sorry that she died and I'm even more sorry that you had to find her." He stroked Ella Mae's hair. "I wish I'd been with you. I want to be with you always."

Ella Mae closed her eyes. She was comforted by Hugh's touch. By the sound of his voice and the familiar way their bodies fit together. "You should get back to Bert," she said.

"I know I should, but I want to stay here a little longer." Hugh kissed her lightly on the lips. "Part of me feels like I never have enough time with you. I don't mean that in a bad way either. What I mean is that what we have is so great that I can't get enough of it."

"At least we had yesterday to ourselves. It was magical," Ella Mae said. She nestled against Hugh one more time. She listened to his heartbeat and ran her fingers over his sun-warmed shirt. Finally, she stepped away from him. Reluctantly, the couple returned to the main hallway.

Outside, Bert was busy speaking with two Gulf War veterans, so Ella Mae gave Hugh's hand a final squeeze and slipped away.

* * *

On the way back to her truck, Ella Mae walked by The Charmed Pie Shoppe. Though her business had been open for a couple years now, the sight of the butter-yellow clapboard cottage with its wide front porch and raspberry-pink front door never failed to make her heart swell with pride.

A blue minivan was parked at the end of the shop's flagstone path. The vehicle was not unusual, but the glittery camellia decal on the rear windshield got Ella Mae's attention. Hustling up the path and into the patio garden, she found a woman seated at one of the café tables.

Ella Mae couldn't see her face because the woman's head was buried in her arms. Her shoulders shook as she sobbed.

"Ma'am?" Ella Mae said softly, not wanting to startle her. She suspected she'd stumbled upon Bea's daughter. "Mrs. Fisher?"

The woman raised her head and swiped at the mascara tracks on her cheeks. "Yes. That's me." She ran a hand through her hair, which was an unkempt mass of mouse-brown curls. "Are you the pie chef?"

"I am." Ella Mae gestured toward the building. "Can I get you something from inside? A glass of water?"

"No, thanks." She sniffled. "I just wanted to see the garden. Mama mentioned it because she knows how much I love gardening. It was one of our few safe subjects." She fell silent for a moment before continuing. "This patio has such a wonderful blend of blooms and herbs. I like how the purple basil is mixed with the black-eyed Susans, and the lavender and rosemary are in the same bed with the wild geraniums. Do you use all these herbs in your food?"

Ella Mae sat on the chair across from Mrs. Fisher. "I do. And what we don't grow here comes from my mother's herb garden. She also has a large greenhouse, so we serve fresh greens throughout the year."

Mrs. Fisher's tears began flowing again. "It sounds like you and your mom are close. You're so lucky."

"We are now, but that wasn't always the case," Ella Mae said. "And I'm sure your mother loved you."

Bea's daughter let loose a dry, humorless laugh. "I was born Elizabeth Grace Burbank, the only child of Christopher and Beatrice Burbank. I was *supposed* to be tall, slim, blond, and accomplished. Above all else, I was *supposed* to be a Camellia. Instead, I turned out to be short, plump, and great at only one thing: motherhood. I'm a good wife too, but I'm most proud of the mom I've become. I never aspired to be a Camellia. What I dreamed of was raising a big, loud, chaotic, happy family." She laughed again, but this time, it was genuine. "And that's exactly what I did."

Smiling, Ella Mae extended her hand. "Well, Elizabeth of the big, happy family, I'm Ella Mae."

"It's just Liz." The other woman managed a small smile. "I'm sorry to show up unannounced. I didn't want to break down at the police station. Mama would have been pleased by my composure. I was able to identify her without crying. I even made it through the interview. But when they gave me her things . . ." Her voice wavered and she stopped.

"I can't imagine how hard that must have been," Ella Mae said gently. "I wish someone had come to Havenwood with you."

"Brady is with the boys. All three of them are Scouts and they're volunteering today. I didn't want them to have to stay at home with a sitter because of this. I thought I could handle it. Brady warned me that it would be awful." Liz pulled a wad of tissues from her handbag and a bunch of other detritus fell onto the ground, including gum, hand sanitizer, toy soldiers, a yo-yo, and a Tide bleach pen.

Liz scrambled to retrieve the items. "I buy these bleach pens by the dozen," she said, showing Ella Mae the large coffee stain on her blouse.

It was hard to believe that this disheveled person with the wild hair, the mascara-streaked cheeks, and the stained shirt was Bea's daughter, but Ella Mae liked her just as much as she'd liked Bea.

"Why don't you come inside?" Ella Mae asked. "I have a great recipe for cheeseburger pie. I bet your sons would love it. When I'm upset, being in the kitchen helps. Talking things over with another woman helps too. What do you say?"

Liz nodded gratefully. "That sounds really nice."

Ella Mae led Liz into the pie shop. She turned on the lights in the kitchen and tuned the radio to an easy listening station. After giving Liz a peach The Charmed Pie Shoppe apron, she set the ovens to the correct temperature and retrieved two balls of pie dough from the refrigerator. As she and Liz rolled out the dough on the flour-dusted worktable, Liz told her what it was like to grow up in Bea's shadow.

"She was top of her class at Emory University. She spoke three languages, was a talented watercolor painter, and played competitive chess, tennis, and golf. She was a skilled pianist and could ride a horse like she was part centaur, but do you know what she *couldn't* do?" Liz held up her rolling pin as though it were a question mark.

Ella Mae shrugged. She wanted Liz to get a few things off her chest, but she didn't want to encourage an hour-long rant about how tough it was to be Beatrice Burbank's daughter.

"She couldn't swim," Liz said sorrowfully. "Isn't that crazy? She grew up in Georgia, for heaven's sake. We have some of the hottest, stickiest summers known to man, but Mama never learned to swim. She was from a small town near the Alabama border, and her family was poor. She never saw the ocean until she married my daddy. She won a scholarship to Emory and that's where she met Daddy, but none of the Camellias know that. Mama always hid the truth about her roots. She was so ashamed of her past that her parents were never allowed to visit."

"That's awful," Ella Mae said, liking Bea a little less.

"She couldn't take the risk of losing her invitation to join the Camellias. To become a member without a legacy status is really difficult. You either have to donate a ton of money, be famous, or have *something* the club wants. An *it* factor."

Ella Mae transferred her pie dough to a dish. She then chopped two yellow onions and swept them into a frying pan to await sautéing. "What did your mother have?"

"She had money. My daddy came from a *very* wealthy family. They were rich *and* had an old Southern lineage. Not long after Mama was invited to join, she became the club's youngest president. She ran the Camellias like a five-star general. The club never raised as much money or received so much attention from the media as when Mama was at the helm." Liz sighed. "If only she'd invested that much time and devotion in getting to know her grandsons."

"That is a shame," Ella Mae agreed as they moved to the stove to sauté the onions and brown the ground beef. Hoping to steer the subject away from Bea, she asked Liz, "What will happen to the club now? Will they cancel the annual retreat?"

Liz shook her head. "No, no. After an appropriate period of mourning, they'll elect a new president. I'm sure the woman who took my place in the club—my surrogate, so to speak—will be in the running. My mother finally got the daughter she wanted in that one." She frowned deeply. "The campaigning will be fierce and furious. Women would kill to be named president of the Camellia Club."

Ella Mae shot Liz a dubious look. "You're kidding, right?"

But Liz wasn't smiling. "No," she said, her gaze fixed on the browning meat. "I'm deadly serious."

Chapter 3

While the pies were baking, Ella Mae and Liz took glasses of mint iced tea out to the patio garden.

Surrounded by blooms and the industrious buzz of honeybees, Liz seemed to relax a little. As the two women chatted, Ella Mae learned that Liz's husband, Brady, was a chemist. Liz also told her how she and Brady left Sweet Briar right after they were married.

"I couldn't wait to get out of that place," Liz said. "Brady and I aren't high-society types. We live in a suburb outside Atlanta. I work part-time for a florist who's also my best friend. Our family hangs out at soccer and baseball games, movie theaters, and parks. We have a rabbit, a turtle, and a goldfish named Cheeto."

"So why the camellia decal?" Ella Mae asked. "I would have expected a stick figure family."

Liz chewed her lip. "I'm not supposed to display that decal

because I'm not a club member, so I guess it's an act of rebellion. Totally juvenile, I know. And now, with my mother's passing . . ." She breathed deeply through her nose and then exhaled slowly through her mouth before continuing, "I stole a bunch of those stupid stickers before driving off into the sunset with my new husband. It was a childish thing to do, but I was angry because Mama didn't care that I was leaving. As long as she had the Camellia Club, she had what mattered most, so I violated the rules by slapping that flower on every car I owned. I even put them on our trashcans."

Ella Mae suppressed a smile. "Did your mother ever notice?"

"If she did, she never let on," Liz said. "She wouldn't give me the satisfaction. Besides, there was no risk of another club member seeing my car because I never returned to Sweet Briar. Mama and Daddy visited us, but we weren't invited to their home."

Hearing the pain in her voice, Ella Mae gave Liz's hand a squeeze. "I think you should scrape off that decal. It might help you say good-bye. Not just to your mother, but to some of your bad memories too."

Though Liz's eyes grew moist, she nodded in agreement.

After checking the oven timer to make sure the pies wouldn't burn, Ella Mae retrieved a sharp knife and a bottle of glass cleaner from the kitchen and met Liz by her blue minivan.

It didn't take long to remove the sparkly flower. When it was gone, Liz sprayed the entire rear window.

"I bet your kids would love to vote on which decals best represent your family," Ella Mae said.

Liz smiled broadly. "I don't know if anyone makes a sticker that combines three different sports, *Star Wars*, Boy Scouts, and *Teenage Mutant Ninja Turtles*, but you're right.

My boys would get a kick out of it. By the time they're done, the entire window will be covered."

Pleased to see that Liz's mood had improved, Ella Mae led her back into the kitchen. They removed the pies from the oven and placed them on cooling racks. While Liz assembled two take-out boxes, Ella Mae wrote down the recipe for her Charmed Chocolate Mud Pie, a favorite among the children of Havenwood.

Finally, it was time for Liz to be on her way. She hugged Ella Mae and thanked her for her kindness. When she was gone, Ella Mae cleaned up the kitchen and sat on the stool for a long moment before picking up the phone and dialing Officer Hardy's number.

"I'm sorry to bother you," she said, "but Liz Fisher just spent over an hour with me and she told me some interesting things about Mrs. Burbank. I thought I'd better share them with you."

"Go on," Hardy said.

Feeling a tinge of guilt, Ella Mae repeated what Liz had said about the Camellia Club.

"She mentioned the club to me as well." Hardy sounded unimpressed. "Bake sales and napkin folding and that sort of thing, right?"

"I think there's more to it than that." Remembering that Hardy was operating on very little sleep, Ella Mae tried to be patient. "Liz said in all seriousness that women would kill to be elected the next club president. What if someone helped Bea finish her term early?"

Hardy grunted. "Are you implying that one of these women committed murder just to be in charge of this club? And that this woman followed Mrs. Burbank to Havenwood because she needn't worry about being recognized?"

"It's possible," Ella Mae said, refusing to back down. "It

couldn't hurt to examine the resort's guest list. Cross-reference the names and make sure none of them have been falsified. Because, if someone from the Camellia Club *did* drive here from Sweet Briar, it's because she possessed certain knowledge about Mrs. Burbank. This fact, which Bea would have probably tried to hide as she saw it as a shortcoming, would have been a *very* useful piece of information for a murderer to have. Especially since Bea was staying at a lakeside resort."

"I'm not following you, Ms. LeFaye, and I'm very busy. Please get to the point," Hardy said testily.

"Bea couldn't swim," Ella Mae said. "Liz told me that her mother never learned. What if someone from the Camellia Club followed Bea as she walked on the dock, or near the lake's edge, and pushed her in when no one was around to witness the act?"

Hardy was silent for a moment. "We're already checking the names on the hotel registry, but in light of this news, I'll get my hands on a list of current club members as well." He paused. "I wonder why Mrs. Fisher didn't mention the fact that her mother couldn't swim."

"I think she was running on autopilot in the police station. She was just trying to survive and get out of there."

"Did she say anything else?" Hardy asked. "Anything that might indicate her mother had issues with alcohol or other substances?"

Ella Mae recounted how Bea's weaknesses seemed to center on her inability to sustain familial relationships. "It sounds like she was too much of a control freak to indulge beyond a glass of wine."

"We'll see about that when the lab results come in." Hardy thanked Ella Mae for the call and hung up.

Ella Mae locked The Charmed Pie Shoppe and drove home. After playing with Chewy for a while, she searched the gardens for her mother. She found her in the greenhouse, watering trays of seedlings.

"You've been gone for ages," Adelaide said, turning off the water.

"I ended up spending time with Bea's daughter." Ella Mae thought about how Liz had never been close to her mother, and felt an overwhelming rush of affection not just for her mother, but also for Reba and her aunts. These women had all played a part in raising her, and whenever something unsettled her—and Bea's death had certainly unsettled her—she wanted to be surrounded by her family.

Her mother must have sensed her need. "Should we have everyone over tonight? We can share a meal under the stars."

Ella Mae smiled. "That sounds like the perfect way to help me move forward after this strange, sad day."

"Didn't I tell you?" Reba cried when Ella Mae told her about Bea's death that evening. "My radar went off the second she stepped in the pie shop. And now she's in a drawer in the morgue. Good thing you can't get involved with her now."

"Reba!" Aunt Dee scolded softly, pulling the sleeve of her filmy blue blouse over the puckered burn scar on her forearm.

"Why do you hide those from us?" Aunt Sissy asked her sister. "You're our beautiful Delia. Those scars could *never* diminish the real you."

Aunt Dee shrugged. "It's become a habit. I see people staring at my arms when I'm at the bank or the grocery store, so I try to cover as much skin as I can. Not because I'm ashamed. I don't care about the scars, but I don't want to make other people feel uncomfortable."

"Too bad for them!" Aunt Verena shouted. Verena, who didn't possess an indoor voice, had a firm opinion on every subject. "It's not like you *chose* to be locked inside a burning barn."

Dee opened her mouth to protest, but Adelaide changed the subject by asking Reba and her sisters what they wanted to drink with dinner.

"I'll guzzle some vino while I'm fixin' the pasta. After all, the recipe calls for wine." Laughing, Reba disappeared into the kitchen.

The rest of the LeFaye women went outside to set the table.

Ella Mae spread a white cloth over the patio table and Sissy distributed plates and silverware. Verena put out wineglasses and then went back inside to retrieve the two bottles of white Bordeaux that Adelaide had purchased to accompany Reba's spaghetti puttanesca. Adelaide snipped pink and purple clematis flowers from a nearby trellis and sprinkled them haphazardly over the surface of the table. Dee lit dozens of tea light candles and placed them on top of the flowers. The effect was magical.

After the table was set, the women rejoined Reba in the kitchen, where they prepared a large tossed salad and two loaves of garlic bread. The room filled with steam, noisy chatter, and laughter. It was the exact balm Ella Mae had been looking for to help her recover from an emotional day.

By the time Reba appeared on the patio carrying an enormous platter of pasta, the rest of the women were already seated. They applauded loudly and raised their glasses to toast the chef, but Reba waved off their compliments and told them to eat before the food grew cold.

"Did you know that, in Italian, *puttane* means the 'lady of the night'?" Sissy asked in a stage whisper. "As in, *prostitute*?"

"My all-time favorite pasta recipe," Reba said, piling a large helping onto her plate.

Ella Mae grinned. "It's true. I remember reading an article

about the origin of the dish's name. The strong aroma is meant to symbolize the perfume of the women who lured men into their houses of ill repute."

"Here's to saucy Napolese sirens!" Verena cried and raised her glass.

Adelaide shook her head in wonder. "I never thought we'd drink in honor of sirens. After all, the only siren we know is Loralyn Gaynor, and she's still our enemy."

Dee shot a nervous glance at Adelaide. "The LeFayes and the Gaynors have declared a truce. You'd better not call Loralyn an enemy in front of the Elders. Verena will overlook it because she's your sister, but the others may not."

A strained silence followed. Eventually, Adelaide dipped her chin in acquiescence and raised her glass. The women clinked rims and sipped their wine.

"Speaking of the Elders, I have a proposition for you!" Verena pointed her fork at Ella Mae.

Ella Mae experienced a strong sense of déjà vu. Suddenly, she was back in The Charmed Pie Shoppe with Beatrice Burbank, listening to Bea describe the Camellia Club's annual retreat.

"Are you all right?" Dee asked softly.

Shaking her head as though to clear it, Ella Mae said, "Yes." She took a large swallow of wine and looked at Aunt Verena. "What kind of proposition?"

"The Elders would like you to be an ambassador, for lack of a better word. There isn't a person on earth who hasn't heard that you found an object of power and sent it back to Scotland, where it was used to restore a ruined grove."

"A magical person, you mean," Ella Mae corrected.

Verena shrugged as though this detail were unimportant. "Now every community hopes to find such an object. Other descendants of Morgan le Fay and Guinevere are joining forces and pooling their knowledge. Wonderful things are happening because of what you did, Ella Mae."

"People are setting out on quests," Sissy said, picking up her sister's narrative. "It's *very* exciting. We might be witnessing a new age of heroes and legends!" She threw her arms wide, nearly knocking over both wine bottles. Luckily, Sissy's dining companions were used to her dramatic gestures and grabbed the fragile items within her reach. "First, King Arthur's sword was brought to light. What will be discovered next? The Holy Grail? The philosopher's stone? The Book of Thoth?"

"Hold it." Ella Mae raised her hand to stop her aunt from continuing. "I'm not involved in that world anymore."

Dee studied her carefully. "And I'd understand if you never wanted to be immersed in it again. Do you remember how you offered me the opportunity to be completely healed and I refused to accept?" At Ella Mae's nod, Dee went on. "I wanted to keep my scars as a reminder of what I'd lost the night of the fire. Despite that loss, I'm doing all I can to move forward. I'm working again. I'm also involved with a kind, generous, and loving man. As are you. And yet what did all those people say the last time you left the grove? After your magic was gone?"

Ella Mae had to pause for a moment before she could answer. The memory was still so powerful that it brought tears to her eyes. "They said, 'You will always be one of us.'"

"Which is precisely what the Elders are trying to convey!" Verena exclaimed. "They *want* you to be involved."

"I'll think about it, okay?" Ella Mae told her aunt. "Right now, I just want to enjoy this beautiful night and the present company."

Adelaide refilled Ella Mae's glass. "You didn't relax much today. Maybe you should let Jenny open the pie shop tomorrow so you can sleep late."

"I'm hoping that Jenny will be too tired from her double date to open for me," Ella Mae said with a smile.

Reba wriggled her brows. "Well, if she can't figure out what to do with that hunky carpenter, she can send him my way. I like a man with a tool belt."

"You like *all* men," Sissy pointed out.

"Not true," Reba argued. "I never found Jarvis Gaynor attractive."

At the mention of Loralyn's father, who was safely locked up in a federal penitentiary, Ella Mae turned to her mother again. "How is Opal?"

Adelaide averted her gaze. "She hasn't been the same since Loralyn left. It can't be easy for her to have no idea where her daughter has gone."

"I think there's more to it than worry," Dee added. "Opal has always been the picture of health, but when I last saw her, she was alarmingly thin. She might be ill."

"That's terrible," Ella Mae said and marveled over the fact that everyone at the table was genuinely concerned for Opal's welfare. Once, not too long ago, they might have been immune to her suffering. But those days were over. The descendants of Morgan le Fay and Queen Guinevere were no longer enemies. Adelaide LeFaye and Opal Gaynor were now neighbors in the truest sense of the word, and Ella Mae felt compelled to see how she was doing.

"I can whip up some chicken noodle soup while I'm preparing chicken potpies tomorrow," she said. "I'll bring her a container after work."

Adelaide looked concerned. "If you drop by, Opal is bound to solicit your help in finding Loralyn."

"How could I be of any use?" Ella Mae was confused.

"By accepting the Elders' offer," Verena answered. "If you located another object of power, Loralyn would undoubt-

edly turn up to seize it. That girl never could resist a piece
of bling."

Ella Mae recalled a promise she'd made to Opal Gaynor
earlier that spring. She'd promised to bring her daughter back
to her. To deliver Loralyn unharmed. And she'd failed to keep
that promise.

"If she asks for my help, then I'll give it to her," Ella Mae
said. "Isn't that what friends do?"

Though her aunts nodded in silent agreement, her mother
looked troubled. Her fingertips pressed against one of the
clematis flowers on the tablecloth and the petals began to curl
inward. Within seconds, the petals had shriveled and turned
into pink dust.

Reba swept the flower detritus off the table and shoved her
chair back. "Come on, gals! Aren't we supposed to be havin'
fun? Drink whatever's left in your glass because I'm goin'
inside for another bottle of wine. It's the unofficial start of
summer. The best time of the year! This is when men wear
the fewest clothes. Shorts. Tight T-shirts. Or no shirts at all.
Can I get a hallelujah?"

Aunt Verena tossed a balled-up napkin at her. "No, but I
second your motion for more vino. What did Horace say?
That the Muses smell of wine?" She leaned over and sniffed
Sissy's neck. "My little sister is a muse, and since she smells
like garlic bread, you'd better get *two* more bottles!"

The next day, Ella Mae felt as though the balance of her
world had been restored. She dropped off Chewy at Canine
to Five, tarrying long enough to kiss Hugh in the privacy of
his office, and then entered The Charmed Pie Shoppe.

Ella Mae was always the first to arrive, but this morning,
Jenny was waiting for her in the kitchen, coffee cup in hand.

"What's this?" Ella Mae asked. "Is there a midweek wedding I don't know about?"

"Nah. I wanted to talk girl stuff with you before the rest of the staff got here." Jenny poured a fresh cup of coffee and put it on the worktable. "I finished the opening chores, so you have a few minutes to relax."

Ella Mae reached for the jug of cream. "How was last night?"

"That's what I wanted to talk to you about. About Finn." Jenny's mouth curved into a smile. "Lord, Ella Mae. I didn't want to like him because he had a thing for you. He swears that he doesn't anymore. He says that he admires you and that he wants to be your friend, but that's all."

Hearing this, Ella Mae felt a surge of relief. "That's good news, right?"

"I guess." Jenny shrugged. "The truth is that I want to believe him because we had a really great time. He had me laughing for most of the night—and you know how important a sense of humor is to me. On top of that, he's sweet, smart, and incredibly cute." She flicked her hair over her shoulder. "Not that I let him know that, of course. I was surprised by how much I liked being with him. And I think he was too."

"Didn't you realize that your brother was setting you and Finn up?"

"No! Had I known, I would have slugged the jerk." Sparks danced in Jenny's eyes and Ella Mae made a show of leaning away from her. Both Upton siblings could exhibit fiery tempers when they were upset. "Calvin said we were going to a party at Finn's place, so I expected to be hanging out with a bunch of people, but when we got there, it was just Finn." Jenny smiled again and the angry glint in her eyes vanished. "Still, it was never awkward. While Calvin was snuggling on the porch swing with Suzy, Finn and I just picked up a conversation we'd been having the last time I stopped by WoodWorks to see what Calvin was making, and the time flew by."

Ella Mae took a sip of her coffee and released a contented sigh. "There's a glow about you this morning—you're even more electric than usual. I think this is wonderful. For both you and Finn."

"You do?" Jenny exhaled noisily. "I was hoping you'd say that. But a small part of me worried that it would make things weird between us. Me having a crush on the guy that had a crush on you."

Ella Mae laughed. "That's life in a small town. Why do you think Reba's always itching to get out of Dodge for a few days? She needs a fresh supply of men."

"I heard that!" Reba shouted from the dining room. She had a key to the front door and had let herself in while Ella Mae and Jenny were speaking.

Giggling, Ella Mae and Jenny stood up, tied on their aprons, and got to work.

That afternoon, Ella Mae biked over to Rolling View, the Gaynors' estate. Though the Georgian manor house, stables, and the sprawling grounds were as meticulously maintained as ever, Ella Mae sensed an emptiness about the place. No one was walking horses or trimming bushes, and Ella Mae waited a full minute before someone responded to the doorbell.

Finally, a middle-aged woman with short, dark hair and a no-nonsense expression cracked the door and peered out at Ella Mae. "May I help you?"

Because the woman was not dressed in the maid's uniform Opal usually insisted upon, Ella Mae was instantly suspicious. "I'm Mrs. Gaynor's neighbor. Who are you?"

"Her nurse. Terri Valdez," the woman replied without opening the door any wider. "Mrs. Gaynor is sleeping right now."

Ella Mae was stunned. Why did Opal require the services of a nurse? How sick was she? "She'll want to see me when she wakes up. I can wait in the library in the meantime. Also, I made her some chicken noodle soup and cheese biscuits."

"Come in," Terri said, a trifle reluctantly. Taking the food from Ella Mae, she headed off in the direction of the kitchen.

Ella Mae shut herself in the library and immediately sent a group text message to Reba, her mother, and her aunts, informing them of the situation. She then busied herself looking for books on objects of power but found nothing. She suspected Opal had hidden the rare and unusual items in her collection prior to Terri's arrival. However, she did locate a book on legendary weapons and managed to read two chapters before Terri entered the library.

"Mrs. Gaynor will see you now."

Terri led Ella Mae to a second-floor sitting room filled with soft furniture, floral fabrics, and pastel hues. Opal sat in a wing chair by a floor-to-ceiling window with a view of the back gardens. In the afternoon light, the skin of her face looked as fragile as tissue paper. She was frighteningly thin—a fact she tried to conceal by dressing in a billowy robe—but one glance at her bony wrists and gaunt cheeks, made it clear that Opal had lost an alarming amount of weight.

"Why haven't you told anyone that your illness was this serious?" Ella Mae asked gently.

Opal flashed a wry smile. "Still acting the queen, are we?" She indicated the chair opposite hers. "Thank you for coming. And for making me soup. That was very thoughtful. Unfortunately, as you've undoubtedly noticed, I don't have much of an appetite."

"Can I do anything to help you?"

"Unless you've found a cure for cancer, you can't help. No one can," Opal said. Ella Mae was struck dumb, but Opal nodded as though she'd spoken and continued, "It took me by surprise too. I thought I had a late-season flu. A very long-lasting flu. I was tired all the time and my body ached." She made a circular motion across her torso. "But the source of my discomfort is tumors. Apparently, they're everywhere."

Ella Mae's eyes filled with tears.

"Don't do that," Opal protested sternly. "Don't make me wish we were enemies again." She beckoned to Terri. "Would you get Ms. LeFaye a glass of water, please?"

The distraction allowed Ella Mae to master her emotions, and by the time Terri returned with the water, she was able to speak calmly. "When did you find out?"

"About a month ago. It's a damned nuisance too. I have so much to do." Opal flicked her wrist dismissively, as though cancer were a fly she might shoo away. But then, a shadow passed over her face and her shoulders sagged. Dropping all pretense of bravado, she clasped her hands in a plaintive gesture. "I want to see my girl. Will you find her for me? I want to make peace with Loralyn before I die."

Ella Mae started to object, but Opal shushed her. "There's no time for platitudes. Look at me."

There was such naked fear in Opal's eyes that Ella Mae could do nothing but nod.

"Good." Opal leaned back in her chair, obviously exhausted. Terri took a step toward her, but Opal asked her to leave the room for a few minutes. Once she was gone, Opal stared intently at Ella Mae. "I knew you'd keep your promise. Do you remember what you said?"

"That I'd do everything in my power to bring Loralyn back to you." Ella Mae's voice was solemn. "However, as you know, I no longer have any power."

Opal smirked. "While that is unfortunate, you *do* have influence. Your fame is widespread and you can use your celebrity statue to find Loralyn and bring her home to me."

She held out her hand, silently imploring, and Ella Mae took it in her own.

"You once said that love is stronger than magic," Opal whispered. "I love my daughter, and I'd trade every ounce of power I possess to see her once more. Tell me. Is there any hope?"

"There's always hope," Ella Mae said, gently squeezing Opal's hand.

At that moment, Terri returned and declared that Opal should rest. Ella Mae said that she'd show herself out and quietly left the room.

As she biked home from Rolling View, tears blurring her vision, Ella Mae prayed that she could keep her promise to a dying woman.

Chapter 4

Throughout the next day, Ella Mae was haunted by the memory of Opal Gaynor's fragility. As soon as the pie shop closed, she met with the Elders and promised to serve as their ambassador in exchange for their help in locating Loralyn.

"We've already been through this with Opal," said one of the Elders, a high school principal. "We put the word out when Loralyn first left Havenwood. Her photograph was sent to Elders across the region. They agreed to forward it to their neighboring communities. However, seeing as Loralyn is unlikely to replenish her magic until the autumn equinox, there's little chance of spotting her unless she enters a grove."

"And the Mabon festival is months away," another Elder, the head of the local library, added. "So Ms. Gaynor could be anywhere."

Verena's mouth formed a deep frown. It was an expression of disapproval that could make even her husband,

Havenwood's mayor, squirm like a chastised child. "Opal was instrumental in mending the rift between our two families," she said. "It's our duty to reunite her with her daughter. If that means waiting until September to locate Loralyn, then we must find a way to buy Opal some time. Isn't there one among us who can heal her?"

A third Elder, who was a physician by trade, shook her head. "Not even the strongest healer can cure disease. We can lessen the severity of wounds. Decrease pain. Speed the natural course of healing. But there has yet to be one of our kind who could rid a body of cancer. Opal's fate cannot be changed by magic."

"But I believe it could be changed by an object of power," Ella Mae said quietly. "Take what I say with a grain of salt because the stories and legends surrounding these objects are as varied and flawed as the tales about us. About you." Her cheeks turned hot over the blunder. "Suzy, who owns The Cubbyhole, has been reading about these objects for years, and when she and I researched Arthur's sword this spring, we learned that most of the objects were created to heal, purify, or unify. I'll ask Suzy to help me find one of these objects. As most of you know, my best friend has a photographic memory. I'd also like permission to inform Hugh Dylan of my activities."

The Elders exchanged anxious glances, Verena included.

"I promised him that there'd be no more lies between us," Ella Mae explained. "Plus, he can help us. Hugh traveled around Europe last year searching for an object. Along the way, he made friends. Those connections could prove valuable if Suzy and I come up with a concrete lead."

Reluctantly, the Elders nodded in assent.

"I'll do whatever I can to find these objects, but I won't allow my business or my relationships to suffer as a result of the search," Ella Mae concluded firmly. She held out her unblemished palm where the burn scar shaped like a four-leaf clover had once marked her skin and then balled her hand into a tight fist. "In the meantime, please find a healer to minister to Opal. There must be someone who can slow the spread of her disease. If she has several months—"

"She has weeks at most," Verena said in an uncharacter-istically soft voice. "But we'll find a specialist. If her pride hadn't kept her from asking for help before you showed up at Rolling View, her fate might have been different."

Following a long moment of sorrow-tinged silence, one of the Elders pointed at the remains of his strawberry cheese-cake tart. "Your food still tastes enchanted."

"Thank you." Ella Mae smiled at the compliment and began to clear the dirty dishes.

After the meeting, Ella Mae walked to The Cubbyhole Book & Gift Shop.

The store was bustling with both locals and tourists. Suzy was busy assisting a mother and her two preteen children make selections from a display called, "Adventures in Read-ing: Better Than Video Games!"

"What's cool about this book is that it's part graphic novel, part thriller," Suzy was saying to the mother, but her gaze was fixed on the boy. "If you like the *Star Wars* or *Avatar* movies, then you'll enjoy the entire series."

"They're okay," the boy said, referring to the films. Despite his bored tone, he reached out for the book and Suzy passed it to him with a nonchalant air before turning to his sister.

"And you're into horses?"

The girl shrugged. "Yeah, but I've read, like, *every* horse book in the world."

Suzy grinned, clearly delighted by the idea of a challenge. She began reciting classic titles like *Black Beauty*, *The Black*

Stallion, *National Velvet*, *Misty of Chincoteague*, and so on. The girl had read them all. Finally, Suzy asked, "How about *The Phantom Stallion*?"

The girl furrowed her brow. "Never heard of that one."

"Come with me!" Suzy beckoned to her. "I have the first three books in the series over here."

A few minutes later, while the grateful mother paid Suzy's assistant for a stack of new books, Suzy joined Ella Mae by the reading chairs in the front of the store.

"Sit down so I can fill you in on Calvin's matchmaking scheme," she said with a mischievous grin. "He has this crazy idea that all six of us will be paired off by the end of the summer. You and Hugh. Me and Calvin. Jenny and Finn. Three couples headed for our happily ever afters."

Ella Mae gestured toward the children's section. "The fairy tales don't explain how unpredictable the *after* part is. Or how a woman's life is made up of more elements than pretty ball gowns and handsome princes. Life is hard, messy, and complicated. It's also beautiful and full of wonder." She waved her hands. "Sorry, I think I'm rambling because I'm facing a major challenge." Lowering her voice to a whisper, she said, "The Elders have asked for my help, and I have no hope of succeeding at this task without you."

Ella Mae didn't finish describing her task before Suzy exclaimed, "Count me in! You know I have tons of material on those objects. When do we start?"

"Tonight? I'll order pizza and buy a bottle of wine."

Seeing a line forming at the register, Suzy moved to go. "You know the way to my heart. I'll bring ice cream. Peanut butter cup or mocha chocolate chip?"

"Both," Ella Mae said. "We have lots of work to do and time is short."

* * *

Two weeks later, Ella Mae's new schedule was already wearing her down. She spent her days working at the pie shop and divided her nights and weekends between researching objects of power, surfing the Internet for traces of Loralyn, and hanging out with Hugh.

She was so busy that she had no choice but to push all thoughts of Beatrice Burbank and the Camellia Club to the back of her mind. It wasn't until Reba told her that Jon Hardy and several of his fellow police officers were enjoying a late lunch on the patio that Ella Mae remembered the investigation.

"Would you ask him to come into the kitchen when he's done with his meal?" Ella Mae asked.

Reba grinned. "Already did. I knew you'd want to talk to him. He's payin' the bill right now, so it'll only be a minute. Also, Jenny's gone off-site to meet with a bride, and I told the college kids to take their break. They went to grab a burger before teatime."

Scooping up a slice of boysenberry pie for another customer, Reba left the kitchen.

She soon returned with Officer Hardy. "I'll be out back havin' a candy break if you need me," she told Ella Mae as she opened the door leading to the parking lot.

Hardy raised his brows. "Is that code for a smoke break?"

"No. Reba's addicted to red licorice twists. She has been since I was a kid." Ella Mae used a dishrag to wipe flour off a stool and waited for Hardy to sit before speaking. "I wanted to ask you for an update on Bea's case. I hope that's not out of line," she hurriedly added. "I know I'm not a family member or anything."

"You're a citizen of this town, so that gives you the right.

And the answer is quite simple. The case is closed. As of yesterday. Mrs. Burbank's death was ruled an accident. The official cause was death by accidental drowning. The medical examiner found a large contusion on the back of Mrs. Burbank's head, so she may have lost consciousness while in the water. Her blood contained no traces of alcohol or drugs. The truth is that we don't know exactly what happened. It's unlikely we ever will."

Ella Mae picked up her potholders and squeezed them. "What if someone hit her hard and then pushed her in the water? Wouldn't that account for the injury and the drowning?"

"Yes," Hardy agreed. "But we found no evidence of foul play. No one saw Mrs. Burbank near the lake. The last time someone at the resort laid eyes on her, she was in the dining room having supper. Her waitress stated that Mrs. Burbank appeared to be in good spirits and that she left a generous tip. All the staff concurred that she was extremely courteous and seemed like a contented person. We discovered nothing unusual in her room."

"What about the Camellia Club?" The ruling perturbed Ella Mae. How could the case be closed? She didn't believe Bea's death was an accident. Not after speaking with Liz. "Were any of its members at the resort when she was killed?"

Hardy released an exasperated sigh. "To our knowledge, none of them were present when Mrs. Burbank met with her tragic end. And before you ask, we did not launch a joint investigation with the Sweet Briar Police Department. I would hardly instigate such an act based on a statement made by Mrs. Burbank's bereaved daughter. People say all sorts of things during moments of acute grief." He paused. "I've spoken with Mrs. Fisher several times since her mother's passing. It's clear that theirs was a complicated relationship. Not only that, but Mrs. Fisher wasn't close to her mother at the time of her death and wasn't familiar with her friends, activities, or movements."

Though Ella Mae hated to admit it, she couldn't find fault with Hardy's reasoning. "But what if Bea's death wasn't accidental?" she asked softly. "I understand the ruling, but it doesn't create closure. Not for me, at least. And I suspect Liz's feelings will be magnified to the umpteenth degree."

"I wish there'd been a different outcome, Ms. LeFaye." Hardy stood. "But police investigations aren't always resolved to everyone's satisfaction. We can't always provide closure. Many times, there are doubts. There are unanswered questions. I have plenty myself. They often keep me up at night."

This unsolicited bit of personal information came as a surprise to Ella Mae, and she smiled to show that she appreciated his candor.

"I didn't mean to imply that you hadn't done your best by Bea," Ella Mae said. "I know that you and your team did all you could. This outcome is just hard to accept."

"Even so, I don't recommend launching an independent investigation, Ms. LeFaye. From the little I did learn of the Camellia Club, their membership is built on a tradition of power and wealth that stretches back for generations. I doubt they'd tolerate meddling from an outsider, and I'd hate to think of how they'd respond to slanderous accusations. My advice? Let it go."

Knowing there was nothing left to say, Ella Mae nodded and walked Hardy into the now empty dining room.

In the brief lull between lunch and teatime, The Charmed Pie Shoppe staff restocked the pie cases, wiped off the café tables, and swept the floors. Ella Mae had hired the same

college students she'd employed during the previous summer, but since neither Maddie nor Royce had returned from
their burger run and Reba was still outside eating licorice
and undoubtedly sexting her latest lover, Ella Mae took care
of the tasks herself.

She was just putting the broom back in the supply closet
when the phone rang. Grabbing an order pad and a pencil,
Ella Mae answered the call. "The Charmed Pie Shoppe, Ella
Mae LeFaye speaking. May I help you?"

"You most certainly may!" a woman declared enthusiastically. "My name is Julia Eudailey and I'm secretary of the
Camellia Club. I thought I should reach out to see if you had
any questions about your contract. I'll be mailing you a hard
copy shortly, and I apologize for the delay. Club business was
put on hold while Bea's estate was being settled. I don't know
how attorneys can wade through all that paperwork. And I
thought real estate was bad!" She laughed, and when Ella
Mae didn't join in, she grew concerned. "Ms. LeFaye? Are
you there?"

Ella Mae had been lost in the memory of the night she'd
handed her contract to the desk clerk at Lake Havenwood
Resort. "I'm sorry. I hadn't realized the retreat was still on."

"Oh, yes! Bea wouldn't want it any other way. In fact,
we've added a celebration of life ceremony to our list of
events. We plan to commemorate Bea's service before we
elect our next president." She paused. "I hope you're still
available for those dates. The Camellias are looking forward
to working with the three chefs Bea selected."

There was a hint of warning in Julia's tone and Ella Mae
sensed she was being reminded that she'd signed a contract.
Julia went on to add, "I'm sure Bea told you that several
young women are depending on our scholarship fund. And
then there's the poor girl who was burned—"

"I wouldn't dream of canceling," Ella Mae cut in quickly. "I'm fully committed to helping that young lady."

"Wonderful!" Julia trilled. "In that case, I'll see you in August. If there's anything you need before then, give me a jingle. In addition to the contract, I'm going to mail you an itinerary and my contact information. Of course, the Camellias would be honored if you'd attend Bea's celebration ceremony. We heard how courageous you were the night you pulled her out of the lake."

"Of course." Ella Mae flashed on an image of Liz in the pie shop's garden, her face etched with grief. "Will her daughter be at the ceremony as well?"

Without the slightest hesitation, Julia answered, "Oh no. It's only for club members. Bea's *public* memorial service took place last Saturday. The church was packed to capacity. I hope Elizabeth realized just how many amazing things her mother accomplished during her time as president."

Despite the knowledge that she'd be helping a burn victim, Ella Mae now regretted her decision to be involved in the Camellia Club's annual retreat. Having spoken with Julia Eudailey, she was reticent to meet the rest of the club members. She remembered Liz saying that she'd wished her mother had invested a fraction of the energy she devoted to philanthropic ventures in forging a relationship with her grandsons, and almost repeated this comment to Julia, but Ella Mae bit back the words. What was the point? Bea was gone. Ella Mae couldn't do anything to repair the damaged relationship between mother and daughter, and she needed to focus on her promise to Opal. To reunite another mother and daughter before it was too late.

Mothers and daughters, she thought. *That's what the Camellia Club's members are. And yet Bea replaced her daughter like she was a pair of shoes that had become too scuffed to wear in public. Had someone else come to the conclusion that Bea was worn out? That she was in need of replacing?*

Because Ella Mae didn't think Bea's death was an accident, she decided to learn more about the Camellias before spending a week with them. After all, one of the women might very well be a murderer.

"Do you have a club directory?" Ella Mae asked Julia. "Something that includes names and faces? I'd like to familiarize myself with your members prior to the retreat. And I'd love to know more about the club's history. Bea gave me a brief introduction, but I'm interested in how it was founded, the membership requirements, and the various events you host."

Julia laughed loudly. "I'd have to send you a box of files to cover all that information, but I think it's wonderful that you want to get to know us before we arrive! I'll include a directory with your contract. Not everyone will have a photograph, however. We had several absences the day of the photo shoot, but we'll be redoing the directory after the August election, so those spots won't be blank for long. Anyway, I'm sure you'll have no trouble figuring out who the ladies with the missing pictures are. I think there were only three or four."

Eager to end the call, Ella Mae thanked Julia and hung up.

That night, she stood in the library at Partridge Hill and stared at the whiteboard she and Suzy were using to trace the magical objects that Ella Mae had once believed were only the stuff of legend.

On one side of the board were the names of the men and women who were credited as being the most notable owners of the objects. There were headings such as "Aaron and the Rod," "Hatshepsut and the Book of Thoth," "Jason and the Golden Fleece," "Bran the Blessed and the Cauldron," "Roland and the Oliphant Horn," and "Bragi and the Harp."

"Biblical, Egyptian, Greek, Roman, Japanese, Indian, Norse, Celtic," Ella Mae murmured, her glance traveling from the board to the piles of splayed books on the table and sofa. Two card tables had been erected to hold the additional tomes Suzy had brought in, and a stack of delicate scrolls had been collected in a large basket near the floor lamp.

"It's pretty overwhelming, isn't it?" Suzy said, entering the room with a jug of milk in one hand and two glasses in the other. Chewy trotted after her, his tail wagging furiously. Suzy put her burdens on the table and pulled a rawhide chew stick and two chocolate bars from her back pocket. She gave Chewy his treat and passed the chocolate bars under her nose, inhaling deeply. "Ready for another night of research?"

"We're not making much progress," Ella Mae said, unable to hide her frustration. "What made the Elders believe I could find these things? People have been searching for them for *centuries* without success." She gestured at the table before her. "Every book we read or scroll we unfurl is filled with contradictory information. What we need is a magical Indiana Jones–type person. Why did the Elders enlist *me*? I'm a pastry chef!"

Dropping the chocolate bars on top of a legal pad filled with notes, Suzy swiveled her laptop screen so that it faced Ella Mae and pointed at the e-mail icon on her screen. "This is why. Because I received over two hundred new messages from all over the world. And that's just today. These people are reaching out to you because you're a household name." She held up her hand. "And don't give me that crap about your not being one of us anymore. It's not like you can forget what you've seen, heard, and experienced. I still believe that magic lives inside you. It's just dormant or something. But that's neither here nor there. What matters is that people want to help you. Scholars. Archaeologists. Scientists. And a few crazies too."

Ella Mae laughed and reached for a chocolate bar. "All right, my pity party's over. What are we focusing on tonight?"

"Symbols. You'll be tracking Greek objects by studying their symbols while I focus on the Celtic ones." Suzy snapped off a square of chocolate and popped it in her mouth. "The theory I'm working on is that, over time, these objects have migrated from the places where they were created. I think they were handed down from one guardian to the next. Either that, or they've been hidden—buried, probably—beneath a symbol that represents them, but not too clearly."

"So the symbol would be like a road sign where all the letters are scrambled," Ella Mae said.

Suzy nodded. "Yes, but not letters. Pictures. Shapes. Take the Book of Thoth, for example. Thoth was an Egyptian god with an ibis head. An ibis looks like a crane. For a long time, treasure hunters searched in tombs by digging behind walls showing hieroglyphs of either Thoth or the ibis, but as time passed, they started looking in other parts of the world, thinking that the book had been secreted out of Egypt. The crane is an important symbol in Asian mythology too."

"But King Arthur's sword never left Great Britain," Ella Mae argued.

"That's true," Suzy agreed. "When Arthur no longer needed it, it was returned to the women charged with guarding it. The priestesses of Avonlea. Learning the real story of that sword has made me approach this research differently. I think the guardians are the key. Who's responsible for each object? Because whenever a magical woman is supposed to keep an object safe, she usually sacrifices everything to do so. And when she is no longer able to fulfill her duty, she passes the job to her descendants."

Ella Mae flipped through the top book on the pile Suzy had given her. "Medea. Circe. Cassandra. Dido." She looked at her friend and smiled. "At least I won't be bored reading about these women. They led colorful lives."

"You know what Mae West said." Suzy poured Ella Mae a glass of milk. "'Good girls go to heaven, bad girls go everywhere.'"

"I hope these bad girls left me a clue." Ella Mae raised her glass and knocked rims with Suzy. "Because even bad girls can keep a secret."

Suzy screwed up her lips. "Are you thinking of Loralyn?"

Ella Mae nodded. "If Opal wasn't sick, I wouldn't go out of my way to locate her daughter. I'm pretty confident that Loralyn will return to Havenwood of her own volition—driven here by revenge. She hates me now more than ever." Ella Mae studied an image of Medea casting a spell with her magical staff. "But she won't just march into town and shoot me. She'll want me to suffer as she's suffered. Which means that she's out there plotting and scheming. She probably married a millionaire on his deathbed and is using his funds to finance her own search for an object of power. And if she finds one, she won't heal her mother with it. She'll free her father from prison and watch him set Havenwood on fire. When every building is ablaze, she'll come for me and the people I love."

Suzy passed her hands over her face. "Good Lord, Ella Mae! If that's what you really believe, we need more help, and we need it now!"

Chewy, who'd finished his treat, sat up on his haunches and whined, alarmed by the shrill note in Suzy's voice. Ella Mae got down on the floor with him and caressed his fur. She continued to stroke him as she spoke to Suzy.

"Who would want to devote hours upon hours to poring over musty tomes and ancient documents?" she asked. "Who's willing to be shut up in a library for days at a time in order to follow vague and improbable leads—tiny threads woven through the tapestry of human history? Who'd volunteer to work on such an insane task other than the two of us?"

"Book Nerds," Suzy said. She gave the computer an affectionate pat. "I've been trading information with a few special people for years. People like me. Bibliophiles whose hobby has been the study of material related to our kind. If I asked, these folks would leap at the chance to be involved in this quest. Put a roof over their heads and keep them fed and they'd see it as a vacation." Suzy's computer dinged, signaling the arrival of another e-mail. "We can't do this alone, Ella Mae. New information is coming in all the time. We need the Book Nerds."

"Call them," Ella Mae said. "We have plenty of room in Partridge Hill and I can certainly provide them with good food. But you have to warn them that there's a risk in being here. People tend to get hurt when they're around me."

Suzy shook her head dismissively. "That was before you lost your magic. They're perfectly safe. The worst that can happen is that someone will sit on their reading glasses or spill coffee on their favorite bookmark."

"I'm sure you're right," Ella Mae said and turned away before Suzy could see the flicker of doubt in her eyes.

Chapter 5

Suzy's "Book Nerds" arrived during the third week of June.
Lydia Park, a petite Korean woman in her early thirties who
owned a bookstore in Northern California, showed up first.
Madge Stutsman, a special collections librarian at Columbia
University, came next. Madge had taken a leave of absence
in order to spend the summer in Havenwood, and she assured
Ella Mae that she'd been looking for an excuse to flee New
York City for a spell when she got Suzy's call.

"I've been working in the same library for nearly thirty
years," she told Ella Mae and Adelaide over cocktails on the
patio. "It's been ages since I took a vacation. There are always
too many books and manuscripts requiring my attention."
She smiled. "I think my boss was glad to see me go. Without
the musty old lady around, I suspect there'll be parties in the
stacks every day."

"Well, we're grateful to have you," Adelaide had said to

their guest. "Is there anything we can do to make your stay more comfortable?"

Madge had one request in particular. "I'd like to Facetime my cats once a day. I am a self-confessed crazy cat lady and I won't be able to work without knowing that they're being properly cared for. I'd rather speak to them without Miss Lulu or Charleston Chew contributing to the conversation. Is there a quiet place for me to make these calls?"

"You can use my late husband's study," Adelaide said. "The dogs aren't allowed inside and the walls are very thick. You'll have all the privacy you need."

The last of Suzy's friends to knock on Partridge Hill's door was a professor of history from Oxford University. Henry Matthews wore silver spectacles and a bow tie. Upon entering Partridge Hill, he bent over Adelaide's hand as though he were a knight and she, his lady. A taciturn man in his late sixties, he lit up like a lamp whenever Adelaide was around. Ella Mae took an instant liking to the professor. A brilliant scholar, he described historical events with such detail and passion that she could readily picture them in her mind.

"Your students are lucky," she told Henry one evening as she studied another obscure book on floral symbols. "You make history leap off the page by infusing every battle, marriage, and diplomatic treaty with energy and color. The topics I once viewed as black and white—all those dates and facts— transform into vibrant people, places, and feelings. Is that your gift? Being able to make people visualize historical events?"

Henry had smiled at her. "No, but thank you for the compliment. My ability is being able to catch brief glimpses of the past. This occurs when I touch certain objects."

Ella Mae wished Henry had been in Havenwood earlier. He could have touched the items in Bea's hotel room. Perhaps he'd have seen what happened to her the night she died.

Believing his ability might still prove useful, Ella Mae had asked Henry if he'd be willing to touch something belonging to Loralyn.

"I doubt my gift would help you find her," he'd answered. "I might see her as a child, as a high school student, or as she was six months ago. Considering she hasn't touched anything in her house recently, I don't think I'd be of much use."

Ella Mae had replayed that conversation many times since then. Even now, as she sat at the end of the dock with Hugh, she returned to it.

"You're drifting away again," Hugh said, sliding his arm around her waist.

Caught out, she smiled at him. "Just a little."

"What are you thinking about?"

Taking his hand in hers, she raised it to the star-filled sky. "When you left Havenwood to search for an object to restore your powers, how did you decide where to go first? How did you navigate?"

Hugh's jaw tightened. He was still reluctant to speak of his journey. "I'm not as smart as Suzy's friends, but there are so many Greek myths about magical weapons that I decided to start my search in Greece. I didn't have access to the materials those book people do, so I had to convince the locals of whichever town I was visiting to trust me. To share their local legends. Loralyn might be doing the same thing. However, she has a magical advantage, and you can bet that she's using her siren's powers to get people to tell her what she wants to know."

"You were friends with her when we were kids—one of the few people she genuinely liked." Releasing Hugh's hand, Ella Mae continued to stare at the stars. "Can you think of something she might have touched before leaving town? Something she felt sentimental about?"

"I'm not sure if she really liked me, Ella Mae, or if she just manipulated me the way she manipulated dozens of other men. It's what she does. And no, I have no idea what she might have touched." Hugh stretched out on the dock and slid his hands under his head. In the moonlight, his face looked like sculpted marble, and Ella Mae touched him to reassure herself that his skin was warm. He grabbed her wrist and pulled her down to him. For a while, neither of them spoke.

A loud splash from the middle of the lake caught their attention.

"Do you miss it? Being a water elemental?" Ella Mae whispered. "Tell me the truth."

"The memories fade a bit each day," he said, sitting up to gaze out at the dark water. "It's almost as though that life belonged to someone else. When I'm at Canine to Five, or hanging out with the crew at the fire station, I can't believe I used to be so different." He turned to her. "What about you?"

Ella Mae glanced up at the hills. "My one regret is that I can't enter the grove again. There's nothing like it in our world, Hugh. It has a lavender sky and velveteen grass. The air is perfumed with jasmine and the trees in the orchard bear gold or silver apples. There's a rolling meadow dotted with hundreds of wildflowers and a veritable rainbow of butterflies. And it's always the right temperature. No matter what the season on this side of the barrier, it's beautiful inside the grove." She paused. "And I'll never see it again."

Hugh squeezed her hand. "I'm sorry."

She shook her head. "Don't be. You gave up an entire world of mystery too. You could explore the depths of any ocean. Any river or lake. But we have a new adventure to look forward to—the one we're taking together."

"I just wish I could help find Loralyn," Hugh said. "Memories of my own search are really fragmented. So are those last days I spent with Loralyn. They're fading too—probably because I was under a spell then. What I do remember is her motive for fighting you. She wants to free her father. And because that's her goal, I believe she'd visit him before setting off on a long journey. I'm not sure if the professor could get a reading from Jarvis Gaynor, but it might be worth a shot."

Ella Mae's eyes widened. "I think you're on to something! I'll ask Verena to have Buddy make a few calls. If we can confirm that Loralyn stopped to visit Jarvis, it would be a start. There's no point in taking Henry to the prison unless Loralyn brought her father an object, and I don't think prisoners are allowed gifts."

Hugh shrugged. "A letter maybe?"

"Which he'd never show me," Ella Mae said dismally. "I'm the reason he's incarcerated in the first place."

"Too bad you don't know the warden. You could have Jarvis's cell tossed," Hugh joked. "Seriously, though. Tackle one thing at a time. Find out if Loralyn stopped by. If so, enlist someone else to talk to Jarvis. He's always had a weakness for pretty blondes."

Ella Mae pursed her lips in disapproval. "So he has. And that weakness tore his family apart. Unfortunately, the prettiest blonde I know would like nothing more than to plunge a dagger into Jarvis's heart."

"Jenny?"

"Yes. Not only did Jarvis reduce her Tennessee grove to ash, but he also killed her best friend. She hates that man more than any person on this earth."

Hugh brushed a strand of hair off Ella Mae's cheek. "But she loves you. If you need her help, she'll give it to you."

As it turned out, Ella Mae never had the chance to ask Jenny. Buddy and the prison warden were college buddies who'd kept in touch through the years. So when Verena convinced her husband to make inquiries about Jarvis Gaynor, the warden was happy to oblige. He told them that Jarvis had received only one visitor since his incarceration and zero correspondence. He spent most of his time reading books from the prison library and, when forced to join the other inmates in the dining hall or exercise yard, kept to himself.

"I wish more of my inmates were like Jarvis Gaynor," the warden had told Uncle Buddy.

Verena had snorted in response to this comment. "He wouldn't say that if he knew about Jarvis's *fiery* temper!"

Buddy learned that Jarvis's sole visitor had been Loralyn. However, her visit had occurred shortly after her father's sentencing and Jarvis had refused to see her.

"He's a cruel man," Ella Mae muttered, recalling the scene in the Gaynors' library when Jarvis had told Opal and Loralyn that he'd tried to sire a son with another woman because he was disappointed with his current wife and child. He'd committed arson and murder in an attempt to replace one family with another. This declaration should have made Loralyn loathe him. Instead, she blamed Opal for the ruination of their family and vowed to secure her father's freedom.

With another plan thwarted, Ella Mae returned to Partridge Hill and told Henry Matthews that his gift was her best and only chance of finding a clue that would lead her to Loralyn.

"I'm willing to accompany you to her home," the professor said after reluctantly closing the book he'd been reading. "But the exercise may prove futile. The young lady could have been thinking all manner of things before she left. You already told me that she was physically weak—drained of her power—and possibly filled with anger and shame as well."

"More like fury and humiliation," Ella Mae murmured.

Henry spread his hands. "There you have it. Should I be

fortunate enough to handle something Loralyn touched prior to her departure, I may only read a tumult of emotions. I don't expect to see a road map with a town circled in red ink."

"I know," Ella Mae said. "And while I realize that what you're doing here is very important, it's already July." She glanced at the wall calendar Suzy had tacked to one of the whiteboards now hanging in the library. "Opal's fading."

Following her gaze, Henry nodded solemnly. "We'll go tomorrow."

Ella Mae hadn't been to Rolling View for two weeks, and she was pleasantly surprised to see a battalion of groundskeepers tending to the lawn and flowerbeds. Horses were being exercised in the rings outside the stables, and a housekeeper in a starched uniform met Ella Mae and Henry at the front door.

"Good morning, Ms. LeFaye," the woman said cheerfully. "Mrs. Gaynor is finishing her acupuncture treatment and asked me to show you to the sunroom. She and Dr. Kang will be down directly."

The housekeeper led them past a center table featuring an enormous arrangement of chrysanthemums. As they walked down the hall, Ella Mae noticed the flowers in every room. She'd never seen so many shades or varieties of chrysanthemums in one place.

"Has Mrs. Gaynor developed a sudden fondness for mums?" she asked the housekeeper.

"The doctor uses them to treat Mrs. Gaynor," the housekeeper answered. "None of us understand exactly how he does it, but we don't care. He's the first person to give her any relief in weeks. She's finally eating a little, and yesterday, she even went for a short walk."

Ella Mae smiled over this news. "That's wonderful."

"I've laid out her favorite treats for tea, but Dr. Kang will decide what she can eat. He says her treatment is about balance." She pointed at a porcelain teapot and a glass pitcher of iced tea. "There's hot English breakfast or cold peach tea. The doctor will have a special herbal tea for Mrs. Gaynor. They should be along shortly."

Henry helped himself to several finger sandwiches and shortbread cookies before selecting a chair near a potted fern. Ella Mae, who was too distracted by the news about Opal and the presence of the mysterious Dr. Kang to focus on the tea spread, walked over to a tall vase of golden chrysanthemums and leaned in to sniff the flowers.

"Good for boosting digestion and increasing blood flow to the heart."

Ella Mae glanced up to find an elderly Chinese man standing in the doorway next to Opal Gaynor. He was small and stooped with powder-white hair, and his gaze was sharp and intelligent. He wore black pants and a red shirt with a dragon embroidered on the lower right side. Though Opal was dressed in similar garb, her moss-green shirt and pants were unadorned and appeared to be made of cotton.

Opal looked much better than she had when Ella Mae had last visited Rolling View. Her face was a touch fuller and her skin wasn't as sallow.

"This is Dr. Kang," Opal said. "He came from China to treat me, and I am very fortunate that he was willing to take my case."

Dr. Kang bowed to Henry, who politely returned the gesture. He then bowed even more deeply to Ella Mae. "It is an honor to meet you, Queen of the Clovers."

"The honor is mine." Ella Mae waved a hand at Opal. "We're very grateful that you've come to help our friend."

"Sit now," the doctor commanded in a whisper-thin voice and Opal instantly complied. "Ruiping will bring tea and mushroom barley broth. You must finish both. Sip slowly. Feel the heat of the liquid enter your body. Feel it warm your mouth, your throat, and your stomach. Feel it penetrate your cells. The herbs are warriors. They are entering your body to defend you. Relax and invite them in."

A tall, slender Chinese woman slipped into the room. She spoke a soft hello to Ella Mae and Henry, served Opal her tea and broth, and then left as silently as she'd entered.

"I practice *Qigong*," the doctor said once he was satisfied that Opal was drinking her tea. "It is an ancient treatment focusing on the energy flow in the body. Cancer interrupts this flow. Imagine a network of rivers blocked by debris. Pieces of trash prevent the clean water from traveling freely. That is what is happening inside this woman." He pointed at Opal. "I use many techniques to restore the flow. Herbs, food, acupuncture, meditation, cupping. I also possess a special gift. I can see which treatment is working and which is not. Therefore, I can customize my treatments for maximum results."

Ella Mae darted a quick glance at Opal, an unspoken question in her eyes.

Opal saw the question and said, "No, he can't cure me. No one can. But he can give me a few more months. Maybe even half a year. I'll be more like my old self. More importantly, I won't be confined to a hospital bed. And when the end comes, I'll go quickly and painlessly. Dr. Kang has promised me that."

If we find an object of power, you can be completely healed, Ella Mae thought.

Aloud, she said, "Professor Matthews is here to help me locate Loralyn." She went on to describe Henry's ability. "We'll need to explore her bedroom, but is there another place she might have gone before she left town? Did she have a favorite haunt? I know Rolling View is full of hidey-holes and secret nooks. Was one of these special to her?"

Opal looked grieved. "I don't know. Loralyn and I . . . we weren't good at talking about personal things. I regret that. I regret that I wasn't a more loving mother, and I want to apologize to my daughter for that. I loved her, but I didn't show it. Not enough. I didn't hold her in my arms or wipe away her tears when she got hurt. I didn't hum her back to sleep when she woke up, frightened, in the middle of the night. I encouraged strength, toughness, and above all else, pride. What did that get me?" She raised her eyes to the ceiling. "An empty house."

"Facing your demons is part of your treatment," Dr. Kang said. "It is good to say these things out loud. It exorcises toxic energy from your body."

After pausing to take a sip of tea, Opal faced Ella Mae again. "As for Loralyn having sentimental places or objects, I have no idea. In recent years, she's been focused on work and doing her part to increase the family's reputation."

"What about her nail salons? The managers haven't heard from her at all. I've called both locations."

"Things are running smoothly and profits are piling up in the bank, but Loralyn hasn't been in touch." Opal turned to Henry. "I'm sorry, Professor Matthews. I wish had more useful information for you."

Setting his teacup aside, Henry got to his feet. "Please don't apologize. It's a pleasure to spend the morning in such a lovely home. I just hope we don't upset the housekeeper too much by moving things around."

At this, Opal grinned. "Rearrange as much as you like. The poor woman is dying of boredom. With just myself, Dr. Kang, and Ruiping living here, she has nothing to do. She's accustomed to biweekly dinner parties, luxurious Sunday brunches, bridge nights, and book clubs. The monotony is driving her mad."

"All right, then, I'll make a real mess of things." Henry winked at Opal and moved to the door, where he waited for Ella Mae to accompany him upstairs.

"Once you reach the landing, take the hallway to the left. Loralyn's bedroom is at the end of the corridor," Opal said.

Loralyn's room was cold and vacuous. Ella Mae glanced from the gray satin sheets and the plum-colored blanket on the waterbed to the floor-to-ceiling mirror positioned on the opposite wall and rolled her eyes. "This is definitely a diva's bedroom."

"Right down to the crystal chandelier and framed prints of designer high heels," Henry said.

Every item in Loralyn's room centered on beauty or fashion. Henry's fingers traveled over makeup cases, jewelry boxes, perfume bottles, hand mirrors, and stacks of fashion magazines.

He suddenly pulled back, frowning.

"What is it?" Ella Mae asked in concern.

"She's not a very nice person, is she?"

Ella Mae couldn't count the number of times she'd been humiliated by Loralyn when they were children. "No, but you heard her mother. I don't think she knew much warmth as a girl. She was rarely praised, hugged, or kissed. And when she came into her gifts and learned that she was a siren and could manipulate people—men in particular—she didn't hold back."

Henry laced his hands together. "I often feel intrusive, catching glimpses of another person's life. In other cases, such as this, I feel tainted." He cast his gaze around the room. "I'd rather only touch things that might lead us to a tangible clue. These other items are clearly unimportant, and quite frankly, they're giving me a bleak outlook on the future of the human race."

"She's not *that* bad," Ella Mae said with a laugh. "Believe me, I've met worse."

There was a collection of framed photographs on Loralyn's dresser and Henry crossed the room to examine them. Curious, Ella Mae followed behind. She was unsurprised to find that most of the images showed Loralyn posing at one of her salons or with a celebrity at a horse race.

When the photos failed to provide useful feedback, Ella Mae pointed at an image of Loralyn and a Hollywood actress standing beside a magnificent chestnut Thoroughbred.

"You know, when Loralyn was in grade school, she was really attached to a particular colt. Her father sold the colt even though he knew the sale would break his daughter's heart. That horse went on to win dozens of major races. I've seen pictures of him in a display case at the main stable. Maybe we should check out that case."

Henry agreed, but he wanted to be certain they hadn't missed anything in Loralyn's room first. He wasn't comfortable searching her drawers, so he focused on the contents of her closet. As for Ella Mae, she had no misgivings about riffling through Loralyn's things.

Fifteen minutes later, she stood up and sighed in exasperation. "If there was anything of personal value here, Loralyn must have taken it with her. This place is like a giant dressing room. That's all it is. It could belong to any woman."

"Let's go down to the stables," Henry said, and Ella Mae could tell that he was eager to escape the glitzy, perfume-scented bedroom.

Ella Mae stopped by the sunroom to give Opal an update, but the housekeeper informed her that Dr. Kang had taken his patient back upstairs for a period of meditation and rest.

Ella Mae thanked her and said that, after dropping by the stables, she and Henry would take their leave.

"If we have any news for Mrs. Gaynor, we'll be sure to call," Ella Mae said as she and Henry exited the house.

The stables, which were cool and clean, smelled of fresh hay. Henry whistled when he saw the row of display cases filled with photographs and newspaper clippings highlighting the success of the horses born and bred at Gaynor Farms.

"They've raised dozens of winners," Henry said, clearly impressed. "Winners on major tracks including the Kentucky Derby, the Preakness, Belmont, Santa Anita, Churchill Downs. Ms. Gaynor is present in most of these photos. Which is the horse she loved most?"

Ella Mae searched for the chestnut gelding with a white blaze and three white socks. "Here he is. Loralyn's Romeo."

"Magnificent animal." Henry opened the glass door. His fingertips stretched out toward the photograph of Loralyn and the horse. For once, Loralyn wasn't posing for the camera. She had her cheek pressed against Romeo's face and her arm curled possessively under his head. A jockey sat on Romeo's back and waved at the camera, but it was obvious that the woman and the horse were lost in a moment that belonged only to them.

Once again, Ella Mae felt a rush of pity for her former nemesis. She was just about to express her feelings when Henry suddenly turned to her.

"I saw her. She stood right here with a duffel bag in each hand. She dropped the bags to open the case. She kissed this picture. Her eyes were filled with sorrow. And a cold anger." Henry gazed into the middle distance as he recited the details of his vision. "She wore jeans and a white blouse and carried a purse stuffed with various items. There was a small notebook sticking out of the purse. It was opened to a page covered with writing. I couldn't read the words, but I was able to spot a flower symbol. I don't know if the symbol means anything, but we should return to Partridge Hill so I can draw it while it's still fresh in my mind."

"There was nothing else?" Ella Mae asked, unable to conceal her disappointment.

Henry gave her a small smile.

"Like I said, it was unlikely that I'd see a roadmap with a town circled in red ink. We'll just have to hope the flower symbol provides us with a tangible clue."

Ella Mae brightened. "Luckily, I live with someone who is an expert on flowers."

"Indeed you do." Henry's smile became so radiant that Ella Mae knew he was thrilled to have an excuse to speak with her mother.

"Tell you what," she said, pulling out her phone and pretending to frown over something she saw on the screen. "Do you mind talking to my mom alone? I have a ton of things to do. I can catch up with you later tonight."

Barely disguising his glee, Henry said, "I should be able to manage."

He whistled all the way back to Partridge Hill.

That night, when Ella Mae, Suzy, and the Book Nerds gathered in the library to conduct their research, Adelaide joined them. She walked to the whiteboard positioned in front of the fireplace and stared at a crude drawing of a flower.

"As soon as Henry showed this to me, I thought of the apple blossom. There are other possibilities, but because he was certain that the flower had five petals and over a dozen stamens, I'm convinced that it's an apple blossom."

Suzy nodded in excitement. "That's a start. What else can you tell us?"

"This flower is related to the rose and is very, very old." Adelaide looked at the drawing with reverence. "There's evidence that apple trees grew in Jordan as far back as 6500 BC. This is an ancient flower. In terms of magic, that means it's very powerful."

"The apple is the symbol of immortality," Henry said solemnly. "In the myths of many cultures, the apple promises long or everlasting life."

Ella Mae groaned. "Not good. This symbol provides us with no leads as to where Loralyn went, but it suggests that she could be searching for an object that grants immortality. I don't think humanity is up to an endless future filled with Loralyn Gaynor's plots and schemes."

Suzy pushed a pile of books toward Lydia and another toward Madge. "Let's get cracking, friends. It's going to be another late night." She then passed Ella Mae the corkscrew. "We'd better skip the wine. Times like this call for coffee. Vats and vats of coffee."

Chapter 6

Henry was right. Apples appeared in the myths of multiple cultures, so the Book Nerds divided the task of researching the assorted versions. Lydia, who was the resident expert on Chinese folklore, volunteered to study the apple myths originating from China. Henry opted to tackle the Norse legends, while Madge and Suzy divvied up the Greek stories.

"Leave it to the Greeks to have three times the number as the rest of the civilizations," Madge said with admiration. "What overachievers."

"What about the apple from the Garden of Eden?" Reba asked. She'd dropped by to deliver the shirts she and Jenny would be wearing for Saturday's Row for Dough rowboat race. Reba and Jenny were representing The Charmed Pie Shoppe and wanted their outfits to be a surprise, but Ella Mae had overheard Jenny exclaim, "I am *not* wearing that!" several times over the past two weeks. Considering Reba liked to show off her assets while Jenny preferred loose-fitting clothing, Ella Mae couldn't imagine how the two women would ever agree on a design.

Suzy glanced up from a thick tome. "The fruit Eve gave to Adam wasn't identified by name in the Bible. It might have been an apple, but it also could have been a pomegranate, date, pear, or quince."

Reba pursed her lips. "I wouldn't have been tempted by a pomegranate. Too many seeds." She sidled up to Henry and ran a finger along his jawline. "What about you, love? What's a girl gotta do to make your heart beat faster?"

Henry's cheeks turned red. "Well . . . I . . ."

"Don't distract him," Ella Mae chided. "He isn't flipping through magazines at the barber shop. He's trying to figure out if Loralyn is tracking an object of power."

"A golden apple, right?" Reba smiled wickedly. "I can show the professor a lovely pair of golden apples."

And though Ella Mae ushered Reba from the room and closed the door, everyone's concentration had been broken. Try as she might, Ella Mae could no longer focus on the Hercules myth she'd begun to read in an effort to help Madge and Suzy.

"Let's take a break," she suggested. "My mother is making chicken and basil stir-fry for supper and I bet it's almost ready. Why don't you all relax on the patio while I make a salad with herbs and feta? I'll bring out some warm flatbread too. Henry? Can I put you in charge of the wine?"

"It would be my pleasure," Henry said.

It was plain that Henry enjoyed being the man of the house. Though Calvin still lived at Partridge Hill, he was rarely home. He was too busy working. This gave Henry leave to play the host opposite Adelaide. He selected and decanted the wine, carved the meat, and pulled out chairs for the ladies. He opened stubborn jars and reached for objects on high shelves. When he needed to step away from the library and its piles of books and stacks of documents, he looked around for things in need of repair. Ella Mae often entered Partridge Hill to find him mending a rent in the window screen, fixing a dripping faucet, or hammering loose floorboards.

Ella Mae was delighted to see how he and Adelaide had fallen into an easy rhythm together. After supper, the pair would wander through the garden or on the paths meandering by the lake's edge. They spent a long time walking and talking every evening, and as the days passed, Adelaide began to glow with secret happiness. Ella Mae hoped that Henry would be the man to finally put an end to her mother's self-imposed solitude.

"Stranger things have happened," Ella Mae murmured later that night as she crossed the lawn leading to her house.

Out of the corner of her eye, she saw a flash of white. It was her mother. Clad in a gauzy sundress, Adelaide had her arm hooked through Henry's. Their backs were to Ella Mae, so they didn't know she was watching when Henry paused beneath an arbor covered with climbing roses and lifted Adelaide's hand to his lips. He pressed a kiss against her skin and smiled tenderly at her.

The roses in the arbor, which had been the palest of pinks, suddenly changed color. Within seconds, Ella Mae saw a dozen shades of pink flow over each petal. The hues moved like wind over water—cotton candy, ballet slipper, blush, shell, bubblegum, flamingo, fuchsia, magenta—until they all shone with such an electrified hot pink hue that they were almost neon.

Is that what love looks like? Ella Mae wondered before hurrying inside to call Hugh. They hadn't made plans to get together that night, but she decided there was nothing she'd rather do than climb into a hammock with Hugh and lie there, whispering—or saying nothing at all—as they returned the resplendent gaze of a million stars.

The town of Havenwood had postponed its official Independence Day celebrations until the fifth of July, ensuring that the majority of its citizens would be able to enjoy the Row for Dough race and the food truck carnival following the main event.

With two members of The Charmed Pie Shoppe staff competing in the race, Ella Mae did something she rarely did on a Saturday. She hung a closed sign on the pie shop's front door. She wasn't the only merchant who decided to take the day off either. From one end of town to the other, storefronts were dark. It seemed as though the entire population of Havenwood, along with hundreds of tourists, had risen early to toss blankets and binoculars into their cars or bike baskets.

The Row for Dough event, which was established to raise money for a different charity each year, also created a flurry of side bets. Though not officially sanctioned, a chalkboard listing the top ten favored teams was erected at The Wicket, Havenwood's pub, and bets were placed up until an hour before the race. As of Saturday afternoon, the two teams favored to win were the Havenwood Police Department and the Havenwood Volunteer Fire Department.

"Damn chauvinists," Reba hissed as she studied the board. "We'll show them, won't we, Jenny?"

"Aw, it's not like that," said Lou, the bartender. "The whole town loves and respects you, Reba, but those donut eaters and hose jockeys have been training for this race for months."

Ella Mae was shocked by the derogatory terms, but she

quickly realized that Lou was trying to get a rise out of the police and firemen gathered near the pool table.

"What was that, Lou?" one of the cops asked.

Lou grinned. "I finally got your attention! Good! You're all going to be late for the beginning of the race if you don't hightail it out of here. You too, ladies," he added, making a shooing motion with his dishrag. "Just don't start without me! With so much money riding on this race, I need to make sure it's a clean one."

"If anyone cheats, I'll knock their teeth out with an oar," Reba said and headed for the door.

Lou saluted her with an empty pint glass. "You're my kind of lady," he said. "Feisty as a chili pepper and sparkly as a firecracker. Why don't you come back after the race? I bet you'll be thirsty."

"Oh, I'll be here." Reba gave him a saucy wink. "But not to drink. I'll need to collect my winnin's."

Ella Mae accompanied Reba and Jenny to the contestant area, where her uncle, Mayor Buddy, was waiting to give a rallying speech. The funds raised that day would help offset the cost of the library expansion.

The Book Nerds had been so impressed by the architectural renderings they'd seen in the community center during their first week in Havenwood that they'd immediately signed up to participate in the race. Though only Henry and Lydia were rowing, leaving Madge to serve as their lakeside cheerleader, all three of them had had custom T-shirts made at the print shop in town. The front simply said, "Book Nerds," while the bold letters on the back read, "Lit Happens."

Over breakfast that morning, Henry let slip that he'd once helped coach the Oxford Men's Crew Team to multiple victories and still competed in races against his peers. Having only seen him in his bookish attire, Ella Mae was stunned when he donned his T-shirt, revealing a pair of wide shoulders and muscular arms. Henry wasn't built like Hugh, who had the physique of a Grecian statue, or Calvin, who was as brawny as a bull, but he was very fit.

"Which team will you root for?" Reba asked Adelaide as she and Jenny headed to their rowboat. "You have to choose between our team and Henry's team."

Adelaide pointed at her daughter. "Ella Mae has no qualms about dividing her loyalties, so I'll root for multiple teams as well."

Ella Mae smoothed her peach-colored T-shirt. The front was embroidered with The Charmed Pie Shoppe's name and logo in green while the back was decorated with an over-sized rolling pin and the text "This Is How We Roll."

Chewy, on the other hand, wore a doggie firefighter costume in support of Hugh and his best canine buddy, Dante. Unfortunately, he'd already wriggled out of the mock helmet and was on the verge of tearing it to shreds when Ella Mae snatched it away.

"That might be a sign," Jenny said, indicating the hat. "Maybe you should have worn a chef's costume, Chewy."

Chewy wagged his tail and trotted closer to Jenny, hoping for a treat.

At that moment, a voice burst through the outdoor speaker system, calling for the racers to head to their boats. Ella Mae was just wondering what was keeping Hugh when she saw him running toward her. His oar was balanced across his broad shoulders, and though he vaulted over an unoccupied folding chair, his eyes never left Ella Mae's face.

"I need a kiss for luck before the race," he panted when he reached her side. He dropped the oar and pulled her in close.

"Traitor," Reba grumbled.

Hugh kissed Ella Mae and then turned to Reba with a

serious expression. "Look, I'll take all the help I can get. Forget about what Lou's board says. You two ladies are the real threat."

Preening, Reba and Jenny hurried off to their boat.

Hugh stole one more kiss from Ella Mae before following them.

The largest boat launch area belonged to Lake Haven-wood Resort, and dozens of rowboats were lined up along the fan-shaped stretch of beach. Behind them, spectators crowded the lawn and docks, shouting encouragement to their favorite teams until the mayor quieted them with three blasts from his bullhorn.

"Welcome!" he bellowed. Buddy could match Verena's volume decibel for decibel. "Welcome to Havenwood's annual Row for Dough! Are you ready to have fun?" People responded with enthusiastic applause, whistles, and shouts. "We have a record number of rowers today, folks," Buddy continued. "So things could get hairy—and a little bit scary—out on beautiful Lake Havenwood today!"

This drew more applause. The onlookers relished the thought of splintered oars or capsized boats. For some reason, their lust for disaster made Ella Mae think of Bea and of the night she'd found the dead woman floating in that water. It seemed so long ago now, especially in the middle of a hot July day, but Ella Mae felt a momentary shadow fall over the festivities, as though Bea's ghost were haunting the shore in search of justice.

Buddy chuckled into the bullhorn, interrupting Ella Mae's maudlin thoughts. "Even though there can only be one grand prize winner, we have some wonderful prizes for the top *five* teams this year. Thanks to the generosity of our Havenwood business partners, we'll be giving away fabulous gift certificates and merchandise. And, of course, the first-place team gets cold, hard cash. A bundle of Benjamins! A group of greenbacks! A mountain of moolah! How does that sound?"

Having successfully whipped the crowd into a frenzy, Buddy paused dramatically. "But the true winner today is the town of Havenwood. Our library has needed updating for a long time—kind of like my hairstyle—and it's getting a serious makeover that will include a new children's wing, a technology center, a career services desk, and yes, tons of new books!"

There was an especially boisterous cheer from the librarians, who'd congregated to one side of the mayor's podium.

"All right, folks. Before my gorgeous wife, Verena, gets her hands on the starter pistol, I'd like to remind you that there is a cornucopia of food waiting for you in the library parking lot. Due to the number of food trucks, the lot has been closed to car traffic, so park in town and walk on over. If you require handicapped access, please continue to the library lot and one of Havenwood's finest will direct you to a special parking area. Okay, I'm going to let my wife's gun do the talking now!"

An anticipatory hush fell over the spectators. Even Chewy could sense the change in atmosphere. He raised his nose and sniffed, his nostrils quivering.

"It won't be hard to track The Charmed Pie Shoppe Team seeing as Reba covered most of her peach baseball cap with rhinestones," Ella Mae told Chewy. "I don't know how she talked Jenny into wearing one of those. And Hugh's team won't be hard to spot either. Not with those Day-Glo yellow shirts."

Pulling her binoculars out of her backpack, Ella Mae scanned the row of nervous contestants. She recognized most of the townsfolk and all of the teams representing local businesses. Nearly every merchant had entered a team in the race. Even Suzy had been talked into competing by one of the high school students she'd hired for the summer. Two boats down from Suzy, the WoodWorks team looked tense and ready to spring into action. Finn Mercer and Calvin Upton certainly had the most unique boat in the race. Hoping to showcase their craftsmen skills, Finn had purchased a rowboat meeting all race specifications and had carved dragonflies and leaping fish along both sides. Calvin, the master electrician, had then wired the boat so that tiny white and blue blinking lights glimmered just above the boat's water line, creating the illusion that Finn's fish were moving.

Another blast from the bullhorn startled Ella Mae and she jumped in surprise. Pivoting, she trained her binoculars on the figure standing at the end of the dock. Draped in a voluminous white dress with a red, white, and blue sash, Aunt Verena looked like a full-figured Greek goddess. And when she pointed her starter pistol in the air, Ella Mae could almost feel a thousand people hold their collective breath.

The report echoed across the lake and the racers leapt forward, shoving their boats into the water and hopping aboard. Some were less graceful than others and capsized within the first minute of the race. The moment it became clear there'd be no more gaffs to witness, the crowd quickly began to disperse.

"Come on, Chewy!" Ella Mae scooped her terrier off the ground, placed him in her bike basket, and pedaled as fast as she could, aiming for the trail that wound around the lake and led into town.

She wasn't the only one hurrying to beat the rowers to a choice viewing spot. The trail in front of Ella Mae was packed with cyclists and more were coming up behind her.

"Hold on to your helmet, boy!" Ella Mae cried, even though she'd already shoved the helmet into her backpack.

Chewy's tongue unfurled from the side of his mouth and his brown eyes glittered with joy. Ella Mae's feelings matched those of her dog. Speeding along with the other cyclists, she felt as giddy as a child. Many people had decorated their bikes with patriotic streamers and American flags while others added to the parade-like atmosphere by ringing bells or tooting horns. Ella Mae rang her own bell or waved hello each time someone passed her, and Chewy barked out a friendly greeting, his tail thumping against the handlebars.

Ella Mae was sweaty and thirsty by the time she reached the community park entrance. All the bike stands were full, so she deployed her kickstand and lifted Chewy out of the basket. After attaching a tire lock, she headed down to the lake's edge. Ella Mae wasn't concerned about her bike being deliberately stolen, but people often rode the wrong bikes home by mistake. This was often due to the amount of beer or hard lemonade the attendees consumed during the carnival portion of the event.

Pulling a beach towel from her backpack, Ella Mae searched for familiar faces and spied Madge sitting with Aunt Sissy; Aunt Sissy's boyfriend, Alfonso; and Aunt Dee and her beau, August Templeton. Aunt Dee had obviously offered to watch Suzy's standard poodle, Jasmine, as well as Miss Lulu, Jenny's Schipperke, until after the race. And while Jasmine was the picture of obedience, Miss Lulu was dancing around in circles. Ella Mae stifled a grin as she watched August try to subdue the high-spirited canine.

"Look here, you little black devil," August scolded Miss Lulu. "Can't you sit for five minutes? How about three? No, no. There's nothing in that basket for you." He pushed Miss Lulu's nose out of his picnic basket, but not before she managed to gulp down a slice of ham.

"Don't get any ideas," Ella Mae warned Chewy before putting him down. He gave Jasmine and Miss Lulu a cursory greeting before snuggling up to Dee. All animals loved Dee.

"We thought you might miss what promises to be a *thrilling* finale!" Sissy patted a rectangle of grass between herself and Madge. "We could have rented this patch ten times by now."

Alfonso chuckled as he stroked his dark beard. "But we never would. We even turned away the mayor."

"He needs to be waiting by the finish line anyway," Ella Mae said, spreading her towel on the grass. "Where's Mom?"

Sissy shrugged. "I don't know. We looked *everywhere* for her. She probably wants to watch her handsome professor in private. She thinks we don't know that she's falling for him, but it's perfectly obvious." Lowering her voice so that no one else could overhear, she went on. "Have you seen what the flowers do when the two of them are together?"

Ella Mae nodded. "The entire garden turns into a kaleidoscope of color. It's beautiful."

"For now, yes," Sissy agreed. "But what happens at summer's end? Oxford isn't exactly close, and Adelaide isn't fond of air travel."

"I hadn't thought of that," Ella Mae admitted, feeling some of her merriment dim. "It's been such a delight to see her happy—to see her open herself up to love after living without it for so long. My father's been dead for over thirty years. I don't want her to be alone anymore."

Sissy squeezed Ella Mae's hand. "Neither do I. And who knows? What's growing between Adelaide and Henry might just be magical enough to overcome an ocean's worth of distance."

"Speaking of water, dear ladies, we should focus on what's happening out on the lake." Alfonso pointed at the rowboats.

Ella Mae raised her binoculars and played around with the focus dial until she was able to find the lead boats.

She instantly recognized the yellow shirts belonging to Hugh and his fellow firefighter, and her heart leapt in excitement. "Hugh's winning!"

Sissy nudged her in the side. "But the team from Village Tire and Service is coming up *fast*."

"As are Reba and Jenny," Dee said. "Reba looks like she just got a second wind. Look at her go!"

Alfonso leaned over to Sissy and murmured, "A second wind or a special energy zap from Jenny?"

Sissy gasped. "She wouldn't dare! That would be *cheating*!" She darted a glance at Ella Mae. "You don't think she'd stoop that low, do you?"

"I hope not," Ella Mae replied in an anxious whisper. "It wouldn't be fair, but Reba's competitive drive can triumph over her common sense."

Peering through her binoculars, Ella Mae began to genuinely worry that Jenny had given Reba a dose of what Ella Mae referred to as "liquid sunshine." With one touch, Jenny could revive a person's flagging energy so that they were suddenly capable of running a marathon. "Or winning a boat race," Ella Mae muttered to herself.

"Don't count Henry out," Madge said. "He might be longer in the tooth than the rest of the leaders, but he's trying to impress a woman. Such motivation could carry him to victory."

"Hugh is trying to impress a woman too," Sissy pointed out.

Chewy barked and Dee placed a steadying hand on his neck. "That's right, Charleston Chew. You're the one wearing the firefighter costume, not your mother."

At this, everyone laughed and the buoyant mood was restored.

"Oh my, it's going to be a close finish!" August cried and

got to his feet. Holding out his hand, he helped Dee to stand. Within seconds, all the spectators were up and cheering for their favorite team.

Don't do it, Reba, Ella Mae thought as she watched The Charmed Pie Shoppe team edge closer to the firefighters and the Village Tire team.

"What happened to the policemen?" Alfonso asked. "So many people expected them to win this race."

"Oh, it was *too* funny!" Sissy exclaimed. "Moments before you got here, the cops collided with another boat and lost an oar. The other team isn't from Havenwood, and you'll never guess what product they sell."

Alfonso gave his beard a tug. "Donuts?"

"Yes!" Sissy squealed. "Isn't that too much? Havenwood PD played bumper boats with Sprinkles Donuts." Her smile disappeared as she squinted at the lake again. "Look! Finn and Calvin are making a final push. They're going to try to squeeze in between The Charmed Pie Shoppe and the firefighters."

Ella Mae saw Reba glance over her shoulder to find more competition coming up from behind and wondered what her longtime friend would do when faced with such difficult odds.

"Come on, Reba! Go, Jenny! Go, Hugh!" she shouted, but her voice was lost amid a cacophony of yelling, screaming, ringing cowbells, barking dogs, and blasting air horns.

Ten boat lengths from the finish line tape, which had been strung between two buoys, another team pressed in from the starboard side of Reba and Jenny's boat, giving them no choice but to angle their bow to port. This forced Finn and Calvin to adjust their direction, causing their bow to scrape along the side of Hugh's boat. It was only the briefest of contacts, but it was enough to reduce the firemen's momentum and the Village Tire and Service team surged ahead.

The noise from the onlookers rose to a fever pitch, and Ella Mae could see Reba shaking her fist in frustration.

But it was too late. The Village Tire team member sitting in the bow broke the finish tape with an oar and the crowd went wild.

As the celebrations continued, Hugh and the other fireman came in second, The Charmed Pie Shoppe took third, and the WoodWorks team captured fourth.

"What a dramatic conclusion!" Madge declared. "I should take more vacations. I had no idea events such as these existed."

"Only in Havenwood," Ella Mae said with a smile. "And wait until you see the assortment of food vendors. They come from all over for this race."

Alfonso cupped a hand around his ear. "I ate a very light lunch in anticipation of this evening's festival, so please enlighten me as to the delights awaiting me."

"If it can be dipped in batter and fried, it'll be for sale," Dee said. "There will also be gyros, Italian sausages, Cuban sandwiches, fish tacos, Korean short ribs, roasted corn, vegetable shish kebabs—"

"My appetite is suitably whetted." Alfonso reached out to take Sissy's blanket and camp chair. "Shall we, my songbird?"

August looked at Dee. "If you'd prefer a less crowded environment, I already prepared a humble dinner at my house. I just need to heat it up."

Dee rewarded him with a grateful smile. "You're so thoughtful. I couldn't imagine anything I'd like more than spending a quiet evening with you." She glanced down at the dogs. "Is it all right if these two stay in your garden until Suzy and Jenny can pick them up?"

August readily agreed then turned to Madge. "Miss Stuts-man, I hope you enjoy your first food truck carnival. Ella Mae, please congratulate Hugh, Reba, and Jenny for me. They provided us with a most thrilling race."

"They certainly did," Ella Mae agreed. She sensed Dee was avoiding the carnival because of her burn scars and wished that her aunt didn't feel the need to shy away from public view.

Their small group parted ways. Sissy, Alfonso, and Madge headed to Sissy's car to drop off their belongings before proceeding to the food truck area. Dee and August packed their things into a large tote bag, took hold of the dogs' leashes, and strode off toward downtown's residential area and August's charming brick townhouse. As for Ella Mae, she unlocked her bike, loaded Chewy into the basket, and pedaled for the library.

However, the paths were so crowded with pedestrians that Ella Mae decided to bike through town. Because most of the spectators opted to park at or around the community center, the business district was nearly deserted. Ella Mae flew down the empty streets, dreaming of all the sumptuous food she and Hugh would soon be sharing.

Suddenly, the ringing of an alarm disrupted her peaceful ride.

The sound was muted at first, but as she drew closer to Perfectly Polished, Loralyn Gaynor's largest nail salon, the clamor grew louder.

Despite Chewy's agitated barking, Ella Mae slowed her pace.

The salon's front door was ajar, and the rhythmic clanging emanated from somewhere deeper inside. Ella Mae peered into the dimness while retrieving her cell phone from her pocket, but she saw no one moving around by the pedicure chairs in the back of the salon. What she did notice, however, was that the door leading to the staff offices and the massage and waxing rooms stood ajar.

Just as Ella Mae was calling the police, a white sedan pulled away from the curb at the end of the block and made an immediate right at the next intersection. Tires squealed and a powerful engine roared as the sedan accelerated so rapidly that Ella Mae was unable to take note of the car's make and model.

However, in the seconds before the sedan rounded the corner, she did catch a glimpse of the decal affixed to the rear window. It was a glittery white flower.

A camellia.

Chapter 7

Ella Mae waited outside with a very agitated Chewy while an officer from the Havenwood PD entered the nail salon.

As she tried to comfort her terrier, Ella Mae focused on the camellia decal she'd just seen. The same decal had been affixed to the rear window of Bea's car. Bea's car had also been white. And like Bea's Cadillac, Ella Mae was quite sure that the car she'd just seen tearing around the corner was also a luxury automobile. The similarities made her uneasy. Did the break-in at the nail salon have something to do with Bea's death?

Ella Mae had little time to mull over this question for the alarm was silenced and the cop reappeared on the sidewalk.

"Was this a robbery?" she asked the officer.

"It's looking that way." The cop glanced down at his notepad. "You saw a white sedan leaving the vicinity, correct?"

Keeping a hand on Chewy's head, Ella Mae nodded.

The officer fixed a hopeful gaze on her. "And you're sure that you can't identify the make or model of the vehicle?"

"I wish I could," she replied with genuine regret. She was about to tell him about the camellia decal when he abruptly thanked her and headed back inside the salon. Deciding not to pursue him, Ella Mae dialed Officer Hardy's number. When he didn't answer, she left him a detailed message.

"I'm sure the responding officer has this well in hand," she added after explaining her reason for calling. "I just thought, considering the doubts we both felt over Bea Burbank's death, that you'd want to know about the decal."

After ending the call, Ella Mae shoved her cell phone back into her pocket. "Good Lord, Chewy! Hugh will think we've stood him up. This is no way to treat the second place winner!"

As it turned out, Ella Mae had missed the entire prize ceremony. And while Hugh was quick to forgive her, Reba was not.

"Who cares about the damned nail salon?" Reba railed. "What's a thief want from that place anyway? Cuticle clippers and emery boards?"

Pulling her aside, Ella Mae told her about the camellia sticker.

The scowl on Reba's face vanished. "Why would one of those club ladies be pokin' around in Loralyn's salon?"

"My question exactly," Ella Mae said. "And I've been so busy helping Suzy and Madge research variations on Greek myths on apples that I haven't gotten around to reading the Camellia Club's directory or the rest of the materials the club secretary mailed me. Tomorrow, after church, I'll be holed up at my house with that package."

"Why not start tonight?" Hugh said from behind her. "Right after we grab a bite to eat, I can put your bike in my truck. I'll be your research assistant." Hugh took her hand in his. "Back before we knew the truth about each other, you couldn't ask for my help when someone threatened our town. Loralyn's gone missing. And now, it looks like a member of the Camellia Club has broken into her salon. That sounds like a threat. Or at least, a mystery. Let me be involved. Let's work as partners this time."

"Because we have no more secrets." Ella Mae smiled at him. "Still, I don't know if I'll be able to concentrate with you around."

Hugh pointed at his chest. "Is it the Day-Glo shirt?"

"More like what's under it," Ella Mae said. "But I can't say no to the second-place winner."

Reba put her hands on her hips and scowled. "Jenny and I would have won if it wasn't for those idiots crashin' into us at the bitter end."

"I'm proud of you," Ella Mae told her friend. "You earned one of the top places without *extra help* from Jenny. Not only that, but you and Jenny will inspire other women to enter the race. No woman has ever won first place."

Reba's mouth curved into a wide grin. "Until today! You missed the award ceremony, so you didn't see the winnin' team in person."

"I know Village Tire and Service," Ella Mae said. "It's the closest gas station to The Charmed Pie Shoppe. The owners, Kevin and April Pillsbury, are good people. He always tells me jokes and she always has recipe ideas to share with me."

"Well, we assumed their rowers were two guys because they were wearin' red shirts and matchin' baseball caps featurin' their logo and a vintage gas pump," Reba said. "April's hair is real short, so it wasn't until she crossed the finish line and took off her hat that everyone realized *she* was the rower sitting in front. For the first time in Havenwood history, a team with a woman has claimed the top spot. And the story gets even better. Tell her, Hugh."

Hugh nodded. "The mayor gave a short speech and tried to hand Kevin one of those giant ceremonial checks, but Kevin sidestepped it and whispered something in the mayor's ear. The mayor had to take a moment to master his emotions before he could speak into the microphone again."

"Really?" Ella Mae couldn't imagine what Kevin had said to move Buddy so deeply.

"The crowd went quiet. No one could understand what was happening. April gave her husband a thumbs-up, but the rest of us were totally confused. Finally, the mayor cleared his throat and said, 'This weekend, we celebrate our nation's independence. And we all know that freedom comes at a price. Freedom must be protected and defended, and sometimes, the cost is very dear. As a way of thanking our servicemen and women, Kevin and April have decided to donate their entire check to the Wounded Warrior Project. Let's hear it for our winners!'"

Ella Mae felt her eyes fill with tears. "I can't believe the noise didn't reach me downtown. That's amazing!"

"It sure was," Reba said. "You know what else is amazin'? Barbecued baby back ribs. I could eat an entire rack after all that rowin'. Finn and Jenny are off somewhere sharin' a picnic blanket, so I need to get some food and then find myself a man for dessert."

"What about Lou?" Ella Mae asked. "He seemed keen on your stopping by the pub later."

Reba dismissed the idea with a shake of her head. "Date the owner of the local watering hole? Never. I like Lou well enough, but what would happen if things didn't work out? I'd never be able to go to The Wicket again." She waved her arm to incorporate the entire parking lot. "Besides, there are hundreds of men here. Men I've never seen before. Strange, exciting men. As different as the fare on the menu boards of these food trucks." Reba's eyes gleamed. "You have fun, kids. I sure intend to!"

Ella Mae and Hugh laughed as Reba disappeared into the throng.

Later that night, after a multicultural sampling that included red curry scallops, polenta bites, barbacoa tacos, shiitake mushroom dumplings, fig tarts, and Nutella pizza topped with chopped strawberries and crushed pistachios, Ella Mae and Hugh headed back to her place.

Hugh showered, fed the dogs, and shooed them outside to play in the garden. Meanwhile, Ella Mae had already opened the package from the Camellia Club's secretary and starting reading about the club's history.

"What's my job?" Hugh asked, joining her on the sofa.

Ella Mae handed him the directory and then patted the laptop on the coffee table. "I haven't looked at the ladies' pictures yet. I'll do that next, but could you try to find images of the ones who were absent during the photo shoot? I'd like to be able to match every name and face before these women arrive. I don't want to be caught off guard by any of them."

Hugh picked up the book and turned to the first group of photographs. "I'm terrible with names. I could never memorize this many by August."

Ella Mae pointed at the photograph of Bea Burbank. "If you'd found her floating in the lake, you could. If Bea's daughter had showed up at your place of work and poured her heart out to you, you'd learn everything you could about these women."

"Why Havenwood?" Hugh mused aloud. "Why did Bea choose this town for their retreat? Why was she killed here? And why was a Camellia in Loralyn's nail salon today?"

Ella Mae shook her head. "I don't know." She gestured at the directory. "Maybe the answer is hidden between the lines of one of the women's bios. Or buried in the club's rich and storied history. There *must* be a connection."

"Then let's find it," Hugh said and fixed his attention on the directory.

Ella Mae returned to her own reading, which proved to be quite fascinating. The Camellia Club was founded in the 1860s as a sewing circle. At least, that was the pretense. According to a reprinted letter from Mrs. Margaret Woodward, the club's founder and first president, the purpose of the Camellia Club was threefold: to broaden women's minds through education; to initiate positive changes in the community; and to perform charitable works.

For the remainder of that century, the Camellia Club was a place women gathered as activists, forward thinkers, and in many ways, rebels. Outwardly, they all played the part of high-society ladies. But behind the closed doors of Margaret Woodward's Sweet Briar mansion, they plotted to secure child labor laws, voting rights for women, and educational opportunities for both women and minorities. Theirs was a group far ahead of its time.

"You were living the Virginia Slims motto during the nineteenth century," Ella Mae murmured. The more she read, the more she admired the tenacity, patience, and passion exhibited by the Camellias. "I wonder if your club still has a hidden agenda or if integral parts of the founder's mission have been forgotten. I don't think the formidable Mrs. Woodward bequeathed her mansion to the club to merely serve as a site for garden parties and weddings. She wanted to be sure there would always be a safe place, a secret place, for the Camellias to meet."

"Are you talking to your book?" Hugh asked.

Ella Mae showed him a black-and-white photograph of Margaret Woodward. The image was small and grainy, so it was difficult to see her face clearly, but Ella Mae had an impression of dark, intelligent eyes; high cheekbones; and smooth skin. Margaret Woodward had one of those ageless faces, much like Ella Mae's own mother, making it difficult to tell whether she was thirty-five or fifty-five. She wore a white day dress with a tight bodice and a full skirt. Her waist was fashionably tiny and her glossy hair had been braided and pinned to the side of her head. A bonnet rested casually against her knee and she stared directly at the camera. Her gaze was challenging and her smile was enigmatic.

"She looks like a woman who could make things happen," Ella Mae said.

Hugh leaned closer to the image. "I swear I just saw her twin. She must be related to this woman." He flipped back to the previous page in the directory and pointed at a set of photographs. "All the women are grouped in mother-daughter pairs. It would be confusing to use this book if you didn't already know them, because most of the moms and daughters have different last names. However, lots of the daughters went with hyphenated surnames after they got married. In this case, you have Cora Edgeworth and Meg Edgeworth-Ryan."

Ella Mae studied the photographs. Cora Edgeworth looked a bit like Jackie Kennedy, but Meg was a dead ringer for the club's founder.

"Meg and Margaret Woodward must be related," she said, shaking her head in wonder. "The resemblance is uncanny. Meg even has the same mysterious smile." Ella Mae examined Meg's biographical sketch. "She's a smart cookie. MBA from Duke. Works as a hedge fund manager at her father's company, Edgeworth Financial. She also has a master's degree in linguistics. Wow. Look at her volunteer experience. When does this woman sleep?"

Hugh shook his head in wonder. "They're all like that. Not necessarily the degrees or the jobs, but the list of charitable works. If I didn't know better, I'd say they were trying to compete with one another—to see who spends the most time giving back."

Curious, Ella Mae looked at Cora's biography and then turned the page and quickly read the bios of another mother-daughter pair. "I wonder if the daughters have kids of their own. And if so, do they ever see them? These women, Savannah McGovern and Blake McGovern-Reynolds, must have been on the committee for every event the Camellia Club hosted over the past year."

"Maybe Savannah or Blake hoped to be elected president one day," Hugh suggested.

"Maybe," Ella Mae said absently. "If that's what it takes to be president, Bea's bio must be really long."

Hugh tapped the directory. "Go back to the beginning. The officers are listed in order of rank, starting with Bea."

Ella Mae turned to the first page, which featured a lovely photograph of Bea in an ivory skirt suit. Behind her, a pair of wrought iron gates opened wide to reveal a Greek Revival–style mansion.

"Atalanta House," Ella Mae read. "This was Margaret Woodward's home," she told Hugh. "Margaret was a wealthy widow when she founded the Camellia Club. Her husband died of yellow fever and they had no children, so she inherited his considerable fortune. According to this book, it was Margaret's idea to build their house in the Greek Revival style. Apparently, she loved all things Greek. The gardens were filled with Grecian art and statuary, and she had a huge collection of urns and other artifacts throughout their home. She sounds like a very interesting lady. I wonder what she would have made of Bea and of this surrogate daughter business. Have you had a chance to look up the names of the women who missed the photo shoot?"

Hugh pointed at a piece of scrap paper on the coffee table. "Helen Lee, Samantha Lee-Singer, and Lyn Croly. I haven't gone online yet. I've been too busy reading these bios and feeling like a poor excuse for a human being."

Ella Mae poked him. "Excuse me. Don't you *voluntarily* enter burning buildings to save people and animals? Dante wouldn't be alive today if it weren't for you. And he's not alone. You're a hero, Hugh. You'd never admit it, but I know who you are."

She leaned over to kiss him. He returned the kiss, and then his lips moved from her mouth to her jawline. When he kissed the soft skin under her ear, she shuddered. Holding her tighter, he whispered, "I'm a small fry compared to you. You saved the whole town."

Ella Mae pushed him away. "This is what I was worried about. How can I concentrate with you around?"

Hugh held up his hands in surrender. "I'll move to the far end of the sofa and place a tower of pillows between us." He hurriedly stacked the pillows until they formed a lop-sided wall. "There. Why are you still looking at me?" He pretended to glare at her. "Don't you have work to do?"

After tossing a pillow at him, Ella Mae finished reading the history of the Camellia Club.

It was clear that the passage of time had diminished the club's identity as a center for political activism and intrigue. By the middle of the twentieth century, the Camellias were mainly focused on raising money for scholarships and supporting the arts in and around Sweet Briar.

Having finished with the history, Ella Mae turned back to the photograph of Margaret Woodward.

It was your hope that all women would receive a quality education. You also strove for equality for women. All women. Not just the upper classes. And yet your club has always been populated by the crème de la crème of society. In your time, that may have been necessary. You needed the cover of propriety to advance your causes, but these days, there's no need to hide, so why is the club still so exclusive? There's no diversity whatsoever. Other than the surrogates, of course.

Ella Mae shuffled through the rest of the papers Julia Eudailey had sent. There was no information about membership guidelines other than a single line stating that membership to the Camellia Club was "granted by invitation only."

Releasing a sigh of irritation, Ella Mae picked up the directory again. Hugh was busy with the laptop and didn't glance away from the screen as she once again studied the photograph of Bea and the magnificent house in the background.

"An unusual name. Atalanta House," Ella Mae said softly, wondering if the title was some sort of play on Georgia's capital city. But then why not just call it Atlanta House? Why the odd spelling?

Ella Mae's gaze moved beyond the live oaks flanking the entrance gates, swept over the neat lawn with its ancient magnolia tree, and fell on the ionic portico, which extended across two-thirds of the façade. She followed the rise of the house upward to the frieze. In the center, a sculptor had carved a flower. "A camellia, I suppose," she whispered, but immediately changed her mind. The flower was the wrong shape and didn't have enough petals. Unfortunately, Bea's head partially blocked the flower's rosette, so Ella Mae couldn't be certain what she was seeing. She needed another view of the front of the house.

"Hugh? How's it going?"

Hugh glanced away from the computer. "Pretty good. I found images of both Cora and Meg and bookmarked them. Would you like to see?" He put a hand on the remaining throw pillows. "Or do we need to maintain our distance?"

Ella Mae laughed. "I can keep my hands off you for now. If you move the pillows, I promise to behave."

Adopting an expression of deep disappointment, Hugh swept the pillows onto the floor. He then opened a new screen and clicked on the page he'd bookmarked earlier. "This is one of the many charity events hosted by the Camellia Club last year. It's called A Shoe Up. It's a clothing drive for women who've faced homelessness, abuse, or other challenging situations. After receiving job training, they need the right clothes to wear to their new jobs. Cora and Meg were in charge of this event. Here they are in *The Sweet Briar Daily News*. It's the online version of the paper, which is great because the photos are in color."

Ella Mae studied the photograph of Cora and Meg. Both women were very attractive, but there was something especially captivating about Meg. Ella Mae's eye went straight to Meg's face. In the photo, Meg handed a young woman a garment bag while Cora looked on wearing an indulgent smile. Meg was completely focused on the young woman. She wasn't smiling, but her expression was sincere. Ella Mae liked that about her.

"Two dark-haired beauties," she said to Hugh. "Any luck finding Lyn Croly?"

"Not yet."

Ella Mae pointed at the laptop. "Mind if I borrow that for a second? I want to see if I can locate other images of the fanciest clubhouse in the South."

Hugh stood up and stretched. "Go for it. I'm going to call

the dogs and get them—and us—something to drink. Any requests?"

"Surprise me," Ella Mae said, her fingers already reaching for the keyboard.

She was so absorbed in her task that she barely noticed the noise of dog nails scrabbling across the floor or of their thirsty lapping as they drank from their water bowls. The sound of a popping cork almost made her glance away from the computer, but just then, an image toward the bottom right of the screen grabbed her attention.

"Is it time for a break?" Hugh asked from what seemed like a great distance.

When Ella Mae looked up from the computer, her eyes were glassy. "It's an apple blossom. The flower on the frieze is an apple blossom. Margaret Woodward was fascinated by all things Greek. Apples were often magical in Greek myths. This can't be a coincidence, Hugh. This is the *same* flower Henry saw in his vision. *This* is the flower Loralyn was seeking."

Hugh carefully put the two glasses he'd been carrying down on the coffee table and touched Ella Mae's hand.

His cold fingers brought her back to the moment. Her eyes came into focus and she grabbed his hand and squeezed. "There *is* a connection, Hugh. It's still not clear, but we're on to something. This is a clue. It must be. I have to find out how this flower fits in."

"How will you do that?"

Ella Mae passed her hands over her face. "By figuring out which Greek myth it appears in, for starters. If Margaret Woodward possessed an object of power, Loralyn might have plans to steal it from Margaret's descendants."

Hugh put his hands on Ella Mae's shoulders. "Slow down, okay? We'll read every myth if we have to. But not now. It's getting late, and I'm half-asleep. That race wore me out." He brushed her cheek with his fingertips. It was a featherlight touch, filled with tenderness. "And you've been burning the candle at both ends for weeks. You need to rest. Come to bed."

Ella Mae couldn't resist the lure of his touch. She shut down the laptop and pointed at the champagne flutes on the table. "What about those?"

"A grapefruit-elderflower champagne cocktail called the Sweet Dreams Sparkler. I found the recipe online and smuggled the ingredients into the fridge when you weren't looking."

Picking up her glass, Ella Mae took a sip. The drink was at once soothing and incredibly refreshing. "I don't think I'm ready to sleep just yet." She slid a hand under his T-shirt. "I guess there's just too much spark in this cocktail."

Hugh raised his brows. "You don't say? In that case, I'd better get you upstairs before it wears off."

And with that, he emptied his glass in three swallows and gestured for her to follow suit. As soon as she was done, he slung her over his shoulder in a fireman's carry and took her up to the bedroom. There was no more talk of camellias or golden apples that night.

The next evening, Ella Mae gathered the Book Nerds in the library and showed them the carving on the frieze on Atalanta House.

"That's the apple blossom I saw," Henry declared softly.

"And the name of the house is reminiscent of a famous female from Greek myth," Madge said, hurriedly reaching for a book. "A headstrong virgin named Atalanta who was tricked into taking a husband."

Adelaide, who'd decided to join the ensemble, cocked

her head to one side. "I'm not familiar with the story. Would you tell it from the beginning?"

Madge settled deeper into her chair. "When Atalanta was born, her father carried her into the woods and left her there to die. She was a girl. Therefore, he didn't view her as a worthy heir to his title or lands."

Suzy growled, causing Chewy to bolt upright in alarm. "Too bad he wasn't mauled by a bear on his way back to his palace."

"*He* wasn't found by a bear," Madge said. "But Atalanta was. The bear raised her, and she spent her childhood in the forest, learning the ways of all the animals. When she grew older, she became a skilled huntress and was chosen to be one of Jason's Argonauts. She was the only female among his crew."

Lydia looked at Suzy. "I bet her dad would have been impressed if he knew that his daughter helped Jason find the Golden Fleece."

With a nod, Madge continued. "Atalanta's prowess as a hunter increased. Her arrow was the first to strike its mark at the famed Calydonian Boar Hunt. Her next triumph occurred when she defeated Peleus, a friend of Hercules, in a wrestling match. It was at this point that her father decided she was worthy of being named his heir and invited her to live with him. She accepted, and he immediately set about finding her a suitable husband."

"It really *is* a shame that he wasn't mauled by a bear," Suzy said.

Henry grunted in agreement. "The father is not a very likable character."

"Atalanta didn't want a husband," Madge went on as though her friends hadn't spoken. "She treasured her independence and the freedom she was accustomed to. However, she thought she could avoid marriage by challenging her suitors to a footrace."

"I remember her now!" Ella Mae exclaimed. "She was really fast. None of the men could beat her. They had to trick her in order to win, right?"

Madge held out her hands, palms up, as though they were scales, and then raised and lowered them. "Tricked or out-smarted, it's a matter of perspective. Besides, if her competitor lost, Atalanta was allowed to cut his head off with a sword."

Ella Mae touched her neck. "Ouch."

"She was the sole heir of a wealthy and powerful man. She was also quite beautiful, so she had no shortage of suitors. Unfortunately, these men were all defeated and killed," Madge said grimly. "Until a young man named Hippomenes came along. He prayed to Aphrodite for aid and was granted three golden apples. These apples were enchanted, and when Hippomenes dropped them, one by one, during his race against Atalanta, she felt compelled to pick them up. The delays allowed Hippomenes to win and Atalanta was forced to marry him."

Suzy smirked. "What a way to begin a marriage. I bet that couple had serious trust issues."

Madge chuckled. "Unlike fairy tales, Greek myths aren't prone to happily ever afters. There are several variations as to what became of Atalanta following her marriage. Some versions say she bore a son who went on to become a great hero. Some say that Aphrodite turned the newlyweds into lions because Hippomenes forgot to thank the goddess for the gift of the apples. But there is a lesser-known ending, such as the one written in this book."

The room grew very still.

With extreme care, Madge opened the dusty tome and turned to a brittle yellow page. "Atalanta outlived her husband by many years. She had the three apples Hippomenes used to win her hand woven into a belt, which she wore at all times, even when she slept. She ruled her father's land with a firm hand, but treated men and women equally. Her people called her the lioness." Madge looked up from the book. "That's it."

"There's no definitive ending to her story?" Ella Mae asked.

"No," Madge said. "An important detail is that the apples were never returned to Aphrodite. In every version, they remained with Atalanta. Whatever magic they contained was hers to control. My guess is that these apples originally came from a Grecian grove. A very old, very powerful grove."

"So we have Atalanta House, the apple blossom, and a connection to Loralyn and the Camellia Club," Suzy said. "But what do we do with this information?"

Glancing around at the others in turn, Ella Mae answered, "I know what I need to do. I need to take a road trip. On Monday, Reba and I are going to Sweet Briar."

Chapter 8

"What excuse will we give the club ladies for showin' up unannounced?" Reba wanted to know when Ella Mae told her that she planned to drive to Sweet Briar the following day.

"Weddings," Ella Mae said. "I'll explain that our catering division is rather new and that we'd love to see how the kitchen and banquet areas are set up at Atalanta House because we're being asked to cater more weddings at private homes."

Reba considered this. "Sounds reasonable except for one thing. Why would you drive all the way to Sweet Briar? There are plenty of places to see in Atlanta, which is much closer. These Camellias aren't dumb. They'll see through your ploy to get into their inner sanctum in a heartbeat, Ella Mae."

"Not if there's a second reason for our being in the neighborhood. You could have a sick relative in Statesboro, for example."

Reba frowned. "Then we'd better find a real person to

visit. I'd bet a week's worth of tips that someone at the Camellia Club will check our story. If they possess an object of power, they'll be suspicious of strangers."

"We'll cover our bases. In fact, Verena found us a patient through a charity she helped establish. It's called Crafting Wishes Foundation. It's an online wish list that matches the needs of patients in hospitals and nursing homes with people willing to donate handmade items. For example, if a patient asks for a quilt, someone with sewing skills can sign up to make a quilt for that person. No names are exchanged because of privacy laws, and each facility takes care of distributing the items, but someone from Crafting Wishes contacts the donor later on with an update on how their donation was received."

"A total win-win," Reba said.

"Yes," Ella Mae agreed. "Anyway, Verena signed us up to fulfill the wish of an elderly woman with Alzheimer's. The poor thing has no family, and she hasn't been eating well lately. She keeps asking for her mama's chocolate or blueberry icebox pie. I'm going to make her half a dozen of each. I figure the nurses can freeze the extras. I can add a little clear gelatin to the whipped cream to stabilize the cream layer so the pies should freeze nicely."

"Good thing we have a refrigerator unit in the truck." Reba watched as Ella Mae stirred a mixture of melted chocolate and sweetened condensed milk in a saucepan for a few moments. "Now I know why you're here on a Sunday, but I'm still worried about gettin' inside the Richest Housewives of Sweet Briar's Clubhouse. When will you call their secretary?"

Ella Mae turned off the heat and moved the pan to an unlit burner to cool. "Right after I get these pies in the freezer. You can help me by pressing the chocolate cookie wafer mixture into the pie pans."

Reba glanced from a huge bowl filled with a chocolate cookie crumb mixture to a second bowl loaded with chocolate morsels before pointing at a large bar of semisweet chocolate that Ella Mae would shave into curls and use to garnish each pie. "This lady must *really* love chocolate."

"The memory of its scent might increase her enjoyment. After speaking with Aunt Verena, I went online and read up on the symptoms of Alzheimer's. Often, people in advanced stages experience dramatic changes to their sense of taste. Sometimes, they can only taste extremely salty or sweet foods. Other times, the food they once liked is no longer appealing. I'm hoping that a strong scent of chocolate will help this lady *remember* the taste of her mama's pie."

As Reba began to press the cookie crumbs into the bottom and sides of a pie tin, she looked troubled. "I wish we could do more for this woman. Nobody should end their days in such a state. It must be scary. If there's comfort in the familiar, in the people and places we know, then what happens when those things vanish like mist? What anchors a person to the world?" She shook her head. "If I thought there was a chance I'd lose my memories of our years together, it would break my heart. Promise to feed me a poisoned pie before you let that happen."

"Stop talking like that," Ella Mae said and moved around the worktable to wrap Reba in a tight hug. "You'll still be filleting people with that knife-sharp tongue of yours when you're a hundred."

After returning Ella Mae's embrace, Reba smirked. "I'm not sure I want to live that long if Loralyn gets her grubby hands on an object of power that will make her immortal."

"Let's worry about finding her first," Ella Mae said. "If a golden apple is somehow tied to the Camellia Club, Loralyn will show up there eventually. If she hasn't already."

"That's what I've been wonderin' since the break-in at her nail salon," Reba said. "What if Loralyn snooped around the clubhouse and the flower ladies caught her? What if some of the Camellias are magical? You found their last president floating in a lake, remember?"

Ella Mae froze. "Believe me, I haven't forgotten about Bea. I'm hoping to learn more about her when we're in Sweet Briar, but finding Loralyn is my priority. If she's being held against her will, we need to free her and bring her home," Ella Mae declared, retrieving the blueberries from the walk-in for the next round of pies.

Reba mumbled something under her breath. Ella Mae caught the phrases "duct tape" and "trussed up like a Thanksgiving turkey" before she switched on the radio.

When all the pies were filled and Ella Mae had covered them with tents of plastic wrap, she called Julia Endailey and expressed her desire to stop by Atalanta House.

"I was utterly captivated by the history booklet you sent," Ella Mae said, hoping she wasn't laying it on too thick. "And since Reba and I will be in the area, I'd love nothing more than to see the house in person."

"Aren't you sweet?" Julia sounded guarded.

Ella Mae, fearing that the Camellias didn't make a habit of rolling out the red carpet for uninvited guests, immediately apologized. "I shouldn't have asked. I'm sure you're all very busy and it was rude of me to suggest it on such short notice. I look forward to seeing you in August."

Ella Mae knew she was taking a risk. It was highly possible that Julia would simply wish her a good day and that would be the end of her chance to get inside Atalanta House. But luck was with her, for Julia said, "We'd love for you to visit. When do you expect to be passing through?"

Suppressing a sigh of relief, Ella Mae gave her an

estimate and Julia promised to meet her at the house. "It's usually closed for cleaning on Mondays," she explained. "That's why I hesitated at first, but I can get a key."

"I'd like to make you a pie for going through so much trouble on my account," Ella Mae said. "What's your favorite kind?"

"Forget about me!" Julia laughed. "I'm counting every calorie until our retreat, but you could bake something for my husband. I've been so preoccupied with club events that he's feeling a little neglected. I've no doubt that a pie made by someone as talented as you would go a long way toward cheering him up. The only hiccup is that he was recently diagnosed as lactose intolerant. Up until a year ago, his favorite pie was key lime. Is it even possible to make a good key lime without milk or cream?"

"If it's possible, I'll find a way," Ella Mae vowed. After ending the call, she considered which substitutions to use in place of the sweetened condensed milk traditionally found in a key lime pie.

"I could use a blend of organic cane sugar, flour, vanilla extract, and either baking soda or cornstarch as a thickener. But figuring out how much will equal a fourteen-ounce can of sweetened condensed milk will be a challenge," she murmured to herself while jotting notes on a grocery list. "I could make a meringue topping. There's no milk or cream in meringue. Just eggs, cream of tartar, and sugar. And I'll change up the crust too. Instead of the typical graham cracker, a vanilla wafer crust would complement the meringue nicely."

Ella Mae spent the rest of the afternoon perfecting her lactose-free key lime pie recipe. It wasn't as easy as she'd initially thought. During her first attempt, she used too much water and the finished pie had a soupy consistency. After that, she was too heavy-handed with the sugar. Luckily, the third try was the charm, and when Reba popped back in to see how Ella Mae's conversation with Julia had gone, Ella Mae cut her a slice.

"I've had key lime a thousand times," Reba said. "I don't need to try it again."

Ella Mae pushed the plate closer to her friend. "Do me a favor and take a bite."

"Fine, twist my arm." Reba popped a loaded forkful in her mouth, chewed, and swallowed. "Same as always. Delicious."

Smiling, Ella Mae reached for the package of vanilla wafers. "Great. Now I can make one for Julia's husband."

Reba gestured at the package. "Why'd you buy those? Are you out of graham crackers?"

"No. I'm making this pie for a gentleman who can't tolerate lactose, so I changed my whole recipe. It was a good exercise too. I'd like to include a dairy-free pie on our menu every day. I'd also like to offer gluten-free and nut-free options. Lots of people have food allergies, and if they can't eat traditional piecrust, there's very little they can order at The Charmed Pie Shoppe other than salad."

"Which is only exciting if you're a rabbit." Reba glanced at her watch. "I'll be at your place bright and early tomorrow morning. As for tonight, I have a date with the dashin' Fernando. Of all the men at the carnival, I knew he was for me the second I saw the name penciled on the menu board of his food truck." She smiled at the memory. "The Naked Chorizo."

Ella Mae grinned. "Fernando? Reminds me of that ABBA song."

"Me too. I even sang a few bars to my hunky Spanish chef while he was fixin' me a special dessert, but he didn't recognize the song. He's too young. Even younger than you." Reba's eyes gleamed with impish delight.

Making a shooing gesture with her potholders, Ella Mae said, "I don't want to hear his age. Have a good time, but don't stay up too late. We should leave around six."

"Not to worry," Reba said. "Fernando can drop me off on his way out of town. That's the beauty of datin' a man with a food truck. His whole summer is booked up with carnivals and state fairs. He can swing through Havenwood every few weeks and light my fire, but other than that, ours will be a relationship without commitment. It's perfect."

After giving Ella Mae a saucy wink, she left the pie shop, singing "Fernando" and playing air drums with two licorice twists.

The next day, Ella Mae took one glance at Reba and knew that her friend wouldn't be doing much driving. "You look like hell," she said.

"I think I'm finally startin' to feel my age." Reba dug her fingers into her temples and moaned. "I can't handle tequila shots like I could when I was younger."

Ella Mae waved at her pink truck. "You should take a nap. I need you to be sharp when we get to Sweet Briar."

Reba slept for most of the trip, her face pressed against the passenger window. She only roused when Ella Mae drove over a speed bump in the hospital parking lot.

"Where are we?" she asked through a lengthy yawn.

"We're about to deliver the icebox pies," Ella Mae replied brusquely. After consuming two large cups of coffee, she desperately needed to use the restroom and there wasn't a parking space in sight.

Slipping on a pair of oversized sunglasses, Reba pointed at a loading dock. "Pull up there. I'll tell the security guard that we need to transfer food straight to a refrigerator. I bet you need to stretch and use the ladies' room after all that drivin'."

Ella Mae didn't argue. While Reba sorted things out with the guard, Ella Mae dashed inside the hospital and took care of business. She then located a nurses' station.

"I'm with the Crafting Wishes Foundation," she told a woman in green scrubs. "We have pies for one of your patients."

The nurse asked Ella Mae to wait while she made a quick call. A few minutes later, another nurse appeared at the desk. "Thank you so much for your donation. I know my patient will appreciate your gift."

"I brought a few extras. They can be kept frozen for up to a week," Ella Mae said. "Is there anything else I can do? This doesn't seem like much."

"But it is, honey," the nurse assured her kindly. "It really is. My patient has been hankering for this pie for ages. One of my colleagues tried to make it for her, but it just wasn't right."

Ella Mae looked at her doubtfully. "My recipe might not be right either."

"Only because what she wants is based on a memory, and memories are always better than what's in front of us," the nurse said. "Memories are golden. Shining. Without flaw. But it's what you put in the pie that matters, hon. The love you put into it. That's what she'll taste. *That's* what she's looking for. The memory of her mama's love. Don't you worry—a stranger's love can make her feel just as good. That's the kind of magic I believe in anyway." She smiled. "If you give me your number, I'll let you know how she reacted to your pie. We have your info in our system, but our computers are running molasses-in-January slow today."

Ella Mae scribbled her number on a piece of paper and handed it to the nurse.

"I have a feeling about you," the woman said as she turned

to go. "I think you're going to make a wish come true today. Bless you, sweetheart."

By the time Ella Mae returned to the loading dock, the icebox pies had been transferred and Reba was behind the wheel, waiting to drive.

"I stopped by the cafeteria. There's a bacon, egg, and cheese biscuit for you on the dash," she said after Ella Mae had hopped into the passenger seat. "Sorry about bein' such a lousy road trip partner, but I'm my perky self again now. I can drive for the rest of the day."

"Was Fernando worth it?" Ella Mae asked, giving Reba a little smile to show that there were no hard feelings.

Reba adjusted the rearview mirror and paused for a moment to examine her reflection. "Oh, he *was*. Did you program the nav system?"

"Yes." Ella Mae reached for her biscuit. "It shouldn't take us long to get to Sweet Briar. I want to get a feel for the place before I call Julia. We need to find a good hub for gossip."

"How about a good truck stop or a donut shop? Or a Waffle House?" Reba suggested.

Ella Mae frowned. "Sweet Briar's too ritzy for those types of places." She took a bite of the warm biscuit and sighed in contentment. Before taking a second bite, she held out her left hand, fingers splayed, and examined her nails. "I know where to go." She shot a glance at Reba. "You're going to relax for a little while longer, my friend. I'm treating you to a mani-pedi."

The nail salon closest to Atalanta House was called Eminence. When Ella Mae called to make an appointment, putting the phone on speaker so she could wipe biscuit grease off her hands, a haughty receptionist informed her that she'd have to wait because all the technicians were booked.

"We won't arrive for another forty-five minutes or so," Ella Mae explained patiently. "Can you put us down for the next available slot?"

"I'll see what I can do," the woman answered in a frosty tone.

Reba scowled, "You need to take the upper hand with the likes of her. She's used to the *Desperate Housewives* type. You'll have to act like one of the Camellias while you're in their flower patch. Basically, you have to be a snob."

"Can't I just kill her with kindness?"

"Nope." Reba tapped the map screen of the navigation system. "Reprogram this puppy to get us to Eminence, would you?"

Ella Mae did, and it wasn't long before they passed a sign welcoming them to Sweet Briar. "Look at that," she whistled. "This community has won the Governor's Circle Award as part of the Keep Georgia Beautiful campaign for the past twenty-five years. That's impressive."

"It's easy to be beautiful when you're rich," Reba said derisively. "Poor folks don't have money for rosebushes and pergolas. They're just tryin' to get by." Her scowl deepened as they drove past one immaculate yard after another. "Where do all the workers live? These people don't mow their own lawns and clean their own houses. There must be a set of railroad tracks someplace in this town, and I can tell you that we're on the right side of the tracks."

Ella Mae had to agree. The tree-lined roads were flat, shady, and clean. Groups of children rode bikes on the sidewalk. Women in straw sunhats pushed baby strollers or stood in their front gardens leisurely clipping snapdragons or gladiolas. The air was perfumed with honeysuckle and cut grass, and a cool river breeze provided relief from the summer heat.

"I wouldn't be surprised if the entire town suddenly burst out in a unified 'Zip-a-Dee-Doo-Dah,'" Reba muttered. "Is this place for real? It's all birds and butterflies. There isn't a speck of litter on the ground or a kid with an untied shoe or a dropped ice cream cone in sight."

"Look." Ella Mae pointed at a sign to the right. "That public lot will take us behind the block where the nail salon is located. Let's park so we can stay undercover for a little while. My pink truck isn't exactly subtle."

Stepping inside Eminence was like entering another world. Everything was white. Gauzy white curtains hung from the white marble floor to the white painted ceiling. They ballooned outward like wind-stretched sails, forming an elegant barrier between each of the pedicure stations. The technicians wore starched white uniforms and used soft white towels. Clients were served cucumber water from white lacquer trays. The only colors that managed to invade the space were the nail polishes themselves, and Eminence had shelves upon shelves of polish in every imaginable hue.

"May I help you?" A young woman whose icy voice Ella Mae immediately recognized glanced up from her iPad screen with a look of unconcealed disapproval.

Before Ella Mae could reply, Reba said, "I hope so. We have a meetin' at Atalanta House and we don't want to be late." Reba flicked her wrist toward the pedicure chairs. "You don't seem booked up to me. And yet you told my friend that you were. I wonder if the Camellia Club member who recommended this salon made a mistake."

Something shifted in the young woman's face. Whether it was Reba's abrupt manner, her mention of the Camellia Club, or both, there was suddenly no longer any wait. Within five minutes, Ella Mae and Reba were comfortably installed in cushy white pedicure chairs. They were then offered cucumber water and a selection of beauty, fashion, and gossip magazines to peruse during their treatment.

"That red is super bright," Ella Mae whispered to Reba when their technicians asked for the colors they'd chosen from the wall display.

Reba handed the bottle to her technician and then leaned close to Ella Mae. "It's called Cherry Bomb. You know I like to go into a strange place armed and dangerous. From my head right on down to my toenail polish. What did you pick?"

"More Than Meets the Eye," Ella Mae answered with a grin.

Reba nodded in approval. "Atta girl."

Their pedicures began and Ella Mae tried to exchange small talk with her technician, whose name was Traci. However, there was an overall hush to the salon and Ella Mae's chitchat was noticeably out of place. It seemed that the only sounds that were encouraged were the instrumental harp music and the gurgling of the wall fountain. And though Ella Mae couldn't see her neighbor because the gauzy curtain obscured her view, Traci glanced in that direction every time Ella Mae tried to initiate a conversation with her.

"We're going to Atalanta House for the first time when we're finished here," Ella Mae told Traci brightly. "Do many of the Camellia Club members patronize your salon? I bet they do. It's heavenly. I love the massage features on this chair."

Again, Traci's gaze slid to whoever occupied the chair to Ella Mae's right.

"We have many loyal clients," Traci answered politely and then clamped her lips together.

"We're meeting with Julia Eudailey. Do you know her?" Ella Mae pressed.

Traci kept her eyes on Ella Mae's toes. "Would you like me to cut these shorter?"

Foiled, Ella Mae murmured her assent and then turned to Reba with a shrug.

Reba, who had a knack for getting people to open up, had no success with her technician either. The women were courteous, but they deflected all questions about the Camellias by focusing on their work. Because Reba had mentioned their meeting at Atalanta House, their skilled technicians gave them quick, but excellent manicures from the comfort of their pedicure chairs. Ella Mae felt utterly pampered.

At one point, when both technicians stood up and explained that they'd be back shortly with hot towels to wrap around Reba and Ella Mae's calves, the client next to Ella Mae pulled back her curtain and whispered, "They're not going to discuss the Camellia Club with you because Traci's daughter has applied for one of the scholarship funds. In fact, she's a finalist."

"How wonderful," Ella Mae said, instantly recognizing the woman from the Camellia Club directory. "I wasn't trying to pry. I just want to get a feel for what they're like because I'm heading over to their house when we're done here. I'm a small-town pastry chef and these ladies are so accomplished. It's a bit intimidating."

The woman smiled. "That's very kind of you to say. I'm a member, actually. My name's Savannah McGovern." She studied Ella Mae for a long moment. "Don't tell me that you're Ms. LeFaye, the pie baker we'll be seeing in a few weeks?"

Ella Mae raised her hand. "Guilty as charged. My friend, Reba, was in the area visiting a sick relative and I asked to tag along in hopes of touring Atalanta House. I've only recently begun catering weddings and I need to learn how to arrange and serve food in an elegant house setting. More and more brides want their receptions in private homes these days."

"Didn't you see our online gallery?" Savannah asked. A shrewd look entered her blue eyes.

"Yes, and it was lovely," Ella Mae said airily. "Unfortunately, there were no photographs of the kitchen. The images reflect what the bride wants to see, but a caterer's needs are completely different."

"Ah." Savannah's glance returned to her decorating magazine as though she no longer found Ella Mae interesting. "Well, I'm sure Julia can satisfy your curiosity."

Recognizing that their conversation was over, Ella Mae thanked Savannah. By the time Traci returned with the hot towels, Savannah had allowed the curtain barrier to fall back into place.

Reba muttered an expletive under her breath, but not so low that Ella Mae didn't catch it.

What am I in for this August? she thought miserably.

When their services were complete and Ella Mae had paid the most she'd ever paid for a manicure and pedicure, she sent a text to Julia Eudailey saying that she could meet her at Atalanta House whenever it was convenient.

"Let's head over there now," Reba said. "Maybe the gates are open."

Ella Mae nodded. "I'd love to take a walk. I've been sitting for far too many hours today."

It was a relief to escape the hushed, whitewashed salon and return to a world of color and noise. After a pleasant, ten-minute stroll, they stood in front of Atalanta House's massive iron gates.

"Locked," Reba said, giving them a firm shake. "Wait here. I want to take a brief survey of the perimeter."

Reba trotted to the end of the block, turned right, and disappeared. Ella Mae gazed around the stunning grounds, but her eyes kept returning to the apple blossom frieze.

"The fence runs around three-quarters of the property," Reba said when she returned a few minutes later. "The third border is a natural one: the river. There are no signs of life anywhere. No gardeners or cleaners. No cars. I didn't see anyone movin' around inside the house either, but there are thick curtains drawn across some of the windows."

"There must be another way in," Ella Mae said. "How would the servants have come and gone during Margaret Woodward's time? They wouldn't have used the front gate."

Suddenly, Reba stiffened. "I heard a door slam. From up at the house. This way!" Reba took off in the direction from which they'd come. As she ran, her gaze was fixed on the wrought iron fence line. Suddenly, she stopped, reached out, and grabbed a clump of ivy. Pushing it off the fence rail, she smiled at Ella Mae. "Hinges! You're right. There's a hidden entrance. This must have been the servants' gate."

A woman's heels striking flagstones could be heard on the other side of the gate, and after exchanging a panicked glance, Ella Mae and Reba ducked behind a car parked by the curb and peeked through the car windows to see who was leaving Atalanta House by the secret exit.

The ivy-covered section of the gate swung outward and a woman with blond hair poked her head around the gate and peered up and down the street. Satisfied that no one was around, she stepped onto the sidewalk and closed the gate behind her. She was already walking away at a brisk pace when Ella Mae darted out from behind the car and cried, "Loralyn! I can't believe it. Thank goodness I found you!"

Loralyn Gaynor swiveled on her heel, her eyes flashing and her lips curling into an ugly snarl. "Damn you, Ella Mae. You always show up at the worst possible time."

Chapter 9

"Hundreds of people are searching for you," Ella Mae continued as though Loralyn hadn't spoken. "Have you been in Sweet Briar the whole time?"

After glancing up and down the street again, Loralyn advanced toward Ella Mae. "Listen to me, you interfering, maddening baker twit. You need to leave. *Now.* You have no idea what you're messing with here. Or who. And if the Camellias catch us talking, the months I've spent in this Norman Rockwell town will be for nothing." She balled up her fist and shook it at Ella Mae. "Seriously. *Get lost!*"

By this point, Reba had joined Ella Mae on the sidewalk. Seeing Loralyn's threatening gesture, she laughed. "What will you do? Poke us in the eye with one of your acrylic nails? For once in your life, act like an adult and have a civilized conversation without your usual pettiness. Your routine is gettin' stale."

Loralyn opened her mouth to respond, but at that moment, a white BMW coupe pulled into the spot in front of the car Ella Mae and Reba had been hiding behind. "Crap, it's Julia," Loralyn whispered and then turned to Ella Mae. "You need to trust me, okay? It's really important that you act like you don't know me. Pretend that we just bumped into each other in town and I was kind enough to show you where the house was, got it?"

When Ella Mae hesitated, Loralyn shot a desperate glance at the BMW. "Please, Ella Mae. You have to do this or I'll face the consequences."

"Because of the golden apple?" Ella Mae asked. "Is that why Bea Burbank was killed?"

A veil fell over Loralyn's features. She had no chance to reply before Julia alighted from her car with a big smile and a cheerful "Hello, ladies!"

Ella Mae turned to shake hands with Julia. "Thank you for meeting us today. This is my oldest friend, Reba. She also works at the pie shop."

"How nice." Julia smiled at Reba and then gave Loralyn an inquisitive look. "I didn't expect to see you here today. What a pleasant surprise."

To Ella Mae's ear's, the latter phrase rang with insincerity.

"I hadn't planned on being in this neck of the woods," Loralyn answered breezily. "But I happened to overhear these two ladies asking for directions to Atalanta House and thought it would hospitable to show them the way myself."

Julia nodded in approval. "Thank you for doing that. I'm about to give them the grand tour, and I'm sure you have a thousand things to do today, so we won't keep you."

"More like a million." Loralyn smiled at Ella Mae and Reba. "I hope you enjoy your visit. I look forward to seeing you again in August."

Wiggling her fingers in farewell, Loralyn pivoted on her high heels and walked away.

"The entrance is actually farther down the sidewalk," Julia said once Loralyn was out of hearing distance. "Did I interrupt something just then? The three of you seemed to be in the middle of an in-depth conversation."

Though Julia kept her tone casual, Ella Mae knew she was being interrogated. "It was my fault we stopped where we did. I was talking about how I'd met Bea and I'm afraid that I got a little emotional. Being here, in her town, has brought back the memory of meeting her . . . and of her unexpected death."

Ella Mae's reply wasn't completely fabricated. Ever since she'd entered Sweet Briar, Bea had been on her mind. When she wasn't thinking about Loralyn, her thoughts turned to Bea. And about Bea's murder. There were secrets hidden inside Atalanta House, Ella Mae was certain of that. The problem was that she had only one opportunity to discover those secrets, and her chance encounter with Loralyn had left her feeling flustered and confused.

You need to be sharper than ever, she told herself. *Julia will be scrutinizing your every move. Assessing your every word.*

Her one comfort was that Loralyn was alive and well. Ella Mae would keep her promise to Opal and bring her daughter home. Assuming she could find Loralyn again before she returned to Havenwood.

And then it struck her. What *was* Loralyn's connection to the Camellia Club? She wasn't in the directory, and yet Julia was unfazed by the fact that Loralyn had escorted two strangers to Atalanta House and mentioned seeing them again during the retreat.

She must be using a fake name, Ella Mae thought. And

yet Loralyn's photograph wasn't in the directory. *How could she become a member without a familial connection?*

"Here we are!" Julia trilled as they reached the front gates.

Ella Mae and Reba exchanged barely imperceptible nods. They were prepared to fight should the need arise. Ella Mae's handgun was in her purse and Reba had an entire arsenal hidden on her person. There were knives in her boots, throwing stars tucked into the waistband of her jeans, and a revolver stashed in an armpit holster.

Julia certainly didn't look threatening in her Lilly Pulitzer shift dress, and as she led them down the short drive to Atalanta House, pointing out interesting architectural details along the way, she was the picture of a gracious hostess.

"What's the flower in the frieze?" Ella Mae asked when Julia paused for breath.

Squinting against the sunlight, Julia said, "An apple blossom. Pretty, isn't it?"

"I thought it would be a camellia." Reba arched a brow at the carving.

"The founder, Margaret Woodward, was fond of all flowers." Julia continued walking toward the front doors. "She was going to call us the Apple Blossom Club, but some of the original members pointed out that apple blossoms weren't as quintessentially Southern as camellia or magnolia flowers. According to club gossip, and this is not the type of thing you'd have read in our history booklet, Margaret had a difficult time fitting in when she first moved to Sweet Briar, so she wisely listened to her colleagues and chose the Camellia Club as the official name. However, this house had been designed and built before the club was established, so her favorite flower is still represented on the frieze."

Ella Mae nodded. "Like I told you on the phone, I found the history fascinating. Margaret and her compatriots lived double lives. From the outside, they were a sewing circle for well-bred ladies. But in reality, they were so much more. Activists. Rebels even. I admire their courage and passion."

Julia made a noise of assent while focusing on the massive key ring in her right hand. Ella Mae noticed that the fob bore a series of Greek letters. Quickly, while Julia was preoccupied searching for the correct key, Ella Mae used her phone to snap a picture of the fob. She dropped her phone back into her bag just as Julia slid the key into the lock and pushed open the door. "Welcome to Atalanta House," she said proudly and ushered them into the air-conditioned vestibule.

Ella Mae immediately noticed the Greek key fret border carved into the baseboard and the plaster pediments over the doorways. Between the doors, small marble statues stood in curved niches. Ella Mae moved to examine the brass plaque attached to the base of the closest one. "Hippomenes," she murmured.

"Are you familiar with the characters of Greek mythology?" Julia asked.

"Only the famous ones," Ella Mae answered. "Like Hercules or Medusa. This man's name doesn't ring a bell. Was he a hero?"

Julia's laugh was derisive. "Hardly. He was a trickster. A cheat. In contemporary terms, he'd be the guy who slips Rohypnol into a girl's drink so she'll sleep with him."

Ella Mae pulled back in disgust. "Why have a statue of someone like that in a women's clubhouse?"

"To remind us not to be deceived or distracted." Julia raised her chin. "As a group, we need to keep our sights on the finish line. On our goal. For us, the goal is to do the most good."

Echoes of the Atalanta myth were evident in Julia's speech, and Ella Mae wondered if the mythological heroine was part of some club initiation rite. Was she used as an example of what could happen if, in Julia's own words, a Camellia was "deceived" or "distracted"? Either way, Ella Mae's pulse quickened. Seeing such obvious evidence of the Atalanta myth meant that an object of power might be hidden in the house. Ella Mae felt that finding the object and saving Opal's life were suddenly very real possibilities.

Reba was just about to wander over to the statue in the center niche—a naked woman either wrestling or embracing a bear—when Julia waved them onward in the direction of the kitchen.

There was no Greek influence in this part of the mansion, nor in any of the areas used for weddings. The rooms were elegantly and tastefully appointed. With their high ceilings and large windows, they created a sense of spaciousness without losing the intimacy of the house setting. Ella Mae could understand why so many brides wanted to hold their receptions at Atalanta House, and when Julia informed them that their spring and summer Saturdays were booked for the next three years, Ella Mae wasn't surprised.

"This garden is part of the reason," Julia said as she led them through the ballroom and out to a terrace. "Guests can relax here or stroll along the paths. There are numerous benches and statues, and when the lights come on at night, it becomes a magical setting—something right out of a storybook."

Ella Mae asked dozens of questions about how the food service was handled and took copious notes. The visit was genuinely helpful in many respects, and she knew that she and Jenny could improve how they set up their wedding buffets based on what she'd seen during her tour. However, it was clear that she and Reba wouldn't be shown the business side of the Camellia Club, for while the ground floor of Atalanta House was open to the public, the second floor was not. Both the main staircase and the servants' stairs were cordoned off with velvet rope and a small metal sign reading, "Private. No Admittance Beyond This Point."

"That's the end of our tour," Julia said as they returned to the front vestibule. She pointed at the staircase, which curved upward in a graceful sweep. "Of course, every wedding photographer wants to pose his or her bride on our staircase, but only a Camellia may pass beyond this point." She patted the banister for emphasis. "We've actually caught a handful of spoiled brides-to-be trying to sneak upstairs despite our express warnings that the second floor is off-limits. Can you believe the rudeness of some people? Their self-entitlement?" She rolled her eyes and then smiled at Ella Mae. "Sorry, I didn't mean to get riled up. Is there anything else I can do for you? Has your time at Atalanta House been well spent?"

Not quite, Ella Mae thought ruefully.

Aloud, she said, "Absolutely. Thanks to you, I have several ideas on how to improve our fledgling catering division. Oh! And I don't want to forget your husband's pie. It's in my truck, which is parked in a public lot in town."

"In that case, I'll give you a lift back." Julia opened her handbag and dug around inside. After a few moments, she became agitated. "Where is the damned thing?" she muttered. Crossing to a side table, she began unloading objects from her purse. As she did so, she cataloged each item. "Wallet, cell phone, sunglasses, mirror, *my* keys, lipstick, checkbook, blotting paper, perfume, protein bar. But no Atalanta House keys!" She looked around the vestibule, her eyes slightly wild, and then fixed her gaze on Ella Mae and Reba. Putting her hand on her chest, she released a nervous little laugh. "You didn't see me put the keys down anywhere, did you? After we came in, I could have sworn I dropped them right in my bag."

Ella Mae and Reba shook their heads in unison.

"We'll just retrace our steps and they'll turn up," Ella Mae said optimistically. "Don't worry about it. I misplace mine all the time."

Julia flashed her a grateful smile. "Really? It's a relief to know that I'm not the only one. Okay, let's head back to the kitchen."

As they walked, Ella Mae darted a glance at Reba, who responded with a mischievous shrug. It was then that Ella Mae knew Reba had stolen the keys from Julia's purse.

This made Ella Mae anxious. After all, Julia would eventually conclude that she hadn't mislaid the keys and that her guests had taken them. From that moment, Atalanta House would be under constant surveillance and they'd never have the chance to search it. At her first opportunity, Ella Mae signaled for Reba to return the set, but it took another three rooms before Reba pretended to discover the keys on the floor.

"Here they are!" she declared triumphantly and handed them to Julia. "It's that heavy fob. It probably got caught on the outside of your bag and just fell out while we were walkin'. We didn't hear them land because this rug is so thick."

Julia nodded absently. "I bet that's exactly what happened. Thank you, Reba. Let's keep this little incident between ourselves, shall we? The rest of the officers wouldn't be pleased if they knew I couldn't keep track of the keys to the castle."

Again, she laughed nervously, and Ella Mae felt sorry for her. Was Julia Eudailey genuinely frightened of her fellow club members? Would she be punished for accidentally losing a set of keys?

If a priceless object is hidden inside Atalanta House, then anyone with access to the mansion carries a great responsibility, Ella Mae thought.

Ella Mae was suddenly torn. Julia had been willing to

do her a favor by showing her around Atalanta House, and Ella Mae didn't want to repay the woman by getting her in hot water with the other Camellias. At this point, there was no hard evidence that a Camellia had killed Bea, and Ella Mae had seen nothing inside Atalanta House to indicate that they were up to anything nefarious. Perhaps it was best to reserve judgment until Loralyn could provide her with more concrete information. Deciding to focus on the fact that she'd found Loralyn, Ella Mae chatted with Julia on the short ride to the parking lot, handed her the key lime pie, and said good-bye. As soon as Julia was gone, Ella Mae got in her pink truck and called Rolling View.

"Mrs. Gaynor is asleep," the housekeeper informed her in a hushed voice. "May I take a message?"

But Ella Mae wanted to speak with Opal herself. "I'll call back in a few hours," she said and hung up.

Reba was staring at her sulkily. "Why'd you make me give those keys back? We could have been searchin' the second floor right now."

"No, we couldn't. Julia would have figured out that we took the keys."

Pulling a dagger from her left boot, Reba said, "And we would have dealt with whatever cavalry she called."

"I have a handgun, but you and I both know that I've never been much of a fighter, Reba," Ella Mae said quietly. "I'll fight *for* people. But hand-to-hand combat? That's your specialty. And as amazing as you are, you're no match for someone wielding an object of power. We need to be smart or we'll be killed." Ella Mae focused on her phone again. This time, she sent a message to Suzy asking her to translate the Greek letters on Julia's key fob. After attaching an image of the fob, she sank deeper into the seat and closed her eyes. "We have to find Loralyn. It's not a very big town. Where would she be?"

"Sitting by the oven in a gingerbread house in the middle of a forest?" Reba muttered. "Nah, she doesn't like children. She likes men." Reba glanced out the windshield. "It's too early for someone to take her out to dinner. So where would she be go to put her moves on the opposite sex? A country club would be my guess."

Ella Mae was impressed. "Good thinking. Let's see how many this town supports." She did a Google search and found two country clubs. One was clearly more prestigious than the second. When Ella Mae noted the name, she barked out a dry laugh.

"What is it?" Reba asked.

"We seem to be plagued by flowers these days." Ella Mae showed Reba the screen. "Magnolia Greens Golf and Racquet Club."

Reba snorted. "We're not exactly dressed in tennis whites. And if Loralyn's usin' a fake name, we can't pretend to be friends of hers. How's this gonna work?"

Ella Mae frowned. "I don't know. There's also a high possibility that other Camellias will be at this country club. If any of the women recognize me, they'll wonder what I'm doing there." She slapped the dashboard in frustration. "We've accomplished next to nothing, but I think we should just head back to Havenwood. I need to go through the club directory again. If Loralyn is a Camellia, she must be listed in that book."

Reba took the truck keys out of her handbag. She bounced them on her palm for a moment as though reluctant to leave Sweet Briar. "What will you tell Opal?"

Ella Mae groaned. "Good Lord. Loralyn doesn't even know about her mother. She has no idea how sick Opal is."

"That's not your fault. She wouldn't let you get a word in edgewise." Reba gave Ella Mae's hand a squeeze. "That's who she is. It's who she's always been. Her agenda has always been more important than everyone else's. Even if you gave her the choice between comin' home or stayin' in Sweet Briar in hopes of findin' an object of power, she'd probably stay here. Loralyn is not a girl with a big heart. Her heart is two times smaller than the Grinch's was at the beginning of the story."

"But his grew. Maybe hers can too," Ella Mae gave Reba a hopeful smile.

Reba shook her head. "Always the optimist. That's you. You kept givin' Loralyn second chances when you were kids too. She'd tease you. Humiliate you. Bully you. And you'd still invite her to your birthday parties. Some folks don't change, honey. Some folks are born mean and they stay mean."

Ella Mae recalled how much Loralyn had loved a chestnut colt named Romeo. All these years later, she still remembered how sad and quiet Loralyn had been at school the week after her father had sold that horse.

"I don't think she was born mean," Ella Mae told Reba. "She wasn't as lucky as me, that's all. She didn't have you. Or three aunts who doted on her. My mother might have been wrapped up in grief over my father's death, but I never felt unloved. Not for a second. I was hugged and kissed every day. I was read to and sung to. I got notes in my lunchbox and care packages every week when I was away at college. I had someone to run to when I was scared, upset, or worried. You were my safe haven, Reba. Has Loralyn ever had someone like that? She lived in a beautiful house, but she's never had a home. Her parents taught her how to be respected and admired, but they kept her at arm's length. It's taken a fatal disease for Opal to recognize the error of her ways, and if she believes there's still hope for a reconciliation, then I choose to believe that too."

Reba shrugged. "Suit yourself. But my throwin' stars will be ready when Loralyn starts misbehavin'."

"That's because you're always looking out for me," Ella Mae said. "Now let's get rolling. By the time we get home, I need to figure out how to tell Opal Gaynor that I found her daughter, and then immediately lost her again."

Reba was just pulling into a gas station to fill up the truck when Suzy called. Ella Mae put the phone on speaker mode again, enabling Reba to participate in the conversation.

"Sorry it took so long for me to get back to you with a translation," Suzy said. "The bookstore has been mobbed and my help called out sick. Somehow, I think her stomach bug had something to do with the cute boy she met at the carnival."

Suzy sounded as tired and grumpy as Ella Mae felt. "Don't worry about it," she said. "None of us seem to be having a spectacular Monday."

"I take it there were no epiphanies in Sweet Briar?" Suzy asked.

"Other than finding Loralyn Gaynor, no."

Suzy inhaled sharply, but Ella Mae began speaking before her friend could assault her with questions. "Before you get too excited, our conversation was about fifteen seconds long and it wasn't altogether friendly. Loralyn was quite flustered." She hurriedly summarized their entire visit.

"She must be after the golden apple. Or apples. There were three apples in the myth. Either way, something magical *must* be hidden in that house," Suzy insisted.

"What makes you so certain?" Ella Mae asked tiredly. "Because I feel like we're chasing shadows."

There was a rustle of paper on the other end of the line.

"The key fob, for starters. The translation of the Greek means 'everlasting.' Or 'eternal.' Take your pick."

Ella Mae stared out the window to where the sky was darkening over the Georgia hills. "Add that to the apple blossom carving on the frieze and the statues we saw inside the house—one of which was Hippomenes and the other of which was undoubtedly Atalanta—and these are either signs pointing to a hidden treasure or just that Margaret Woodward was a big fan of the Atalanta myth."

"Even if a treasure does exist, is it magical?" Reba interjected. "Or just something pretty, shiny, and dipped in gold?"

Ella Mae mulled this over. The Camellias were obviously interested in wealth. They married rich men and encouraged their daughters to marry rich men. It was only within the last two decades that the women had started acquiring wealth through their own means. They now sought high-paying careers in addition to well-bred spouses. They wanted it all: the impressive job, the happy home life, and a membership in the Camellia Club. They were greedy for success and fiercely competitive among themselves. But Ella Mae didn't think a golden apple would impress these women unless it had special powers.

"It must be magical. An object with healing powers. Or the ability to grant immortality to the possessor." She furrowed her brows. "So what's the meaning behind the fob? Is the Camellia Club everlasting? Or just a particular member?"

"The only way to discover that is to get your hands on club directories from ten, twenty, or thirty years ago," Suzy said. "The Book Nerds and I will start looking around for those. You'd be surprised by what comes up for sale on the book black market."

Reba sniggered. "Like what? Grimoires? Satanic spellbooks?"

"Of all varieties," Suzy answered seriously. "Drive carefully now."

Ella Mae hung up and pointed at the truck stop's convenience store. "I'll buy you a pack of Twizzlers while I'm getting our coffee. It's been a helluva day."

"Better make it two packs." Reba examined her freshly manicured nails. "After what you paid for our beauty treatments, it'll be more economical for me to chew on licorice instead of my nails. And I need to chew on somethin'. There's too much to think about, and as somebody famous once said, we have miles to go before we sleep."

That night, moments after Ella Mae entered her dark and empty house, the phone rang. She was tempted to ignore it. All she wanted to do was collect Chewy from her mother's place, take a shower, and climb into bed. However, when she looked at the caller ID and recognized Julia Eudailey's number, she felt compelled to pick up the phone.

"I'm sorry to bother you," Julia began. "You probably haven't even had time to wash off the road dust."

"That's all right," Ella Mae said without much conviction. "What can I do for you?"

Julia laughed. "Actually, I'm calling to thank you. My Howie was just wild about his key lime pie. He had no idea that it was a lactose-free version. After two slices, he was like a new man. He put a record on our vintage turntable and we danced around the living room. We haven't done that in years! It's because of your pie that we shared such a lovely evening together."

Ella Mae smiled over the image of Julia and her husband

kicking up their heels in the living room. "I'm so glad he liked it, but I'm sure there were factors other than my pie that influenced him to dance with his bride."

"Aren't you sweet?" Julia's voice sounded light and bubbly. "I don't want to keep you. I just called to express my gratitude and to encourage you to make that pie again. It was certainly a hit in the Eudailey household."

"I definitely will," Ella Mae promised. "May I ask you something before you go?" Without giving Julia a chance to refuse, Ella Mae went on. "The woman who was kind enough to direct us to Atalanta House. I'm afraid I didn't catch her name. Could you fill me in?"

There was a slight pause. "Oh, that's right! Lyn Croly showed you the way. I'd already forgotten." She laughed again. "I'm really not this flaky. Between this and the key incident, you must wonder what kind of secretary I am."

"An excellent one, I'm sure," Ella Mae said, reaching for the club directory on the kitchen table. She remembered that Lyn was one of the three members who'd been absent the day photographs had been taken of all the Camellias. "I now know why I didn't recognize Ms. Croly." She told Julia that Lyn didn't have a photograph in the directory. "And I don't see her mother's name either. Am I missing something?"

"It's a little complex for those outside the club to understand, but Lyn is a surrogate," Julia explained patiently. "Not all Camellias give birth to daughters, and there are times when our natural-born daughters prefer not to follow in their mother's footsteps. In those rare instances—and believe me, they are *very* rare—a woman may adopt a surrogate. This woman will become her true daughter in the eyes of the Camellia Club."

"Fascinating," Ella Mae said. "Who adopted Lyn?"

Again, Julia hesitated and Ella Mae held her breath.

Finally, Julia said, "Bea Burbank. Bea chose Lyn a few months before she passed away."

Ella Mae swallowed hard and did her best to keep her tone casual and cool. "Thanks for explaining this to me. At least I'll be able to greet Lyn when she arrives in August. She'll be joining the rest of you for the retreat, right?"

"Of course," Julia said. "In fact, she's one of the three women running for—oh, I don't need to go into our club minutiae. You must be exhausted. I look forward to baking with you in a few weeks."

Ella Mae wished Julia a good night and then collapsed on her sofa. "I don't need to hunt down Loralyn anymore," she murmured to the ceiling. "She's coming back to Havenwood. And when she does, she will make peace with her mother or I'll threaten to expose her to the Camellias. Whatever she's after, she won't get it if she's thrown out of the clubhouse."

Satisfied by how the day had ended, Ella Mae headed to Partridge Hill to say a quick good night to her own mother and to fetch her dog. She couldn't wait to spend the next seven or eight hours snuggled up in bed with her terrier, dead to the world.

Chapter 10

Ella Mae paid a visit to Rolling View after work the next day. In the privacy of Opal's sunroom, she told her everything that had happened in Sweet Briar. Not only was Opal Loralyn's mother, but she was also an Elder. Therefore, she had to be apprised of the possibility that an object of power could be hidden inside Atalanta House.

The rest of Havenwood's Elders were present as well, and when Ella Mae finished speaking, Verena turned to Opal and, in the softest voice Ella Mae had ever heard her use, said, "I'm overjoyed that your daughter is safe. And so very close."

Opal's eyes filled with tears, but she blinked them back. "All this time, she's been in Georgia. And yet she might as well be on the moon. I can't believe that I have to wait until August to see her." And then, to Ella Mae's surprise, Opal grabbed Verena's hand and clung to it. "What am I supposed to do in the meantime?"

"Keep getting stronger," Verena declared stoutly. "Prepare to fight for your daughter. We don't know what we're dealing with in regard to these Camellias. They might be coming to Havenwood for the sole purpose of enjoying their annual retreat and producing their centennial cookbook, or they could have a more nefarious purpose. We won't know their true agenda until I hear Ella Mae ask them about it. If they lie to her, I'll hear the lie."

"Can you explain why the Camellias pose a threat to our community?" another Elder asked. "Because if they possess an object of power, we should tread very carefully."

Ella Mae nodded. "This is a complicated situation, but in light of what Bea Burbank's daughter told me, I've come to believe that Bea was murdered by a Camellia. And because her murder took place in Havenwood and her killer wasn't apprehended, the return of the Camellias to Havenwood should put us all on high alert. A murderer is undoubtedly accompanying the rest of the Sweet Briar ladies on their annual retreat."

After exchanging a flurry of low murmurs, the Elders told Ella Mae to continue.

She balled her fists in frustration. "I've been unable to gather concrete clues to prove my theory about the murderer, so our best chance of solving the mystery of Bea's death lies with Loralyn. She's spent months among the Camellias." Ella Mae uncurled her fingers and looked at Opal. "She'll be home before you know it. Until then, stay strong. Keep fighting."

Opal thrust out her chin in a show of determination. Once, the expression would have irritated Ella Mae, but now, she was glad to see it, for it was a sign of Opal's strength.

"I have something more effective than medicine. More powerful than any enchantment," Opal told Ella Mae after the meeting had adjourned and the other Elders were gone. "And you gave it to me."

Ella Mae, who was also on her way out, paused in the doorway. "I did? What's that?"

Though the meeting had clearly drained Opal, she managed a small smile. "Hope. No matter what happens with Loralyn, I will never regret the day I pledged my loyalty to you. Whether you realize it or not, you are still magical, Ella Mae LeFaye."

The weeks leading up to August were marked by long, hot, humid days, but Ella Mae barely noticed the weather. Her time was spent inside The Charmed Pie Shoppe, where she conducted a flurry of baking experiments.

Creating reduced-sugar, dairy-free, and nut-free pies proved to be far easier than coming up with a gluten-free piecrust. Ella Mae, who felt that she'd perfected her buttery, flaky piecrust years ago, had to start from scratch. Not only did she have to try different flours—and these ranged from almond flour, bean flour, sweet and brown rice flour, a sorghum flour blend, tapioca flour, and millet—but she also had to figure out how those flours interacted with corn or potato starch. Sometimes her dough was too crumbly. Other times, it stuck to her worktable like glue. Once, when she foolishly thought she'd discovered the perfect blend, she tasted a piece of the dough and instantly spit the mouthful into the nearest garbage can.

"Another one bites the dust, eh?" Jenny asked, entering the kitchen with a catering order in hand.

Ella Mae sighed in frustration. "It tastes like egg cartons. I don't know what I'm doing wrong. I feel like I'm getting closer to the right combination, but close isn't good enough."

"You'll get it." Jenny settled down on a stool. "Do you remember how long it took me to roll out a decent piecrust? I was terrible, but you were such a patient teacher. Be patient with yourself. What you're doing is part cooking, part science, and part art." She tapped the order form. "So what I have here will either be a source of inspiration or a source of stress."

Ella Mae wiped her hands on her apron. "Is this a glass half-empty or half-full scenario?"

"Yep," Jenny said cheerfully. "It's a proposal for a wedding dessert bar, but the bride has asked for a selection of bite-size gluten-free pies. Apparently, the catering company handling the wedding is providing a gluten-free meal, but the couple wasn't wild about the company's dessert options, so they've turned to us. I told them you were working on a gluten-free menu, but that I wasn't sure we could commit to a contract right now."

"When's the wedding?"

Jenny glanced at the proposal. "October."

Ella Mae studied the mess she'd made. Flour covered the table and speckled the floor. Bits of dried dough stuck to her rolling pin, her hands, and her face. She was certain there were small pieces in her hair as well. "It'll be August in two days, which gives me two days to perfect this crust. If I fail, I'll have to tell the ladies of the Camellia Club that I can help them create nut-free, dairy-free, and low-sugar pies, but not gluten-free pies. You'll also have to turn down this bride."

"And if you succeed?" Jenny asked.

"Then my confidence in my abilities as a pastry chef will be restored," Ella Mae grumbled. "Because right now, I feel like a rookie. I don't think I could operate a can opener correctly at this point."

Jenny came around to Ella Mae's side of the worktable. "Close your eyes," she whispered and put her hands on Ella

Mae's shoulders. "Let me tell you about this bride and groom.
They're high school sweethearts and are super cute. They're
the kind of couple that finishes each other's sentences. They
laugh so loud and freely that you end up laughing with them.
The bride told me how, back in high school, the two of them
were teased because of their food allergies. She also told me
how the groom's parents once believed his diet was a ploy for
attention. And about how her best friend thought she was avoiding gluten just to stay slim. She said the strife made them
stronger as a couple. Earlier this summer, this darling couple
attended a friend's wedding where your pies had been served.
Seeing the guests' reactions, they decided to read up on you.
They love that you use fresh ingredients, grow your own
herbs, buy produce from local farmers, and get honey from
area beekeepers. They knew you could make their dessert
bar unforgettable. So don't let them down."

Suddenly, a powerful heat flooded through Ella Mae's
body and she knew that Jenny had used magic on her. Bolts
of Jenny's liquid sunshine electrified Ella Mae's blood and
gave her an incredible surge of energy. She felt like she could
run a marathon. Or two. Opening her eyes, she spun around.
"You didn't need to do that."

"I know, but my shift is over, and Finn and I are going to
see a movie. By the time we sit through the ads, twenty
minutes of previews, and a two-hour film, I'll be completely
recovered." She pursed her lips. "Unless I gorge on popcorn
and Milk Duds—which I shouldn't do on a date—but probably will. I have no discipline once I get a whiff of that
movie theater butter. I'm already planning on buying a huge
tub and I might not share a single kernel with Finn. How's
that for starting off a relationship on the wrong foot?"

Ella Mae laughed. "Thank you, Jenny. Not just for the
energy boost, which is far better than a six-pack of Red Bull,

but for painting that picture of the couple. You reminded me of why I became a chef in the first place. I lost sight of that somewhere between the white bean flour and the Asian tapioca."

"Glad to be of service." Jenny gestured at the worktable. "Would you like help cleaning up? Everyone else has gone home."

"No, thanks. I'm going to give this gluten-free piecrust another whirl. Hugh's sleeping at the fire station tonight so I won't see him until tomorrow." Ella Mae put her hands on her hips and surveyed her messy kitchen with a grin. "I'm going to crank up the radio, cook myself some dinner, and wipe off this worktable. When I literally have a clean slate, I'll think about that sweet couple while I experiment with a flour blend I've yet to try. For some reason, I have a feeling that it might be the combination I've been looking for."

Ella Ma's hunch proved true. Though still challenging to roll out—a problem she solved by first refrigerating the dough for an hour before gently rolling it between two layers of flour-dusted wax paper—the piecrust came out of the oven with a lovely golden-brown hue. And when Ella Mae tasted it, she was pleased to discover that the crust had the same buttery, flaky texture as her traditional crusts.

"Hallelujah!" she shouted and danced a little jig in front of the cooling racks.

With Jenny's liquid sunshine still flowing through her veins, Ella Mae was too wired to sleep, so she made another dozen gluten-free dough balls. After carefully wrapping these in plastic wrap, she placed them in the refrigerator and cleaned the kitchen until it shone.

"Tomorrow, the first gluten-free pies will appear on The Charmed Pie Shoppe's menu board," she announced to the empty room.

Feeling incredibly satisfied by her day's work, she headed home, only to find her mother waiting on the front porch swing. Chewy's head was on her lap, and though he opened his eyes at the sight of Ella Mae, he couldn't quite wake up enough to greet her properly. She whispered a hello to him, smiled when he thumped his tail once against the swing cushion, and then lowered herself into a rocking chair with a weary but contented sigh.

"You're home late," her mother said.

"I am, but the extra time was well spent. I finally mastered a gluten-free piecrust." She let out a little laugh. "After all the things I've been through, you wouldn't think I'd find the task so daunting, but it was getting the better of me. Luckily, Jenny came along and gave me the perfect pep talk." Ella Mae picked a piece of hardened dough out of her hair. "I could use a shower, but I have a feeling that you need to tell me something."

Her mother's gaze strayed toward Partridge Hill. She looked as though she was searching for the right words. The hesitation put Ella Mae on edge.

Maybe she wants to voice her feelings about a certain professor, Ella Mae suddenly thought. She certainly hoped so. Over the last two months, she'd grown very fond of Henry Matthews. She could see that Henry made her mother happy, and it was obvious that Henry was smitten with Adelaide LeFaye. Should the couple ask Ella Mae for her opinion, she'd encourage them to take a chance on love—to work out a way to be together. Because what they'd found in each other was far more important than anything they stood to lose.

"Mom?" Ella Mae prompted.

She expected her mother to smile shyly or to begin by saying that Henry's time at Partridge Hill was nearing an end, but she did neither of these things. "Someone came to me requesting a Luna Rose ceremony for the month of August." Her mother paused. "It's an unusual circumstance— one I never expected to have to deal with."

"So it's complicated?" Ella Mae couldn't help smiling. "The person who made the request—do you know him well?"

"Well enough," her mother answered.

"And the woman he'd like to marry? Are you two . . . close?"

This time, her mother simply nodded.

Ella Mae pretended to mull the matter over before saying, "What's the nature of your concern? Are you worried about the outcome—that the rose won't bloom for this couple?"

In the silence that followed, Ella Mae recalled the first time she'd unintentionally witnessed a Luna Rose ceremony. It had occurred shortly after she'd moved back to Havenwood, before her own magic had been awakened. Something had prompted her to leave her bed in the middle of the night. She'd looked out her window to find a man and a woman clasping hands in the middle of her mother's rose garden. However, the rosebush they stood in front of bore no flowers. Its tight, colorless buds yielded no clue as to the type of flower it might produce.

Ella Mae had watched, too entranced to be frightened, as a figure in a white robe and cowl had stepped out of the darkness and raised both arms in a beckoning gesture. Instantly, a cloud of fireflies had descended from the sky and covered every visible inch of the rosebush. When they'd withdrawn, a single rosebud had unfolded. It had sparkled like a candle flame, though its light was a much purer, far more radiant white. It was the most beautiful flower Ella Mae had ever seen.

The robed figure had nodded at the couple. As one, they'd stretched out their clasped hands toward the glimmering rose. However, the moment their fingertips had touched its petals, its light vanished and the garden had been plunged into darkness. Later, Ella Mae's mother had explained that the Luna Rose ceremony predicted whether or not a couple was destined to be together. The couple Ella Mae had seen had failed the test.

Suddenly, Ella Mae understood her mother's predicament. "I see the problem now. How can you officiate the ceremony if you're one half of the couple?"

Her mother's brows shot up. "Me?"

"Yes. If Henry wants to be with you and has proposed a Luna Rose ceremony, then—"

"I didn't meet with Henry today, Ella Mae," her mother said very softly. "I met with Hugh."

All the air rushed out of Ella Mae's lungs. Her head felt balloon-light and tiny stars winked along the edges of her vision. "No," she whispered. "It couldn't have been Hugh. I told him about the ceremony because I wanted him to know everything about my life. About my family. But . . ." She shook her head. "Why? Why does Hugh want to use magic now? We've been just fine without it. We're doing great."

"Because he wants to marry you, Ella Mae," her mother said. "He wants to build you a house overlooking the lake. He wants to start a family with you. But the past haunts him. The fear that either of you might one day regret your choice to give up magic haunts him."

Ella Mae's anger flared. "Other people don't get to know for certain if their relationships will last. They rely on faith, trust, and love—not on glowing insects and enchanted flowers!"

Unfazed by her daughter's outburst, Adelaide LeFaye gently moved Chewy's head aside and got to her feet. "Perhaps that's their loss. Look how many marriages fail these days. More than half. I have to admit, Ella Mae, that when Hugh first asked me to perform the ceremony, my immediate reaction was to refuse him. But when I sat back and considered his request, I realized that he never would have come to me if he didn't truly love you. I've doubted Hugh's sincerity in the past, but I now believe that he would walk through fire for you. In a way, the Luna Rose ceremony is a test of faith, trust, and love. You need all of those, and a great deal of courage besides, to stand before that bush and await your destiny."

Ella Mae bolted to her feet. "*I* am in control of my fate! If Hugh Dylan wants me to be his wife, then he can get down on one knee and propose. I'm not entirely sure I'd say yes, considering how furious I am right now, but it would be a good place for him to start." She blew out a long, slow breath. "The only ceremony I want is the kind where vows are spoken in the presence of the people we love, rings are exchanged, Hugh kisses me, and after a declaration by the officiant, Hugh and I belong to each other for the rest of our days. It's a simple and beautiful act. Why complicate it with magic?"

Her mother didn't respond.

Feeling suddenly drained, Ella Mae opened her front door. "It's time for me to turn in. It's been a long day. Good night, Mom. Chewy, come on, boy. Bedtime!"

Before Ella Mae could enter her house, her mother's voice held her in check. "Promise me you'll think about it. Just take a few days before you reject the idea."

Ella Mae sighed. "All right. But only if *you* promise to tell Henry how you feel about him. He's scheduled to return to England in two weeks and I know you don't want him to leave."

"It doesn't matter what I want. He has commitments—"

"Just tell him. Let *him* decide how to handle his commitments," Ella Mae insisted. "Do we have a deal?"

Her mother raised her hands in surrender. "Yes, yes. But

I'm going to wait for the right moment. This is not a conversation I want to have in front of my sisters, Reba, and the Upton siblings."

Ella Mae swept her arm in an arc, indicating the gardens spreading out behind Partridge Hill. "I'm sure you'll find the perfect place."

When Ella Mae saw Hugh the following night, she was tempted to rail at him for speaking to her mother about securing a Luna Rose ceremony, but she'd promised to consider it and she kept her word. However, she'd also made a vow never to lie to Hugh again, so when he asked her if anything was wrong, she was torn. They stood side by side at the sink, cleaning up after a supper of chimichurri skirt steaks, corn on the cob, and watermelon slices. Ella Mae dried her hands on the dish towel and looked at Hugh.

"Last night, my mom told me about your request. It made me really angry." Unbidden, tears filled her eyes. "I'm not looking for a shortcut. Other people take chances and go forward blindly believing in their love. That's what I want to do. I don't want to rely on magic to predict our future."

Hugh opened his mouth to reply but Ella Mae put her fingers to his lips.

"Hold that thought for just a second." She moved to lower her hand but he grabbed it instead. Laughing, she went on. "I promised my mother that I'd weigh my options. To do that, I need to know what motivated you to ask for the ceremony. So convince me that it would be good for us. Why should we, the two people who have deliberately turned our backs on magic, use it to decide whether or not we should spend the rest of our lives together?" Her voice trembled. "Because you know what happens if we touch the rose and its light goes out? It means that we won't make it. Sooner or later, we'll fall out of love."

"Never," Hugh whispered hoarsely and enfolded Ella Mae in his arms. He pressed her so hard against his chest that she could feel his heart hammering as though it might break through his rib cage. "I don't doubt what we have," he said into her hair. He then released her and cupped her face with his hands. "But I fear what the past has done to us. The scars it's left on us. In places we can't see. It's these holes in my memory, Ella Mae. I know they're the result of magic and I don't want them to hurt us later on. After we're married and have our own family. I can't let that happen. I need to know that there isn't something terrible lurking inside me like some sort of latent time bomb. Your happiness is all that matters to me, and the Luna ceremony is the only way I can be sure I'm the man who can deliver that happiness."

Ella Mae let her tears fall unchecked. "Damn it, Hugh. Why did you have to present such a practical and yet incredibly romantic argument?"

Hugh smiled. "We have two weeks until the full moon. Just think about it, okay? I know the Camellias are coming tomorrow and you'll probably be too busy to give this serious thought, but if those women start driving you crazy, I want you to picture this." He pulled out a folded piece of paper from his pocket and set it on the counter. "Go on, open it."

When Ella Mae unfolded the paper and flattened it with her palm, she saw that it was a real estate listing for a lot overlooking Lake Havenwood. It was just under an acre and included a dock.

"I was thinking of a craftsman-style house with a big back deck," Hugh said. "We could have coffee there in the morning and a cold beer or a glass of wine at night. The dogs would love it. They'd have room to run and swim. We could get a little boat. And later, I could put a play set with a sandbox here." He pointed to a spot on the paper. "Or hang a tire swing."

Ella Mae glanced up from the listing and caught Hugh's faraway look. She could see that he was imagining their lives as though they were pages from a scrapbook, and she liked the picture he was painting. She wanted to climb into the vision with him, to sit on their deck at sunset, to cradle their firstborn child in a rocking chair as dawn broke over the mountain, to watch the dogs chase dragonflies during the summer and snap at snowflakes come wintertime. "I love it," she said, sliding her arms around his waist. "And I love you too."

The next morning, Ella Mae rose especially early. Leaving Hugh to sleep in, she put on her running clothes, fed Dante and Chewy, brewed a pot of coffee, and then ushered the dogs outside into the pale August light.

The dogs immediately spotted a brace of ducks by the lake's edge and raced off to chase them, leaving Ella Mae free to enter the trail leading into the woods without company. It wasn't that she didn't enjoy having the dogs with her, but they tired too quickly and she needed to burn some energy in order to be calm and collected before facing the members of the Camellia Club.

Beneath the canopy of the pine trees, the air still held traces of the night's coolness and Ella Mae maintained a steady pace over the packed dirt trail. She ran to the watering hole, where she'd seen Hugh swim like a dolphin so many times in the past. Deciding to take a brief water break, she leaned against the large boulder that teens had spray-painted for as long as Ella Mae could remember.

Every year, someone from the park service would drive

out to the swimming hole, clean the spray paint off the boulder, and post signs warning against vandalism. And every year, the signs would be uprooted and the initials of young lovers would appear in a rainbow of colors on the rock.

Ella Mae looked at the entwined letters and hearts, and decided that the boulder was wonderful. The kids knew that it was only a matter of time before their initials would be painted over again, but they didn't care. They wanted their declaration to be public for as long as possible—in neon orange and swirls of deep purple and electric blue.

They'll take what they can get and celebrate it, she thought. *Boldly. Beautifully.*

Because the rock wasn't ugly. Each pair of initials had been meticulously drawn. And every set of lovers had their own style. No two hearts were the same. Some were surrounded by rainbows or butterflies. Others were decorated with gold lightning bolts or silver stars. There were Gothic designs as well. Black roses with sharp thorns and dark hearts bound by chains. Dozens of initials. Dozens of proclamations. Ephemeral pledges in paint.

Ella Mae cast one last glance at the tableau before sliding her water bottle into her runner's belt and starting down the trail, back the way she'd come. When she cleared the woods and reappeared on the lawn behind Partridge Hill, she found her mother standing on the dock, tossing sticks into the water for Dante and Chewy.

She waved Ella Mae over. "I saw Hugh's truck in the driveway, so I take it things are okay between the two of you."

Ella Mae's gaze moved across the lake to where the lot for sale was located. "We're better than okay. I've agreed to the ceremony, Mom. I've given it plenty of thought, and I'm willing to go through with it, though I'm really scared."

Her mother nodded. "Most things worth doing come with

a risk." She smiled at Ella Mae. "Like having a child, for example. The worry never really ends, no matter how old the child is. Be sure to keep Reba close today. I've made arrangements to bring Opal to the resort first thing tomorrow morning. Until then, don't let your guard down."

"I really hope Opal and Loralyn can reconcile," Ella Mae said quietly. "There has to be more to Loralyn than what people like Reba see. Because if Loralyn Gaynor is as cold and heartless as she seems, then she could prove to be the most dangerous enemy Havenwood has ever known."

Chapter 11

After receiving a surprisingly warm hug and a detailed itinerary from Julia Eudailey, who looked every inch the ladies club secretary with her tortoiseshell clipboard, fountain pen, and designer reading glasses, Ella Mae headed to one of Lake Havenwood Resort's multiple kitchens to meet the other chefs.

Maxine Jordan, the organic chef from Charlottesville, Virginia, was a short, stocky woman with a mass of ginger hair. She had a laid-back, unhurried manner about her that instantly put Ella Mae at ease.

"Isn't this setup amazing?" she asked, coming around a prep counter to shake Ella Mae's hand. "My entire café could fit inside this space."

"Mine too," Ella Mae said. "And this is one of the *small* kitchens. The larger ones are undoubtedly being used to prepare breakfast for hundreds of guests."

At that moment, a petite blonde wearing cat eyeglasses and a sky-blue, 1950s-style dress popped out from behind a stack of produce crates. "Not hundreds." Seeing the look of confusion on Ella Mae's face, she went on. "Didn't you hear? The Camellia Club rented the *entire* resort! These gals must have some mighty deep coffers. I'm Caroline James, by the way. Of Carolina's Cakes."

Ella Mae was taken aback. Having seen the total number of members listed in the club directory, she knew the Camellias would occupy less than half the resort. Why did they feel the need to have the place to themselves?

Reba, who'd entered the room in time to catch Caroline's remarks, shot Ella Mae a quick glance of triumph. Earlier that morning, she and Ella Mae had argued over which weapons to hide among their cooking tools. Ella Mae hadn't been comfortable with the idea of stashing handguns and Tasers in with her rolling pins and spice canisters, but Reba had been adamant about arming themselves as thoroughly as possible.

"You can't talk me out of bringin' them," Reba had insisted. "We have no clue what will happen over the next few days and I plan to be prepared for all kinds of crazy."

After waiting for Reba to slide a cardboard box marked "Perishable" on a nearby shelf, Ella Mae introduced herself and Reba to Maxine and Caroline. The other two chefs had also brought female assistants, and before long, the kitchen reverberated with the pleasant din of women's voices and the sound of utensils, pots and pans, and dry goods being arranged just so.

At one point, Maxine held up the itinerary they'd all been given and said, "This might be the only time we'll be able to chat. I worked at a D.C. law firm before I opened my bakery, and I've seen entire case files that were less detailed than this itinerary. I half expected to find bathroom breaks penciled in."

Caroline laughed. "I'm wondering what will happen if one of my sessions runs late. When it comes to baking cupcakes, it's good to get a little carried away. And these ladies will make mistakes. They won't produce the perfect Cleopatra cupcake right from the start. They'll need time to make them at least twice."

"What are Cleopatra cupcakes?" Ella Mae asked.

"Honey cupcakes with mascarpone frosting and caramelized figs," Caroline said. "Cleopatra loved honey and figs."

Ella Mae tossed her apron on the counter. "That settles it. I'm playing hooky and coming to your class."

"Don't worry, I'll make extras." Carolina examined the itinerary. "It looks like we're all teaching at the same time. When the ladies aren't cooking with us, they'll either be having spa treatments, wining and dining, attending meetings, or engaging in some type of group exercise. I guess that last part makes sense, seeing how many desserts they'll be tasting over the weekend."

"What's this dockside ceremony they're having tonight?" Maxine asked. "We're invited to join them for drinks and dinner, but after that, we're supposed to make ourselves scarce. We're not permitted near the back terrace or dock between nine and eleven. Isn't that weird?"

Ella Mae knew that the ceremony was a final farewell to Bea Burbank, but she didn't share this information with the other chefs. "Secret club business, I guess," she said. "I've never been in a club before. Have either of you?"

Caroline smiled. "I started my own Nancy Drew Club when I was a girl. I handed out toy magnifying glasses and notebooks to my friends, and we met in the shed behind my house once a month to report on suspicious activity. All we did was gossip about the neighbors and eat cookies. It was a very Southern club!"

The women laughed.

"I was involved in several political clubs back in D.C.," Maxine said. "That was before I fell in love with a farmer named Aaron. To be closer to him, I quit my job, sold my condo, and moved to Charlottesville. Aaron taught me about living organically, and I began to cook and bake practicing those ideals. We opened From Scratch on our third wedding anniversary."

Caroline clapped. "That's so sweet! I never get tired of hearing how people fell in love with food. What about you, Ella Mae? How did you end up with a pie shop?"

Ella Mae, Maxine, and Caroline spent another hour getting to know one another while setting up their kitchen spaces. Finally, it was time to head to Café Soleil, the resort restaurant that served only breakfast and lunch.

The Camellias had ordered a lavish brunch buffet and the café was buzzing with activity. The waitstaff bustled around the room delivering orange juice, coffee, Bloody Marys, and mimosas. At the far end of the buffet line, one resort chef manned an omelet station while another served smoked salmon. Both the buffet tables and the dining tables were decorated with elegant floral arrangements of white magnolia blossoms and green viburnums presented in silver punch bowls.

Catching sight of Ella Mae and the other bakers, a willowy blonde made her way to their side. Ella Mae had already met Savannah McGovern at the nail salon in Sweet Briar, but having now memorized the directory, she also knew that Savannah was the club's current vice president.

"Ladies!" Savannah beamed at them. "It's such an honor to have you with us. I'm Savannah McGovern." She pointed at her gold nametag. Her age and fashion sense reminded Ella Mae of Bea, but Savannah lacked Bea's warmth. "After we've all had a bite to eat, I'll ask each of you to say a few words about your individual styles and what we can look forward to learning today. We'll then break up into groups and get started with the first session. Is that acceptable?"

The three women murmured their agreement, and when Savannah turned away, Maxine whispered, "Why do I feel like saluting?"

Caroline pushed her glasses back onto the bridge of her nose and surveyed the room. "Don't worry, sugar. I've seen my fair share of divas and debutantes. They all put on airs at first, but the instant I get these ladies in the kitchen and put a cupcake in front of them, they turn into little girls again. Little girls who are dying to lick pink frosting off their fingers and pour rainbow sprinkles onto everything. They'll bounce on their toes and giggle. You'll see. Your food will have the same effect on them. That's why we're here. We work a special kind of magic."

Ella Mae let the other two chefs go ahead. When she and Reba were at a safe distance from everyone else, she nudged Reba in the side. "Did you hear what Caroline said?"

"Yeah, but I didn't catch any vibes off her, Maxine, or their assistants." Reba lowered her voice. "Some of the Camellias have special abilities, but it's too crowded in here for me to sort out which ones. When they break into smaller groups and come into the kitchen to work with you, I can get a better read on them. Then we'll know who to keep a closer eye on. Savannah already has my hackles up. She's got a reptilian stare."

Ella Mae sighed as she helped herself to some turkey bacon. "As much as I enjoy Caroline's image of these women becoming playful during our cooking classes, there's obviously more to this retreat than the creation of their centennial cookbook. I remember Julia telling me back in May that the Camellias would be electing a new president this weekend. If someone murdered Bea to become the next president, then that woman will stop at nothing to gain that position. Anything could happen over the next few days."

"I have a feelin' that it won't be all giggles and rainbow sprinkles either," Reba grumbled while proceeding to load her plate with enough bacon and sausage to feed a high school football team. She then led Ella Mae to their assigned seats, which happened to be at the same table as Julia Eudailey and her daughter.

Julia introduced her offspring as Anna Katherine, but the young woman waved off the name with a smile. "Just call me Annie," she said and turned to the other two women at the table. "This is Mary Grace Smart and her daughter, Shelby Smart. Shelby and I have known each other since preschool."

Ella Mae recognized the Smarts from the directory, but it was clear that she wasn't going to learn much about them during brunch because Annie wouldn't let anyone get a word in edgewise. She prattled on about the Eudailey family business, which was real estate, while Shelby sat back in her chair looking bored. Mary Grace inserted a polite comment or two, but in general, she seemed anxious for the meal to be over. She kept glancing around the room, as though she were missing out on more important conversations. At one point, Annie mentioned that Mary Grace served as the Camellia Club treasurer and that both Mary Grace and Shelby were math whizzes.

"Between the Smart women and the Edgeworths' financial acumen—Cora and Meg are sitting right over there by the window—we were able to add another scholarship this year," Annie said proudly.

After locating the Edgeworths, Ella Mae focused on Annie

again. "That's amazing," she said. "I think I recognize all the club officers now. Savannah McGovern is the vice president. Julia, you're the secretary. Mary Grace, you're the treasurer. Is there anyone else?"

Mary Grace held up two fingers. "We actually have a *first* and *second* vice president. Cora Edgeworth is the second. We also have a parliamentarian. Her name is Lyn Croly. She's the tall blonde flirting with the waiter by the coffee station. Lyn is a relative newcomer to our club." Her eyes narrowed slightly. "And yet our former president was convinced that Lyn held the key to our future." Suddenly catching a warning glance from her daughter, Mary Grace added, "I suppose Lyn has promising ideas for fund-raising and such." She suddenly seemed eager to leave. "If you'll excuse me, I believe I'll freshen up before the next bit of fun begins."

Mary Grace didn't head for the restrooms, however, but stopped to chat with another table of Camellias. The women bent their heads together and began whispering, drawing hostile stares from other groups of women in the room.

"Oh, Lord," Reba whispered. "It's worse than the cliques in a middle school cafeteria."

Ella Mae's gaze swept over Mary Grace and landed on Loralyn. Appearing in her Lyn Croly persona, Loralyn wore a wrap dress that revealed far less décolletage than usual. She'd also forgone her sexy stilettos, opting for a trendy pair of Jimmy Choo pumps instead. Her hair was modestly styled, her accessories were classy, and her movements were so deliberate that they looked choreographed.

The whole thing's a dance, Ella Mae thought. *A political dance. And by Sunday, one of these women will be crowned Belle of the Ball.*

For a moment, Ella Mae was nearly overcome by the soft whisper of female voices. By the blend of so many perfumes, the sparkle of diamonds and twinkle of gold, the sheen of silk, and above all else, the undercurrent of anticipation, hostility, and excitement. The sensation that something incredibly dramatic was about to happen, that they were all walking a tightrope, was almost palpable.

"Too much estrogen," Reba muttered in Ella Mae's ear. "We need to get in the kitchen so you can breathe a nice, healthy dose of cinnamon or orange peel. These women must have bathed in Chanel No. 5 before they got dressed."

"Thank goodness for you," Ella Mae said, looping her arm through Reba's. "You smell like bacon and eggs. And toast spread with strawberry jam. Like home."

Later, after the chefs had finished their short speeches, the Camellias broke into three groups and followed Ella Mae, Maxine, and Caroline into the kitchen.

Having seen her fellow chefs prepare for their lessons, Ella Mae knew that Maxine's class would focus on several varieties of organic pound cake while Caroline was going to kick off the weekend with two types of cupcakes. The first was called Let's Hear It for Chocolate, and the second was Vanilla Bean Dream. Ella Mae told her group that there was no point in addressing fillings, toppings, or decorations until her students had mastered the most difficult step of pie baking.

"It must be the crust!" Annie Eudailey declared. "I tried to make a homemade crust once. It was a disaster. After that, I stuck with the frozen kind."

"We can't list frozen crust as an ingredient in our cookbook," Julia admonished her daughter with a grin. "Roll up your sleeves and tie on your apron. We can do this."

As it turned out, Julia and Annie were attentive students. Ella Mae had sixteen women in her first group, and they all managed to follow her directions for preparing basic piecrust dough using a food processor.

"Ice water and very cold, unsalted butter are the key ingredients," she told them. "Using the pulse option until your dough forms pea-sized balls will help create the perfect curst. Cora's looks just like mine. See?" She pointed at a food processor and then went on to inspect the other women's results. They'd all managed to correctly blend their ingredients. Except for Loralyn. She'd been too heavy-handed on the pulse button and had overblended her dough.

"Don't worry," Ella Mae told her. "Unlike life, everything in the kitchen can be fixed. There's always a chance to start over again."

Ella Mae showed her students how to shape their dough into balls and then cocoon the balls in plastic wrap. The dough would chill in the refrigerator for thirty minutes while she taught the ladies the art of making a gluten-free piecrust. Annie was particularly excited about this next activity because her husband had celiac disease.

"Unfortunately, our workspace is now contaminated, so our crusts wouldn't be safe for someone like your husband," Ella Mae explained. "Therefore, I'm going to demonstrate on a different workspace using totally clean equipment. By the time I'm done, the dough we just put in the refrigerator will be sufficiently chilled and you can roll out your piecrusts."

The afternoon passed pleasantly. Once the Camellias had lined glass pie dishes with their dough and put them in the oven to blind bake, Ella Mae taught them how to blanch, skin, and slice fresh peaches. She then led them through the steps required to create a sumptuous salted caramel peach pie. The sliced peaches were tossed in a salted caramel sauce, poured into the pie dish, and then covered by a crumble layer. After the pie was fully baked—and Ella Mae had premade several for the ladies to sample—it was cut into wedges. Each wedge was garnished with a drizzle of warm caramel.

"This is heaven on earth," a woman named Ethel declared after her first taste.

"It most certainly is," Julia agreed. "And we can include this recipe in our cookbook?"

Ella Mae said that she'd come up with a dozen new recipes for the Camellias to use in their centennial dessert cookbook. Her announcement was received with a burst of applause.

"Bea knew what she was doing when she hired you," Meg Edgeworth told Ella Mae. "If the rest of our pies turn out like this, and the breads, cakes, and cupcakes are equally as good, we might want to invest more money in the production and marketing of this cookbook. What do you think, Mom?" She turned to her mother and the two women engaged in an excited bout of whispering.

Up to this point, Meg had been fairly quiet, so Ella Mae was glad to see her opening up a little. Meg wanted to know what other recipes Ella Mae had in mind and the two women spoke quietly for several minutes. Ella Mae was on the verge of asking Meg if she was related to the Camellia Club's founder when the ringing of a bell interrupted her.

"Time's up, ladies!" Savannah stood in the center of the kitchen, a hand bell raised in the air. "I hope you enjoyed your first session. Let's hear it for our fantastic chefs!"

After another round of applause, the Camellias began exiting the kitchen.

"Lyn?" Ella Mae called out. "Could you spare a few minutes? I wanted to give you a quick one-on-one lesson so you'd be ready for our next class."

Seeing as Loralyn had blatantly failed to make piecrust dough, Ella Mae thought her request was a reasonable one.

Apparently, Julia agreed. She gave Loralyn a gentle push. "Go ahead. I'll tell the spa that you'll be a bit late."

Ella Mae didn't wait for the rest of the ladies to clear the room before ordering Loralyn to cut a stick of cold butter into cubes. While Loralyn obeyed, glaring at Ella Mae from beneath her lashes, Ella Mae whispered, "The reason I came looking for you all those weeks ago—and was so surprised to find you in Sweet Briar—is that your mother is very sick."

Loralyn's knife stopped moving. She stared distrustfully at Ella Mae. "What do you mean?"

"I'm sorry to have to tell this way." Ella Mae waved at the flour-dusted space. "I wanted to speak with you in Sweet Briar, but you didn't give me the chance."   .

"Just spit it out," Loralyn hissed and plunged the knife back into the butter.

Ella Mae swallowed. "Your mother has cancer. It's incurable. A Chinese healer is taking care of her right now. He has special abilities and has been able to build up her strength, but her time is running out. I'm sorry to have to say this so bluntly, but she's dying." Ella Mae reached out, gently took the butter from under Loralyn's hands, and dumped it in the food processor.

"What's next?" Loralyn wiped her fingers on her apron. Her voice was hollow and her eyes were glassy with shock. "How many times do I press pulse?"

"I'll show you." Ella Mae used the machine to cover up her words. Only Loralyn could hear what she was saying. "More than anything in this world, your mother wants to see you. She misses you and has so much to tell you. Before it's too late."

Ella Mae scooped out the dough, formed it into a ball, and guided Loralyn's hands on the rolling pin. Working together, they created an even disk. For a fragile moment, Ella Mae felt connected to her oldest enemy.

She's a woman, just like me, Ella Mae thought, feeling a powerful rush of sympathy and tenderness toward Loralyn. *A woman in need of a friend.*

Suddenly, Loralyn shoved the rolling pin aside, plunged her nails through the circle of dough, and tore it apart. "I don't miss her," she seethed. "And *I* have *nothing* to say. I went out and found another mother. My father taught me that family members are replaceable. Wives. Daughters." She shrugged. "I learned that mothers are replaceable too. We can all be traded in for better models."

"Okay, so you met Bea and somehow convinced her to name you as her surrogate," Ella Mae whispered urgently. "But she's gone, so why not reunite with your *real* mom? She knows she's made mistakes. She wants to make amends while she can."

Loralyn cast an anxious glance around the kitchen. Seeing that all the Camellias had left, she relaxed. "I won't need a mother once I'm president. Family will be totally irrelevant after that. In a way, my mother is doing me a favor by dying." She untied her apron. "Thank her for me, would you?"

As she watched Loralyn wipe flour and wet dough off her hands, Ella Mae wanted to slap Loralyn's cheek, but she kept the urge in check. Still, she couldn't let her leave. Not just yet.

"What about your father? Is he irrelevant too? I thought you wanted to free him from prison?"

Loralyn's face darkened. "He can rot there for the rest of his days for all I care. I gave him an opportunity to apologize and he blew it." She squared her shoulders. "As far as I'm concerned, I'm an orphan. And if you care about *your* family, Ella Mae, you'll stick to the retreat itinerary. Bake your pies and stay out of my way." She held up a single finger. "The only reason I'm warning you is because I believe that you did mean to tell me about my mother when you were in Sweet Briar. Not many people would have gone through the trouble of searching for me." Something softened in Loralyn's eyes. She suddenly seemed torn and Ella Mae took advantage of her hesitation.

Putting the lid back on the food processor, Ella Mae hit a random button. Over the whir of the blade, she said, "Maybe the apples could heal her. If they're capable of granting immortality, perhaps they could be used for good. Their magic might save your mother's life."

Instantly, as though a switch had been thrown, Loralyn stiffened. Her anger and hostility returned, even more intense than before. Sneering, she leaned close to Ella Mae and said, "That would be such a waste of magic."

Tossing her soiled apron on the counter, she walked out of the kitchen.

Later that night, after dinner and drinks, Maxine and Caroline announced that they both planned to retire to their rooms for the rest of the evening.

Ella Mae, on the other hand, had been invited to attend Bea's celebration service, so she lingered on the back terrace with Reba.

"I can't believe that Loralyn," Reba groused for the third time. "Is Opal still comin' first thing tomorrow? Because Loralyn is gonna break that woman's heart."

"Opal must have the chance to speak to her daughter in person. No matter how Loralyn responds, I need to get mother and daughter in the same room."

Reba looked up at the lit windows of the resort. "Which room? I thought the Camellias booked the whole place."

"They did. However, none of them are staying in the private bungalows in the woods. Like most resort guests, the Camellias wanted rooms with a lake view with convenient access to the amenities, so my mother made arrangements for Opal to wait inside one of the bungalows."

"How will you lure Loralyn there?"

Ella Mae smiled. "I helped myself to some of Julia's official Camellia Club stationery during cooking class. I saw a box sticking out of her tote bag and grabbed a few sheets when no one was looking. An early wake-up call from the front desk combined with a note from the Camellia Club secretary delivered to Loralyn's guest room should do the trick."

Reba tapped her temple. "Smart. If Loralyn's vyin' for the presidency, she'll want Julia in her corner."

"I hope so," Ella Mae said and then fell silent as the Camellias slowly exited the resort and joined them on the terrace. Every one of them had changed from the cocktail dresses they'd been wearing at dinner into simple white dresses. They'd also exchanged their designer heels for nude ballet flats.

"What's with the Mr. Rogers act?" Reba whispered.

At that moment, Annie Eudailey sidled up to them. "We're going down to the dock. Mom has a box of flower-shaped paper lanterns waiting there. We'll each light one and put it in the water as a tribute to Bea."

"Am I supposed to say something?" Ella Mae asked anxiously.

"Only if you want to," Annie replied. "Anyone who felt compelled to speak already did so at Bea's funeral. Tonight's ceremony is more of a symbolic act. We're bidding farewell to one president and preparing to welcome a new one on

Sunday. The candidates will be the first to release the lanterns. There are three of them."

"Why are you wearing white?"

Annie glanced at her dress and murmured, "It's a long-
standing tradition. From Greece." She then turned away,
obviously unwilling to expound on the matter.

Down at the dock, the Camellias arranged themselves in
mother-daughter pairs along the edges and waited for the
ceremony to begin. The officers stood at the far end with
the lake glistening behind them. It was clear that Savannah
and Cora were at odds. The two vice presidents glowered at
each other until Julia and Mary Grace positioned themselves
between the other two women in an attempt to maintain
peace. As for Loralyn, she kept herself slightly apart, radiat-
ing an air of cool confidence.

"She acts like she's above it all," Reba whispered. "It
makes her seem more like a leader and less like a sulky
teenage girl. She's showin' up the other candidates. Makin'
herself look classy while they look like fools."

It soon became obvious that the majority of the Camellias
agreed with Reba, for when Savannah and Cora began bick-
ering over who would light the first lantern, Loralyn
responded by shaking her head in disapproval. The rest of
the Camellias soon mimicked the movement.

Finally, Savannah grabbed a lantern and the lighter and
intoned, "For Bea, who left us too soon. May her successor
be willing to make similar sacrifices." She knelt, placed her
lantern in the water, and gave it a little shove.

Next, Cora lit her lantern and, in a voice far louder and
more theatrical than Savannah's, declared, "For Bea, who
gave her all to the Camellias! May her successor be worthy
of the apples."

Julia elbowed Cora. "We have outsiders among us, remember?"

"As if they'd understand," Cora answered coldly and pushed past Julia.

The ceremony continued, and the flower-shaped lanterns began to float farther and farther from the shore. The more they fanned out in the indigo water, the more the burning flowers looked like reflections of the stars above.

This would have been such a beautiful tribute without all of the tension, Ella Mae thought.

When it was Ella Mae's turn, she found that her hand was shaking. Memories flooded her mind. She recalled how much she'd liked Bea the day they'd met. But that memory was instantly replaced by the horror of seeing Bea's moon-pale face bobbing just below the surface of this same lake. And then, Ella Mae remembered how angry she'd been after meeting Liz and learning how deeply Bea had wounded her own daughter. Everything she felt about Bea was a jumble. However, she knew one thing. Bea deserved a better ending than the one she'd received. She deserved more than a ruling of accidental death and a scattering of paper flowers that would be gone by morning.

Ella Mae took her lantern from Julia and turned to face the Camellias. "Right after I dragged Bea's body out of this very lake, all I wanted was to find my mother and hold her tight," Ella Mae said in a voice thick with emotion. She didn't look at Loralyn, but she directed her words her way. "No mother is perfect. No daughter is either. But family is more precious than gold. More important than power. These relationships are irreplaceable. They're what define us. They're what our memories are made of." Ella Mae paused. She wanted to hint at Bea's murder. If ever there was a time to shake up the complacent Camellias, it was now. And yet she felt severely vulnerable at the end of the dock. Reba was a force of nature, but she couldn't take on fifty women at once.

Suddenly, there was a collective gasp at the other end of the dock, where the wood gave way to grass. Mothers and daughters parted, ashen-faced and whimpering, to reveal the figure of Liz Fisher.

Liz stood with her feet planted hip-width apart. Her eyes glittered with cold rage, and her arms were held out in front of her, as stiff and unbending as fence rails. In her hands, a black gun shone beneath the dock lights.

"I want to know who murdered my mother," she demanded in a low, powerful voice that swept over the women like an icy wind. They stared at Liz in shock and terror, and retreated one step. Then two.

Liz pointed her gun at the woman closest to her, but she kept her gaze fixed on the officers near Ella Mae. "Give yourself up, murderess! Give yourself up right now or I'll start shooting, and I won't stop until I run out of bullets!" Without turning her head, she shuffled sideways and pressed her gun against the woman's temple. "You came to say good-bye to my mother, but *I* came for justice. And I'm not leaving without it!"

Chapter 12

Loralyn began walking toward Liz.

"Stay where you are!" Liz shouted. She pressed the gun against the Camellia's temple with more force and the woman cried out in terror.

Loralyn slowed her pace, holding out both hands in a gesture of supplication. "You don't want to do this, Liz. Think of your boys. Your three lovely boys."

Loralyn's voice was musical, but the sound was far from melodious. It was eerie and dissonant, like a carnival tune being played on a rusty pipe organ. The phrase "three lovely boys" echoed over the surface of the lake and Ella Mae knew that Loralyn was using her siren's powers. A siren's voice was most effective on men, but because Liz wasn't magical, she was very susceptible to magic.

"Don't talk about my sons!" Liz shook her head as if to clear it. She then pointed the gun at Loralyn. Finding herself free from immediate danger, the woman standing next to Liz fell into a crumpled heap on the dock.

Liz didn't so much as glance at her.

As for Loralyn, she continued to advance toward Liz. Behind her, Ella Mae and Reba also crept forward, hoping to prevent bloodshed if possible.

"What will your boys do if you go to jail?" Loralyn's tone was infused with concern and tenderness. "What will your husband say when they ask, 'Where's Mommy?'" Her voice changed. It became a young boy's voice, plaintive and frightened. "Where are you, Mommy? I can't find you."

Again, the sound reverberated over the surface of the water. It seemed to be everywhere at once. The air was haunted by the boy's repeated pleas, and many of the Camellias began to cry without knowing why. Though Loralyn's magic was directed at Liz alone, Ella Mae realized that she could hear the full spectrum of Loralyn's siren song.

"What is it?" Reba whispered.

"I can hear Loralyn's magic," Ella Mae said. "Not just the words, but the magic infusing each syllable. In the past, I've only sensed when she was using it. This is different. I can almost see it working, but it doesn't influence me."

Liz, however, was definitely being influenced. She gaped at Loralyn, her eyes round with shock.

"Stop it," she whimpered. The hand holding the gun began shaking violently.

"I want my mommyyyy!" the boy's voice wailed pitifully, and Liz's shoulders sagged. Her hand went limp and the gun clattered harmlessly onto the dock.

Genuinely spooked, she began to take a few steps backward, but Loralyn pointed at two women near the end of the dock and commanded, "Cassie! Jillian! *Grab her!* No one touch the gun!" She turned, glanced past Ella Mae and Reba, and signaled to Annie Eudailey. "You're a runner. Sprint to the lobby and call 911. We'll watch over the nutcase until the cops come. *Go!*"

Annie didn't hesitate. She dashed toward dry land, the dock boards thudding as she raced over them.

"Reba and I will take Liz to a secure location inside the resort and wait for the police there," Ella Mae said, infusing her voice with the authority she'd recently possessed as the leader of her kind. "She came to see me after her mother died, so she knows me. She won't try to escape. Take her arm, Reba."

With a mumbled "Step aside," Reba inserted herself between Jillian and Liz. Cassie, the other woman holding Liz, looked at Loralyn for guidance.

Loralyn shrugged. "Fine by me, pie girl. Just make sure to send the police down to us as soon as you've handed the whack job over. We all witnessed what happened tonight, and I want to see that Liz Fisher is suitably punished for threatening the Camellias."

The rest of the women began murmuring in angry agreement and Reba shot Ella Mae an urgent glance. It was time to take Liz back to the resort before the Camellias formed a lynch mob.

Liz didn't say a word as Ella Mae and Reba half dragged her over the lawn, the terrace, and into the resort, where they led her to a small reading room.

After guiding Liz to a leather sofa, Ella Mae asked her if she wanted a glass of water. Instead of answering, Liz fixed her gaze on the blue Aubusson rug. Ella Mae covered Liz's hand with her own and was shocked by the coldness of her skin. She mimed to Reba to fetch a drink and knew that Reba would return with something stronger than water.

"You took a terrible risk coming here," Ella Mae said softly.

Liz didn't answer. For several minutes, the only noise in the room was the rhythmic ticking of the mantel clock. In the silence, Ella Mae paced in front of the fireplace, wondering what would happen to Liz once the police took her into custody. She feared the Camellias would pull every string to ensure that Liz was heavily penalized for what she'd done.

Ella Mae was about to use the reading room phone to call Uncle Buddy and ask him to intervene on Liz's behalf when Reba returned.

Reba knelt in front of Liz and held a coffee cup to her lips. "You need this, honey. Drink it down in one go. That's a girl."

Mechanically, Liz complied. Within a few seconds, her vacant stare dissipated and she was able to focus on Ella Mae's face. "I didn't take that much of a risk. The gun isn't real."

"What?" Ella Mae and Reba cried in unison.

"It's a toy. A plastic accessory from my son's Halloween costume. He was a zombie hunter." A ghost of a smile appeared on Liz's face, but quickly vanished again. "It was originally bright orange. I painted it black."

Ella Mae exhaled loudly. "Well, that's a relief. The charges against you will certainly be less severe considering your weapon was a toy, but you still made formidable enemies tonight. How did you even know about the ceremony?"

"I heard some Camellias talking about it at my mother's funeral. I thought of all the events she'd missed in my life and of all the ones I'd missed in hers. This was to be her last event, and I was *not* going to be excluded." She paused to set the empty mug on a side table. "I'm her daughter. Nothing my mother said or did changes that. She wronged me, but I've forgiven her. And in forgiving her, I've learned that I can't accept the ruling that her death was an accident. So I came to find out who killed her."

"Why are you so certain she was murdered?"

Liz let loose a humorless cackle. "You were standing on the dock! You saw those women. Not one of those ice queens protested her innocence when I accused them of murder. Either the Camellias know the exact identity of my mother's murderer or they don't know who she is, but they realize there's a killer among them and don't want to be her next victim. They don't care about justice. To protect themselves and their precious club, they're more than willing to turn a blind eye to murder."

"All this just to be the next president?" Reba shook her head. "We're not talkin' about the election of a world leader here. The perks of runnin' this club can't be that great."

Ella Mae knew that Reba was trying to provoke Liz into revealing whether she possessed any knowledge of the golden apples, but Liz clearly believed the presidency was motive enough.

"I know I sound crazy," Liz answered sharply. "To people like you and me, to *outsiders*, it *is* just a club. But to them"— she pointed in the direction of the docks—"being a Camellia is *everything*. It's a cult. There, I said it. Those women are brainwashed. From a very early age. Trust me, I know. My mother tried to brainwash me, but it didn't take. Generation after generation. The white dresses. The rich husbands. The way they research the men they plan to ensnare. They have spreadsheets on the state's most eligible bachelors, for heaven's sake. They don't enter into relationships based on love. Everything they do is for the club. It's sick."

"I take it you didn't marry the man your mother selected for you," Ella Mae said.

Liz laughed. "Look at me. I never stood a chance at catching one of those princely bachelors. Of course, my mother had a solution. She suggested I have plastic surgery. Several surgeries." She spread her hands. "You see how twisted the culture is. By the age of twenty, over half the Camellias have already been nipped, tucked, or enhanced."

Reba curled her lip in distaste. "That's shameful."

"I didn't want surgery, and I didn't want to marry a man I didn't love. My mother and I had horrible fights over both subjects. Luckily, I met my husband soon after I graduated from college and we fell hard and fast in love. Within three months, we were living together. I've never regretted my choice." She rubbed her wedding band with her thumb. "I lost my mother because I turned my back on the Camellias, but I gained a beautiful family of my own."

In the distance, the sound of police sirens cut through the night's tranquility.

Lifting her head, Liz's face drained of all color. "My boys. I heard them out there on the dock. I heard their voices."

"No. It wasn't your sons." Ella Mae knew she had to convince Liz of this or she could end up in the psych ward. "What you heard was Lyn Croly's voice. She's your mother's surrogate. I grew up with her and I can assure you that her voice becomes very high and shrill when she's upset. The way it carried over the water made it seem much younger. But it was *her* voice. Do you understand?"

It took Liz a long moment to process Ella Mae's words, but finally she nodded. "The water," she repeated. "It can distort the way things sound."

"It sure can," Reba said. "Now, you tell the cops that you're sorry—that you regret coming here and that you were out of line."

Liz stared at her. "But I still want to know what happened to my mother."

They heard men shouting in the hall. The crackle of walkie-talkies.

"As do I," Ella Mae declared softly. "And I'll do everything

I can to discover the truth. The Camellias won't suspect me. After all, I'm only a baker. I pose no threat, so let *me* take the risk." She took Liz's hands in her own. "You're a wife and a mother. When the cops come in, you need to be contrite and cooperative. Do whatever it takes to get back to your family."

"My husband will think I've had a nervous breakdown," Liz muttered miserably. "Maybe I have. I must have been nuts to think I'd get these frost princesses to crack. I've only made things worse for myself." After casting a fearful glance at the doorway, she began to sob.

When Jon Hardy entered the reading room followed by two other officers, he found Reba rocking Liz in her arms like a child.

Leaving Reba to minister to Liz, Ella Mae hurried forward to block Hardy's path. "The gun Liz was carrying is a toy. A plastic prop. She said her intent was to scare, not to injure, and she's prepared to do whatever it takes to rectify this situation." Ella Mae turned back to the couch. "It's time to speak with the police, Liz."

Reba helped Liz to her feet.

"She won't need to be restrained. She's not violent," Ella Mae whispered to Hardy.

"Until I see the weapon for myself, I can't take any chances," Hardy said and gestured for his female officer to secure Liz's wrists and Mirandize her.

Ella Mae was about to argue but decided she wouldn't be doing Liz any favors by aggravating Hardy.

"Mrs. Fisher can keep her hands in front," Hardy conceded when the officer was done reading Liz her rights and moved to cuff her. "Put her in the car, Officer Parks. As soon as Officer Hutchins and I have retrieved the weapon, you can take Mrs. Fisher downtown. We'll remain on-site to conduct preliminary interviews." He paused briefly to look at Ella Mae and Reba. "Did you both witness the entire scene?"

"Yes," Ella Mae and Reba answered together.

"Tell me what you saw. Quickly now," Hardy ordered as Officer Parks escorted Liz out of the room.

Ella Mae gave Hardy a succinct account—punctuated by several colorful remarks from Reba—which he listened to without interruption.

"Are you staying at the resort or going home for the night?" he asked when Ella Mae was finished.

"We're going home," Ella Mae replied.

With a nod, Hardy told them they were free to leave and that he'd be in touch if he had additional questions. He and Officer Hutchins then marched down the lobby toward the terrace. Ella Mae and Reba followed at a safe distance. They wanted to make sure Hardy retrieved the gun.

Suddenly, Savannah appeared from the mouth of the corridor leading to the business center. She strode up to Hardy and thrust out her hand.

"I'm Savannah McGovern, vice president of the Camellia Club. As the highest-ranking officer, I'll be serving as my organization's spokesperson. I will provide the official statement on behalf of my club members, and I'll also accompany you to the station in order to press charges against Liz Fisher."

After briefly shaking her hand, Hardy pointed toward the rear exit. "I'd like to bag the weapon. Could you lead me to it?"

"Certainly," Savannah answered.

Savannah paraded down the lobby like a queen at her coronation, and when Cora and Loralyn stepped into the lobby from outside, Savannah raised a regal finger to silence them before they could speak. "I'm acting as Officer Hardy's liaison, ladies, and will be representing the Camellias in this matter. Why don't you round up the rest of the ladies and tell them to wait for us in the café? That way, the officers can address us as a group."

Without waiting for a reply, Savannah turned back to the policemen. "We're heading for the dock, Officers," she said. "One of our members is standing guard over the gun. No one handled it other than the assailant."

Cora shot Savannah a venomous look and, ignoring her directive, followed Savannah and the two officers out to the terrace. Loralyn stayed where she was, but the glare she cast at Savannah's back was murderous. Spying Ella Mae, she spoke in a whisper laced with such icy menace that it raised the fine hairs on the base of Ella Mae's neck.

"I warned you to stay out of my way. That fool Savannah needs to listen to the same warning." Loralyn's eyes were dark with anger. "If she knows what's good for her health, she'll withdraw her candidacy. If not, she could be the next bloated body you pull out of the lake."

While Officer Hardy interviewed several of the Camellias, Officer Hutchins returned to the station to examine Liz Fisher's gun. The female officer had driven off with Liz well before the interviews got under way, and Ella Mae was concerned that by the time Officer Hutchins confirmed the gun was a toy, Liz would be condemned to a night in lockup.

Unfortunately, Ella Mae's efforts to secure an audience with Hardy were fruitless. Savannah made it clear that she wasn't welcome in the café and that she should go home without delay.

"I guess you've been lumped in with your fellow chefs," Reba said as they headed to the kitchen to retrieve their handbags and cell phones. "Whatever special treatment you got because you dragged Bea out of Lake Havenwood is over."

"Fine by me. I don't care how much charity work those women do. Theirs is one club I wouldn't be caught dead joining," Ella Mae grumbled.

As they approached the kitchen, they heard the clink of metal on metal. Reba stiffened and put a hand on Ella Mae's arm.

"Who's bangin' pots and pans at this hour?" she whispered. "Unless someone decided this might be a good time to search through the chefs' things."

Ella Mae's eyes widened. "Like the weapons you hid in that special box?"

Grinning, Reba reached under her T-shirt. "Don't worry. There's plenty more where those came from. If somebody's lookin' for those, they're about to see one real close up. Come on."

They tiptoed to the doorway and peered into the room, where they saw Caroline James tinkering with a row of chocolate fountains.

"Trouble sleeping?" Ella Mae entered the kitchen wearing a friendly smile.

Startled, Caroline put her hand over her heart. "There wasn't much chance of that once I heard the sirens and watched the cop cars pull up out front. Do you know what's going on?"

"A woman threatened one of the Camellias," Ella Mae said. "But it turned out to be more of a prank than a threat."

Caroline was stunned. "And someone felt the need to call in the cavalry?"

Ella Mae shrugged. "I guess so. The whole thing's been diffused by this point. The cops are just taking statements." She pointed at Reba. "We missed all the action because we were hiding in the reading room, but we're ready to leave now. It's way past our bedtimes."

"Yeah, maybe you should try to get some shut-eye instead of messin' with, what, seven chocolate fountains," Reba told Caroline. "What are you doin' with so many? Manufacturin' chocolate body peels for the spa?"

Caroline laughed. "Actually, the Camellias requested this activity. They host tons of parties and asked me to help them create desserts to accompany a chocolate fountain. Apparently, every member owns her own fountain. Can you believe that?"

"Yes," Ella Mae and Reba answered in unison.

"Not this size, however," Caroline added, touching the commercial fountain on the floor. "This thing's so heavy that my assistants will have to help me lift it in the morning. It weighs ninety pounds and is nearly five feet tall. It's the biggest fountain you can buy. It's not mine either." She eyed the apparatus with longing. "The resort was kind enough to let me borrow it for the day."

Ella Mae scooped a bottle of oil-based food coloring off the counter. "Are you using this blue in your lesson?"

Caroline nodded. "We'll be dyeing the white chocolate. I have purple, pink, blue, yellow, orange, and red. I thought it would be fun to show the ladies how to dye the chocolate while it's running through the fountains. It creates an incredible showpiece for holiday parties and baby showers. The big fountain will be the exception. That'll be regular milk chocolate. I've set it up for a test run because I've never used one this big before. The head chef told me that this beast goes through twenty-five pounds of chocolate at a time."

"Must be a female fountain," Reba quipped, and the three women shared a companionable chuckle.

Caroline held up an extension cord. "Anyway, all I have to do before tomorrow's class is go online and double-check the ingredients of the chocolate melting wafers. The lettering on the bag is smeared and I can't make it out, but two of the Camellias have nut allergies and I need to be sure that it wasn't packaged in a facility that processes nuts."

"That's right," Ella Mae said. "Alisha Kerns has a mild tree nut allergy, and Cora Edgeworth has a serious peanut allergy. She carries an EpiPen with her at all times. Because of that, I'm not using any peanuts in my recipes this weekend."

"Neither are Maxine and I. We both compared notes and we only have a few recipes containing nuts. Mine include a chocolate hazelnut recipe with Nutella frosting and a banana walnut cupcake with a honey vanilla buttercream. I've modified both recipes for Alisha and Cora. They can bake nut-free versions from their own workspaces. No sense taking chances."

"Exactly," Ella Mae agreed. "I'm doing a pecan pie and a lemon tart in a pine nut crust, but that second pie can be made using a traditional or even a graham cracker crust."

Reba smirked. "But you can hardly find a substitute for the pecans in your pecan pie."

Ella Mae grinned. "You can, actually. Pretzels mimic the color and crunch of a pecan and are the perfect ingredient for a faux pecan pie."

"That's brilliant!" Caroline clapped. "May I steal that idea for my caramel pecan brittle cupcakes? If I offered a nut-free version, I bet they'd fly out of the display case."

"Sure, but I can't take the credit," Ella Mae confessed. "A mom whose son had a nut allergy came up with the idea."

Caroline smiled. "That doesn't surprise me. There's no stopping a mother determined to make her child happy. Believe me, as the owner of a cupcake shop, I've seen it all. From sweet, caring parents to over-the-top, lost-their-marbles parents."

She scooped her room key off the counter and took a

final glance at the chocolate fountains. "I guess I'm feeding into the over-the-top theme with tomorrow's activity, but it's what these ladies want." She saluted Ella Mae and Reba. "I'm going to bed. I hope this is the only time I look out my window and see a bunch of cop cars parked out front."

"Me too," Ella Mae said, collecting her own things. "Good night."

After Caroline was gone, Reba examined her box of weapons. Satisfied that nothing had been touched, she replaced it on the shelf.

"I have to put in a final word on Liz's behalf before we leave," Ella Mae told Reba as they turned off the lights.

"Do you?" Reba asked. "She might be safer at the station. You saw how mad the Camellias were. It might not be a luxury suite, but no one can touch her in that holdin' cell. By tomorrow, she'll be free to go."

Ella Mae chewed her lip. "She could stay at Partridge Hill."

"You'd have to sit around waitin' for hours before she was released." Reba tapped her temple. "That's not a good idea considerin' you need to be back here at the crack of dawn to get Loralyn and Opal together. How sharp will you be if you've spent half the night sittin' in one of those plastic chairs in the police station?"

Though Ella Mae knew Reba was right, she still tried to speak with Hardy. However, Savannah once again refused her access to Café Soleil.

"I'll tell Officer Hardy that you asked for him," Savannah said before firmly shutting the door in Ella Mae's face.

"That's that," Reba declared. "Time for bed." Seeing Ella Mae's hesitation, she added, "You aren't responsible for Liz's actions. It wasn't smart, but she can't be in too much trouble, no matter how much power these women have. In the mornin',

Liz will go back to her family and we can focus on the Gaynor reunion, solvin' Bea's murder, and findin' those mysterious golden apples." Reba put an arm around Ella Mae's shoulders. "Like Scarlett said, tomorrow is another day."

"And another chance to make things right," Ella Mae whispered. "But we're running out of time. If Opal fails to soften Loralyn's heart, then we'll have to use force to get Loralyn to tell us everything she knows about the Camellias. Things could get ugly, Reba."

"I hope they do," Reba said, her eyes shining with a wicked gleam.

The next morning, well before the August sun had risen above the hills surrounding Lake Havenwood, Ella Mae pulled into the resort's parking lot. With the letter she'd typed using the stationery pilfered from Julia Eudailey safely tucked away in her handbag, she took the stairs to Loralyn's room, pushed the letter under the door, and then hurried back down to the lobby.

After stopping by the front desk and placing an order for a coffee tray to be delivered to Loralyn's room, Ella Mae waited for Reba to show up.

"I need two things before we head over to the guest cottage," Reba informed her upon her arrival. "An IV drip of the strongest coffee in this hotel." She yawned loudly. "Or several Red Bulls. And I also want to get a few choice items from my box in the kitchen."

"We can get weapons and coffee in the same place," Ella Mae said in a low voice. "But we should hurry. I want to be with Opal and my mother long before Loralyn arrives."

Reba snorted derisively. "Oh, please. She'll have to shower, dress, and put on twelve layers of makeup. We have tons of time." Despite her words, Reba walked to the kitchen at a brisk pace. "I'll just brew us half a pot of coffee, grab a Taser and a Beretta, and consider us prepared for our showdown."

At the kitchen doorway, she came to an abrupt halt.

When Ella Mae stepped around Reba to see what the problem was, she had to choke back a scream.

There was a woman on the floor. Her face was completely submerged in the bowl of the largest chocolate fountain. Her dark brown hair, which hung over one shoulder, had merged with the pool of milk chocolate congealing around her inert form. Her body was prone, her arms and legs splayed, while the fountain sputtered and gasped, as though in the final throes of asphyxiation.

In contrast to the noisy machine, the woman was eerily still. And when Ella Mae and Reba rushed forward to pull her face out of the fountain, they both quickly realized that she was beyond saving. Her lips and tongue were so swollen that they gave her an alien appearance, and it was clear that it had been some time since she'd last drawn a breath. Her body was stiff to the touch and her skin was cool and rubbery.

"She was obviously murdered. People don't drown themselves in chocolate fountains," Reba whispered. "Do you know who she is?"

"Cora Edgeworth," Ella Mae said. "And you're right. This was no accident. There are only two presidential candidates now. Savannah and Loralyn. I hate to do this, Reba, but we'll have to leave Cora as we found her. We need to meet with Opal and my mother as planned because Loralyn is no longer just Opal's estranged daughter or an eyewitness to activities inside Atalanta House. She's now a murder suspect."

Reba frowned. "For which murder? Bea's or Cora's?"

"Maybe both." Sickened by what she was doing, Ella Mae

gently placed Cora's chocolate-crusted face back into the fountain's bowl. Anger coursed through her in searing waves and she sprang to her feet, eager to find an outlet for her rage. "Remember when I said that things might get ugly?" When Reba nodded, Ella Mae pointed at Cora's body. "This is as ugly as it gets. This wasn't done by a lady. This is the work of a monster."

Chapter 13

Ella Mae and Reba took the exit at the far end of the western corridor and headed for the trail leading to the bungalows.

"I hate leaving Cora like that," Ella Mae muttered angrily. "But if we'd stayed a second longer, even to get weapons, someone might have seen us. Then, we would have been tied up with the police, leaving Loralyn free to continue doing as she pleases." Ella Mae let loose a growl of frustration. "I should have listened to you, Reba. I should have been more assertive with her. We should have driven back to Sweet Briar weeks ago and forced her to talk to us. It would have been simple enough. All we had to do was threaten to expose her as an imposter to the Camellias."

"We waited because she asked you to trust her. Loralyn came as close as a Gaynor comes to beggin'," Reba said. "I was there, remember? She almost had *me* convinced that it was best to let her finish with her business. Lookin' back, I wish I'd knocked her over the head and thrown her in the bushes. We could have trussed her up like a turkey and brought her home to her mama. Instead, you gave her the benefit of the doubt. We won't make that mistake again."

Ella Mae glanced over her shoulder at the main building. "It won't be long before the other chefs show up in the kitchen to prep for their classes. I feel terrible that Caroline or Maxine will discover Cora's body."

"There's no avoidin' it," Reba said. "And once they raise the hue and cry, all hell is gonna break loose."

The women approached a stone and clapboard cabin. The cabin, which was nestled in a copse of pine trees, allowed for the upmost in privacy while still being within a short walk of the resort. Ella Mae's mother had been granted temporary access to the cabin because the resort manager owed her a favor. Adelaide had delivered a large supply of cut flowers for an important society wedding after the original florist had the misfortune of being involved in a car accident en route from Atlanta. Adelaide's fee had not only been more modest compared to the florist's, but her arrangements were also the loveliest and most fragrant the guests had ever seen. The bride's father, who owned several magazines, was so pleased that he published an article on the stellar service provided by Lake Havenwood Resort.

Since then, the manager had been looking for a chance to repay Adelaide's kindness. Therefore, he didn't hesitate when Adelaide asked for permission to use one of the woodland cabins for an hour or two that Saturday morning. The manager wasn't concerned about breaking the clause in his contract with the Camellia Club—the one stating they'd be the only guests at the resort—because Adelaide wasn't checking in. She was only borrowing a vacant space for a short time.

Now, as Ella Mae raised her hand to knock on the cabin

door, she realized that her initial reason for securing the cabin was no longer paramount. A reconciliation between Opal and Loralyn was far less important than discovering whether or not Loralyn was a murderer.

Rapping once, Ella Mae called out, "It's me!" and listened to the sound of the deadbolt being withdrawn.

Ella Mae and Reba entered the cozy cabin and were greeted by Adelaide, Opal, and Henry. If Ella Mae was surprised to see Henry sipping tea in a wing chair by the window, she was even more stunned to find Ruiping, Dr. Kang's taciturn assistant, standing like a statue in the far corner of the sitting room.

"Isn't this a bit overcrowded for a meeting between estranged family members?" Ella Mae asked, still too upset over finding Cora to be tactful.

Opal, who sat in the chair opposite Henry, shook her head. "Professor Matthews knows more about the golden apples than any of us. If Loralyn is seeking the enchanted objects Atalanta collected during that famous footrace centuries ago, then he's the best person to speak with her about their benefits and dangers. I know what my daughter desires. She's hungry for power. She'll do anything and everything to get her hands on a magical object with the potential to transform her into something above and beyond humankind. Or our kind. Her pain has driven her to this point. She has been deeply wounded. By her father first. Next, by me."

Reba opened her mouth to protest but Opal lifted a finger to silence her. "It doesn't matter how anyone else views my actions. *Loralyn* saw my choice to join with the LeFayes as a betrayal of our family name. It confused her. Her confusion turned to anger. That anger has festered into a cold and calculated fury. But I have to believe that I can still reach her—that I can stop her from taking this too far."

Ella Mae crossed the room until she stood before Opal's chair. "I don't think anyone can stop her now," she said gently. "Reba and I just found the dead body of a woman named Cora Edgeworth. Cora, who was obviously murdered, was one of two candidates running against Loralyn in the race to become the next Camellia Club president. Loralyn's only remaining opponent is Savannah McGovern."

Opal, who was already pale, grew ever paler. There was a gray cast to her skin, and the signs of vitality Dr. Kang had helped her gain seemed to be eking away. "And you believe Loralyn is responsible for this woman's death?"

"I can't say for certain, but yes. The apples and the election are somehow linked. Whoever is elected will come in contact with the object of power," Ella Mae said. "Last night, when all the Camellias were gathered on the dock, Cora said that she hoped the next president would be worthy of the apples. She clearly forgot that Reba and I were present and was immediately shushed by another club member. The apples may actually be in Havenwood. I don't know any details about the ritual, however. This is the kind of information I wanted to elicit from Loralyn."

Opal inclined her head. "I also think the object of power is here. If not, Loralyn would never have bothered with this charade. She wouldn't have created a false persona, sought membership to this club, or run for president. She is too impatient for such things. If there were any other way for her to have obtained the apples, she would have done so. She *had* to attend this retreat. She *had* to become a candidate." Opal's gaze landed on Reba. "You can protect us from my daughter should she turn violent, but Ruiping has a role to play as well. Not only is she highly skilled in multiple martial arts disciplines, but she can also read deceit in someone's body language the same way Verena can detect a lie in a person's speech. Verena wanted to come too, but your mother and I decided that she lacked the subtlety needed for today's venture."

Instead of replying, Reba cocked her head as though listening to a distant sound. She then ran to the door and looked through the peephole. "You'd better decide how you want this to play out because Loralyn's hustlin' down the path," she said to Ella Mae. "Should I grab her when she knocks? She's expectin' Julia to prep her on some club ritual, so she won't be ready for me to jump her."

Ella Mae shook her head. "You and Ruiping wait in the bedroom. Stay out of sight. Mom, go with Reba and Ruiping. Henry can open the door. Having grown up with a large household staff, Loralyn will assume he's an employee of the resort. She'll be inside before she realizes that his jacket and bow tie don't match the uniform." Ella Mae turned to Opal. "At that point, the floor is yours. I hope . . ." She trailed off. She hoped for an outcome that wouldn't bring Opal any more grief, but that seemed so unlikely that she was unable to complete her thought.

"Thank you for trying," Opal whispered quietly.

Ruiping moved into the bedroom while Henry took up his position by the door. Ella Mae's mother murmured something into Opal's ear, told Ella Mae to be careful, and then joined Ruiping in the bedroom. Reba looked at Ella Mae and hesitated.

"I don't like leaving you," she said. "What if Loralyn has the apples?"

"If she had them, she wouldn't have gotten out of bed this early. She would have reduced the hotel to rubble right after the wake-up call." Ella Mae smiled at Reba. "I'll be all right. I'll stand behind Opal's chair. That's as close as I can get to you."

Mollified, Reba made herself scarce just as the sound of Loralyn's impatient knock reverberated through the sitting room.

"Good morning, Ms. Croly," Henry said, performing a deferential bow. "Won't you come in? There's coffee on the table."

Henry used both his body and the door to block Loralyn's view of the room's occupants, so she was halfway across the sitting room before she noticed her mother and Ella Mae.

"What the hell is going on?" She directed her question at Henry, who'd smoothly closed the door and fastened the dead bolt.

"Won't you sit down?" He gestured at the chair facing Opal's. "Your mother would like to have a conversation with you. May I offer you some coffee? Or would you prefer tea?"

Loralyn glowered at him. "I'd prefer to watch you thrown out of an airplane without a parachute, but since that's not going to happen, I'll just leave. And if you try to stop me—"

"You may go when your mother is finished," Henry said, an edge of steel creeping into his voice. "I am one of your kind, Ms. Gaynor. For the sake of your overall health, I suggest you not provoke me into using my ability. The few who have survived the experience are usually too traumatized to speak of it."

Ella Mae worried that Loralyn might take one look at Henry's spectacles, bow tie, and silver hair and call his bluff, but she didn't. Having found his speech convincing, she opted to sit in the vacant chair. With an irritated sigh, she turned to her mother and said, "I don't have time for this. You have no idea what's at stake."

"My dear, I know exactly what you're after. The three golden apples Hippomenes used to win Atalanta's hand. You want this object of power for yourself. You're tired of being a pawn on other people's gameboards. You're ready to cut all ties. You want to start afresh in a new place as a new person. You don't ever want to grow old. Or weak. Or sick. You want to be strong. Stronger than I ever was. Stronger than your father ever was. You want to show us how wrong we were about you." Opal's words were soft. A gentle caress. "And we *were* wrong. About *so* many things. Your father and I were so blinded by pride that we didn't take care of our family. We spent our energy increasing our profits and our reputation when we should have been focusing on being good parents. I failed you as a mother, Loralyn. For that, I am truly sorry."

The lengthy speech had clearly drained her, but Opal took a shallow breath and went on. Her eyes never leaving Loralyn's, she spoke as though they were the only people in the room. "I'm sorry that I didn't hug you. That I didn't read you stories or put notes in your lunchbox. I'm sorry that I never once brushed your hair or baked you cookies. I'm sorry that I didn't stop your father from selling Romeo. I barely listened when you talked about your school day, and the advice I doled out wasn't helpful. If I'd spent half as much effort on being a good mother as I did on being a successful businesswoman, then you would have had a better childhood. For letting you down all those years, I am truly sorry."

Opal reached for Loralyn's hand, but Loralyn pulled back. She was obviously shaken by her mother's confession. The Gaynors didn't speak to one another with such openness, with such earnest emotion, and Loralyn didn't know how to deal with it. Sitting there, with the early morning light washing over her, she suddenly looked like a frightened and vulnerable young girl.

"It's not too late for us to get this right," Opal continued quietly. "Even though my time is limited, we can spend what's left of it together. I want to leave you in charge of the business. I'd be happy knowing you were caring for the horses. You could change things, Loralyn. Make everything better."

Something in Loralyn's face was loosening. She was reacting to the idea of running Gaynor Farms. Ella Mae held her breath. Was Opal getting through to Loralyn?

But then, in a flash, her eyes turned hard again. "No," she hissed.

"Why not?" Opal's question came out as a plea.

"Because I want more." Loralyn's words cut through Opal's hopes like a sickle. "You said it yourself. You don't have much time left. So if you really care about me, then let me get what I want without standing in my way."

Opal stared at Loralyn for a long moment. Most people would have flinched or squirmed in the face of such a penetrating gaze, but not Loralyn. Returning the stare, she asked, "Are we done now?"

"Did you kill that woman?"

Loralyn's lips twitched. "Which woman?"

"Cora."

At the sound of Cora's name, Loralyn's brows shot upward. "Cora's dead? Since when? And how do *you* know about it?"

Ella Mae knew that Loralyn was capable of deceit, so she didn't buy her act for a second. "Her death leaves only you and Savannah in the presidential race," she said, joining the discussion. "You must believe the apples are tied to the presidency. Did Bea tell you about them? Did you use her to get in with the Camellias and then murder her so could you take her position?"

Loralyn snorted derisively. "I have no interest in being their president. Growing up Gaynor, I've had my fill of politics and photo ops. And I didn't kill Bea. I liked her. She *chose* me to be her daughter." Loralyn cast an accusatory glance at her mother. "She thought I had admirable qualities."

Seeing the hurt on Opal's face, Ella Mae recalled what she'd been told about surrogates. "You've been a Camellia for months, but I've learned a few things about them too. For example, to become a member without having been born the daughter of a Camellia, you have to offer them something truly special. A great deal of money, fame, or political clout. Of those three, the most likely in your case is money." Ella Mae watched Loralyn closely, but her old nemesis revealed nothing. "You left Havenwood in a hurry," Ella Mae continued. "You didn't have time to get your affairs in order, so my guess is that you invented Lyn Croly—a rich, young widow searching for a worthy cause in which to invest her fortune."

"Oh, *puh-lease*." Turning to Henry, Loralyn gave a languid wave at the coffeepot, which was no more than a foot away. "If she's going to indulge in wild fantasies, I might as well keep my hands occupied."

"Of course." Henry nodded amiably and poured her a cup of coffee.

Ella Mae pressed on. "Tell me. Were you in Havenwood during the Row for Dough event? Did you break into Perfectly Polished?"

"It's hardly breaking in when you're the owner," Loralyn declared acerbically.

Though Ella Mae felt a rush of triumph for being correct, she kept her feelings in check. "I suppose you'd run out of money by then. Whatever clothes, cars, and jewelry you had to buy to create Lyn Croly's persona had drained your resources. You needed to refill the well and you didn't want to leave an electronic trail. You must have kept a wad of cash or loose gems in the salon safe for emergencies."

"Aren't you a clever baker? I'm sure your deductive powers

will prove very useful the next time you need to make a lemon meringue pie." Loralyn set her cup down and folded her arms. "What's your point?"

Ella Mae took a step toward Loralyn. "What's *your* point? You've invested months of your life as well as a great deal of money ingratiating yourself to these women. Why? To get your hands on the golden apples. You wouldn't make such major sacrifices and leave anything to chance. To ensure success, you'd have to eliminate the current president, Bea Burbank. After that, you'd have to get rid of any woman foolish enough to run against you. Luckily, there are only two candidates. Cora Edgeworth and Savannah McGovern. You're almost there, Loralyn. One more woman and those apples will be yours." She shrugged, hoping to bait Loralyn with her next line. "Though how you can be confident they're in Havenwood is a mystery to me."

"You wouldn't know because you're not a Camellia," Loralyn snapped. Her eyes glittered with rage. "When a new president is elected, she is presented with the symbols of the office. They are purely ceremonial, and she is only allowed to handle them during her swearing in, which takes place immediately after the tallying of the ballots. Another Camellia safeguards the presidential symbols the rest of the time. It's never the same woman twice, and no one knows her identity. Cora's mother, Maisie, presented the apples to Bea and reclaimed them immediately following the ceremony. Maisie passed away years ago, and only her attorney knows which Camellia she bequeathed them to. That woman must keep that secret under penalty of expulsion. These stupid cows don't have a clue that the apples have power, but they're smart enough to realize that they're valuable."

Opal cocked her head. "Because they're made of gold?"

Loralyn frowned. "It's more than that. The apples serve

as a reminder of Atalanta's folly. Each newly elected president is supposed to hold them up and give a speech about using a woman's power to bring about positive changes in the world. That was the mission of the club's founder or some altruistic crap like that."

"If I might interject." Henry cleared his throat. Without waiting for permission, he picked up a book from a side table and opened to a color illustration of a woman in a Grecian gown. Her long hair curled in dark ringlets and she wore a quiver filled with arrows on one shoulder. She stood on a mountain overlooking a city and was studying it with a proprietorial air. "Atalanta may have been distracted by the enchanted apples and thereby tricked into marriage, but she never again lost focus of her goals following that legendary race. In fact, she became a powerful landowner and respected leader long after her father and husband faded into obscurity."

"How marvelous for her," Loralyn mumbled. "And while I love mythology as much as the next person, I'm afraid I have far too much to do—"

"Allow me to finish, please." Henry didn't raise his voice, but Loralyn responded to his authoritative demeanor and fell silent. Tapping on the illustration, he brought the book closer to Loralyn. "You can be like this woman. Not the young girl sidetracked by shiny golden apples, but the woman who ruled for decades. An independent woman admired by her people. A woman who was known as the Lioness due to her wisdom and fortitude."

Ella Mae could tell by the way Loralyn leaned forward that she was listening closely.

Henry pressed his advantage. "You could run Gaynor Farms the same way Atalanta managed her holdings. The employees would depend on you to lead them into the future. With that kind of power, you could effect all sorts of change. You could be a lioness of the modern era. You don't need the apples. Learn from this woman's mistake. Your mother is offering you the chance to become powerful, respected, and immortal in name without enchantment. And without the costs that come with possessing an object of power. Seize this opportunity, Ms. Gaynor. I implore you. Take the path of the wiser woman, not the path of the foolish girl."

Loralyn reached for the book and Henry gingerly set it on her lap. Raising the illustration close to her face, Loralyn studied Atalanta with such intensity that no one dared speak.

After a full minute of scrutiny, she began to smile. It was a small, crooked smile. A cruel smile. It made Ella Mae's heart sink, for she knew they'd failed to convince Loralyn to forget her quest. She was utterly fixated on her obsession and no one could lure her away from it.

"Immortal in name is not enough," she said, slamming the book shut. "But I have to thank you, uh . . ."

"Professor Henry Matthews of Oxford."

Loralyn got to her feet and handed the book back to Henry. "Thank you, Professor Matthews of Oxford, for confirming my theory that the apples are worthy of any sacrifice." With an aura of genuine happiness, she moved to stand in front of her mother. "I'm sorry things didn't work out the way you'd hoped, but I have bigger plans than Gaynor Farms. I won't apologize. I've waited a long time for the chance to show the world what I'm made of." She hesitated for a moment, and then, with lightning quickness, she kissed her mother's cheek. "Good-bye, Mama."

Loralyn had turned for the door, her mind already fixed on people and things outside the walls of the cabin, when Ella Mae raced forward to block her path.

"Tell me the truth," Ella Mae demanded. "Did you kill Bea?"

"No."

"What about Cora?"

Loralyn stepped closer. "Not me either. I don't care that she's dead, but I didn't kill her." She poked Ella Mae in the shoulder. Just once, but the touch conveyed a lifetime's worth of hatred. "I warned you to stay out of my affairs, pie girl. You didn't listen, and because of that, you and yours will pay the price."

"Your mother is dying!" Ella Mae cried. "The apples might heal her. Are you so heartless that you won't at least find out if their power could save her life?"

"It's better this way," Loralyn said in a near whisper. "You see, I don't want to be a lioness. I want to be a phoenix. I want to rise from the flames with my past totally forgotten. You're a part of the past too. You belong in the fire with all the rest."

And with that, Loralyn moved around Ella Mae, unfastened the dead bolt, and opened the door. Ella Mae glanced toward the bedroom. Reba stood in the threshold next to Ruiping. Both women were tensed and ready to spring.

"She wasn't lying," Ruiping said. "She didn't kill those women."

By the time Ella Mae turned her attention back to the front door, Loralyn was gone.

"She didn't hurt anyone, but she thinks she knows who the murderer is," Ruiping continued. "It came to her when she was looking at the book."

Reba strode toward the front door. "Should I run her down?"

"She won't tell you anything," Opal said wearily. Sorrow had deepened the creases bracketing her mouth and heightened her pallor. She seemed to have aged several years in a matter of minutes. "Not even if you use force. She's too close to her prize to fail now."

Ella Mae had to agree. "Let her go, Reba. We don't need

to rush back either. We won't be teaching today." She passed her hands over her face. "The killer has made it that much harder for me to investigate. What I don't get is why the murderer wasn't more careful. She's practically invited the cops to descend on the resort. It's almost as if she *wants* everyone to be stuck here." She gestured at Henry's book. "Henry? Can you open to that illustration again?"

"Certainly," Henry said and hurried to comply.

Carrying the book to the window, Ella Mae studied the image under the direct light. She'd only caught a glimpse of Atalanta's face earlier, but now, as she examined the classical features—the proud brow, sharp cheekbones, full lips, and lovely, intelligent brown eyes—she knew what Loralyn had seen. "Not what," she whispered. "Who."

Putting the book down on the coffee table in front of Opal, Ella Mae grabbed her handbag and pulled out her copy of the Camellia Club directory. She turned to the image of Margaret Woodward and laid it next to the illustration of Atalanta. The two faces were almost identical.

As Ella Mae's mother, Henry, Reba, and Ruiping looked on, Ella Mae pointed from one image to another. "Margaret Woodward, the founder of the Camellia Club, must be a descendant of Atalanta. I believe she also possessed the golden apples. But that's not what got Loralyn so excited."

Flipping ahead in the directory, Ella Mae stopped at the page showing Cora Edgeworth and Meg Edgeworth-Ryan's photographs. "What do you see?"

"Margaret Woodward and Meg Edgeworth-Ryan—they could be twins!" her mother exclaimed.

"Not twins," Ella Mae said. "The same person."

Reba pressed her fingers against her temples. "What? How's that possible?"

"Because she has the apples, she doesn't age. Margaret

and Meg are essentially the same name. They look exactly the same. Margaret *is* Meg."

Adelaide put a hand over her heart. "I think you're right."

"Maisie is another form of Margaret," Opal said weakly. "Didn't Loralyn tell us the apples were presented to Bea by Cora's mother, Maisie? Maisie could have been Margaret as well."

"Hold on," Henry said. "If the murderer is an immortal woman who has gained her immortality through the possession of an object of power, then why would she need to kill Bea and Cora?"

Ella Mae shook her head. "I have no idea."

Opal reached out and grabbed Ella Mae's arm. "Loralyn is going to get hurt. She can't fight this woman. There's only one way to defeat someone with this kind of power, and I know exactly how to do it. You must listen to me, Clover Queen. You were willing to sacrifice everything to save us all, and you succeeded. Now it's my turn."

Chapter 14

Ella Mae headed back to the resort's main building in a daze. She glanced from the clear summer sky to the shimmering lake and wondered how it was possible to be surrounded by such beauty when it felt like the entire world was unraveling, one thread at a time.

Seeing no other alternative, Ella Mae had reluctantly agreed to Opal's plan even though every cell in her body rebelled against it. She wanted to bring down Margaret Woodward on her own. And as much as she wanted the woman who'd killed Bea and Cora to be punished for her crimes without putting anyone else in harm's way, she knew she couldn't overcome someone who was basically immortal.

Why did *Margaret kill them?* Ella Mae thought angrily. *She already possesses an object of power, and she's already lived several lifetimes.*

"I know you're simmerin' like a teapot on the stove. That's

a good thing," Reba said. "Hold on to that steam. We've got enemies comin' at us from all sides. This Margaret creature. Loralyn. The cops won't be too happy with us either."

Ella Mae stopped just outside the staff entrance. "You're right. They're going to wonder why we weren't in the kitchen this morning. I have no choice but to tell Hardy that I arranged a meeting between Opal and Loralyn."

"What if you blow Loralyn's cover?" Reba asked, opening the door and waving Ella Mae inside the cool hallway.

"I could be saving her life. If she can't run for president, she's no longer a threat."

Reba touched Ella Mae's arm. "Except to you. She'll try to claw your eyes out if you ruin her chance to get those apples."

"I don't think she'll wait until tomorrow," Ella Mae said as she glanced around the lobby. "Now that she knows Margaret Woodward has the apples, she'll go after them at the first possible opportunity."

Gesturing between the police officers guarding the front door, the main stairwell, and the elevator banks, Reba muttered, "It won't be easy. I think the resort just became a five-star holdin' cell."

"Let's find Hardy," Ella Mae said. "The sooner we clear ourselves with him, the sooner we can focus on Margaret Woodward."

"Can't we just call her Meg?" Reba grumbled. "Even if it is a young-soundin' name for that bag of bones."

"Sure," Ella Mae agreed absently.

Recognizing Officer Hutchins from the previous night, Ella Mae approached the policeman and asked to see Hardy.

"He's been looking for you," Hutchins scolded her before escorting Ella Mae and Reba to a small conference room. He knocked on the closed door and, without waiting for permission, cracked the door and said, "I have Ms. LeFaye and her assistant."

"Give me five minutes," Ella Mae heard Hardy say.

Hutchins pointed at a row of plastic chairs pushed up against the wall. "You can wait there."

Exactly five minutes later, a Camellia named Luanne was ushered out of the room by a female officer. Luanne paused in the doorway, put her hand on her hip, and glared back at Hardy. "Just how long do you intend to keep us prisoners in our rooms? I have a spa appointment at one, and I really need that massage!"

Ella Mae was stunned by the woman's arrogance as well as her complete lack of concern over Cora's death. Hardy, who'd probably heard similar remarks all morning and was tired of them, merely signaled to his officer to move Luanne along and called out, "Send them in, Hutchins."

"I'm sorry if our absence caused confusion," Ella Mae said as soon as she and Reba were seated. Hutchins stood by the door with his arms crossed over his chest and arranged his face into a mask of disapproval.

Hardy nodded in acknowledgment but didn't reply to Ella Mae. Instead, he pressed a button on the recording device in the center of the table and noted the date, the time, and the names of those present.

He then looked at Ella Mae and asked, "Did you kill Cora Edgeworth?"

"What? No!" she spluttered.

Hardy repeated the question to Reba, who calmly replied in the negative.

Hardy's gaze returned to Ella Mae. "What time did you arrive at Lake Havenwood Resort this morning?"

Ella Mae answered him.

"And what did you do upon entering the premises?"

Omitting the detail about going to the kitchen to check on Reba's weapons and discovering Cora's body, Ella Mae explained her scheme to trick Loralyn into appearing at the designated woodland cabin.

"For what purpose?" Hardy demanded.

Ella Mae hesitated. She didn't think Opal would be strong enough to execute her plan after enduring a taxing interrogation, but if Hardy caught Ella Mae in a lie, she would no longer be free to move around the resort.

"Ms. LeFaye?" he prompted impatiently.

"I don't like discussing another person's medical issues, but I can see there's no avoiding it," Ella Mae said. "Opal Gaynor has terminal cancer. She and her daughter, Loralyn, have been estranged since last spring. It's Opal's dying wish to reconcile with Loralyn before she . . . passes. Opal asked me to find Loralyn and I did. Purely by accident. I bumped into her while I was visiting the town of Sweet Briar. At the time, Loralyn made it clear that she didn't want to talk to me, so I was forced to wait until the Camellias came to Havenwood to get Loralyn and her mother together. I lured Loralyn out early this morning by pretending that she was engaging in a Camellia Club ritual. It sounds very underhanded, I know, but I only did it to help a dying woman reunite with her daughter."

Hardy frowned as he took this all in. He then picked up his pen and started reading a list of names.

"You won't find Loralyn Gaynor's name on that list," Ella Mae said.

"You need to look for Lyn Croly," Reba added. "Loralyn's pretendin' to be somebody else with the Camellias."

Hardy circled the name. "Why?"

Ella Mae gave an innocent shrug. "If I had to guess, I'd say that she wants to start over again. Her father, who she once idolized, is in prison, and she had a major falling-out with her mother last spring. Loralyn responded to her familial troubles by moving to a new town and joining this club under a false name."

"Though she *did* return to Havenwood in July to grab cash out of the safe in her nail salon," Reba said. "Set off her own alarm and didn't give a hoot. She must have figured no one would hear the noise with the rowboat race goin' on. I suppose she forgot to pack her salon keys when she left town in a huff last spring."

Now it was Hardy's turn to be stunned. "Ms. Gaynor was responsible for the break-in? When did she tell you this?"

"About an hour ago," Reba said placidly. "Ella Mae and I were in the cabin with Opal the whole time she and Loralyn talked. We wanted to be on hand in case she started feelin' sick. I stayed in the bedroom to give mom and daughter their privacy, but I could hear every word. I have ears like a bat." She touched her fingertips to her lobes.

Hardy jotted a note on a legal pad. "Were you hiding in the bedroom as well, Ms. LeFaye?"

"No. I was there as mediator," Ella Mae said. "And to be honest, I had an ulterior motive."

Hardy gave her an appraising look. "Which was?"

"To find out what Loralyn could tell me about Bea Burbank." Raising her hands in a defensive gesture, Ella Mae quickly continued. "I know I wasn't supposed to conduct an independent investigation, but I couldn't waste this opportunity. As it turns out, Loralyn knew her *very* well. In fact, she became Bea's surrogate. In Camellia Club terms, Loralyn effectively *replaced* Liz as Bea's daughter, and immediately after Bea's death, Loralyn announced that she was joining the race for club president."

Hardy and Hutchins exchanged befuddled glances.

"I find it difficult to believe that two women have been murdered over this position," Hardy said. "However, the facts belie my doubt. Mrs. Edgeworth was also a candidate. I learned that from her daughter."

"Poor Meg!" Ella Mae exclaimed with mock concern. "How is she holding up?"

Hardy looked troubled. "She's numb with grief, I'm afraid. She couldn't supply much in the way of information other than to tell us that the chocolate in the fountain, which was a blend of peanuts and milk chocolate, would have certainly sent her mother into anaphylactic shock had she swallowed a single spoonful."

"Cora obviously trusted the person who offered her that spoonful," Reba said. "And that person must have come up with a mighty compellin' reason for gettin' Cora out of bed so early. Doesn't this joint have cameras?"

"It does, but only in certain areas." Hardy drummed his fingers on his pad. "Were you aware of Mrs. Edgeworth's allergy, Ms. LeFaye?"

"Yes," Ella Mae said. "All the chefs were notified beforehand. In fact, Caroline James and I were discussing that very subject last night. When Reba and I saw Caroline setting up the fountains, she'd yet to do a test run using the milk chocolate because she wanted to check the ingredient list on the Internet first. The words on the bag of chocolate melting wafers were smeared, and she didn't want to take any chances, considering the seriousness of Cora's allergy." Ella Mae shook her head. "Caroline must be so upset. I hope she doesn't blame herself."

Reba narrowed her eyes at Hardy. "*You* don't suspect her, do you?"

Hardy returned Reba's stare. "As of this point, no one is above suspicion." When Reba grunted in disgust, he reluctantly added, "Ms. James doesn't strike me as a killer. Neither she nor her assistants appear to have a motive. The same goes for Ms. Jordan and her assistants. This crime is personal. Based on the scratches on the victim's neck, the ME believes Mrs. Edgeworth ingested the peanut-tainted chocolate. The moment she did so, her lips, tongue, and throat began to swell. When she could no longer breathe, she must have panicked and clawed at her own neck. Once she lost consciousness and fell to the floor, her assailant positioned her, facedown, in the bowl of the fountain."

"How terrible. And cruel." Ella Mae shuddered. She hadn't seen the marks on Cora's neck because her skin had been covered in chocolate, but she remembered Cora's swollen lips and her bloated, protruding tongue.

"Is there anything else you can tell us that might aid in our investigation?" Hardy asked.

Knowing the longer Loralyn was tied up with the police, the safer she'd be, Ella Mae nodded solemnly. "I don't want to implicate anyone, but considering what's happened, I can't leave without repeating what Loralyn told me last night. I thought it was said in the heat of the moment because Loralyn *can* be dramatic. But now . . ."

"Go on," Hardy prompted.

"She made a threat. It wasn't directed at Cora, but toward the other candidate, Savannah McGovern," Ella Mae explained. "Loralyn said, and this is a direct quote, 'If she knows what's good for her health, she'll withdraw her candidacy. If not, she could be the next bloated body you pull out of the lake.'"

From his position near the door, Hutchins shifted impatiently. He looked more than ready to haul Loralyn into the conference room for a nice tête-à-tête with Officer Hardy.

"Thank you, Ms. LeFaye." Hardy took down another note and spoke into the recording device, indicating the time before he hit the stop button.

Ella Mae hesitated at the threshold. "May I see Meg? I could bring her some hot tea or a little soup. She shouldn't be alone right now. She should have company. Maybe someone who isn't a Camellia."

Hardy briefly mulled this over. "One of my officers is with her, but I don't mind your checking in on her. I'll let Officer Parks know you've been cleared to enter Ms. Edgeworth-Ryan's room."

"Thank you," Ella Mae said.

Out in the lobby, Reba breathed a deep sigh of relief. "That went as well as it could. Loralyn will be very busy with the men in blue for the next hour or so, and I expect Hardy will put a few extra officers outside Savannah's door too."

"*And* he's given us permission to visit Meg."

Reba scowled. "Yeah. Poor, sweet, grief-stricken Meg. Let's bring her some chicken broth laced with arsenic. Then, when she busts out the apples to heal herself, we can grab them."

"As appealing as that sounds, we have to prove that Meg and Margaret are the same person, and that she's responsible for murdering Bea and Cora, before we can start poisoning her food," Ella Mae said. "After all, I have no idea what would motivate a woman who already owns an object of power to commit murder in the first place."

"Give her cream of mushroom, then," Reba said with a grimace. She'd never cared for mushrooms.

In the kitchen, they saw that Cora's body had been removed, as had the largest of the chocolate fountains. Two police officers were busy cataloging the items in the kitchen. Maxine and Caroline each stood behind their stations as a police officer examined every one of their pots, pans, utensils, and dry goods.

Ella Mae threw Reba an anxious look. Once the cops had finished with the chefs' belongings, they'd catalog the supplies on the shelves next. And the moment they opened Reba's box of weapons, Ella Mae and Reba would be in a heap of trouble. Unless they could come up with a distraction—something to draw the officers away from that side of the kitchen long enough for Reba to relocate the box.

Just then, Caroline looked up and exclaimed, "Oh, Ella Mae! Isn't this awful?"

Maxine put an arm around Caroline's shoulders as she began to weep. Ella Mae stepped forward, intending to provide Caroline with whatever comfort she could, when one of the cops blocked her path with his meaty arm.

"Are you the pie chef?" he asked. When Ella Mae introduced herself and Reba, the officer pointed at her station. "Please stand behind the counter until we're done here."

Ella Mae read the officer's nametag. "Listen, Officer Tippit, I don't know if you've had a chance to investigate the walk-in yet, but I could have sworn I saw a bag of chocolate melting wafers mixed in with my stuff. I didn't think anything of it yesterday, but considering what happened to Mrs. Edgeworth, it might be relevant. Maybe it contained peanuts. Should I show it to you?"

This was a complete fabrication, but Officer Tippit took the bait and followed her to the other end of the kitchen. Ella Mae risked a backward glance and was pleased when Reba responded with a slight nod.

Inside the refrigerator, Ella Mae walked past dough balls

wrapped in plastic, pints of strawberries, and bags of lemons and key limes. She paused, suddenly realizing that she wouldn't be using any of these items today. There would be no key lime cream cheese pie, rhubarb peach cobbler, strawberry pie in a pretzel crust, faux pecan pie, or lemon tarts with a pine nut crust. Not a single pie would be baked. Ella Mae doubted she'd be instructing the Camellias tomorrow either. She'd have to pack up all this food and bring it back to The Charmed Pie Shoppe to keep it from going to waste.

"Ma'am?" Officer Tippit was gazing at her expectedly.

"Sorry, I was just thinking about the lesson I was supposed to be teaching now." She turned to face the policeman, who was about ten years her senior. "All of the chefs were cautioned about Mrs. Edgeworth's peanut allergy, so we didn't bring peanuts with us. However, I'm sure peanuts are a staple in every resort kitchen. If the killer didn't take them from the dry goods shelf, she could have had a baggie of crushed nuts in her pocket and simply poured the contents into the warm milk chocolate flowing through the fountain. The nuts would have blended in like that." She snapped her fingers.

Officer Tippit began to look annoyed. "Yes, ma'am, but where is the bag of chocolate, er . . ."

"Melting waters?" Ella Mae smiled at the officer. She hoped she'd bought enough time for Reba to act, because not only was her ruse coming to an end, but she was also getting quite cold.

"Yes. Where are they?"

Ella Mae pushed two tubs of mascarpone cheese aside and poked around behind a bag stuffed with rhubarb. "I thought it was back there," she murmured, continuing to search between boxes of butter and gallons of milk.

Officer Tippit interrupted her endeavors by tapping on

her shoulder and indicating a section of empty shelf space on the opposite side of the refrigerator. "Is that where you saw the bag?" he asked tersely.

Ella Mae pretended to be confused. "Maybe. It was white." She held out her hands. "And about this big."

"The chocolate wafers belonging to the resort were stored up there," Officer Tippit said. "We've already collected those as evidence, so unless you saw *another* bag in a *different* location, you're wasting—"

The rest of his sentence was cut off by the sound of an alarm.

Officer Tippit slammed into the refrigerator door, shoving it open wide. The piercing shriek of the alarm was even louder in the kitchen, and when Ella Mae exited the refrigerator, she saw the other officer shooing the other chefs and their assistants into the hallway.

"What's going on?" Tippit shouted to his partner.

"Fire alarm!" the officer called back. "It's no drill either. Orders are to take the civilians to the rear lawn!"

Reba was the only "civilian" left in the kitchen. Her eyes met Ella Mae's and she shrugged as if to say, *It wasn't me.*

"We need to clear out." Tippit waved Ella Mae forward.

There was no choice but to do as he commanded. Within minutes, everyone was outside.

Shielding her eyes against the glare of the August sun, Maxine turned to the first officer and yelled, "Where are we headed?"

"Follow the signs for the docks! We're gathering everyone near the magnolia on the back lawn."

"We'll get sunburn," Maxine's assistant complained. She had very fair skin and her freckled cheeks were already becoming flushed.

Maxine reached into her handbag and pulled out a ban-

danna. "Wrap that around your face. Sunburn is better than a
fire burn, if that's what the alarm is all about." She glanced
up at the higher floors of the resort. "I don't see any smoke."

Now that they'd moved away from the main building,
there was no longer the need to shout. Ella Mae leaned over
to Reba and murmured, "Loralyn said that we all belonged
in the fire. Do you think she planned on starting one?"

"It would be a smart way of gettin' everyone outside and
generatin' chaos." Jerking her thumb at Officer Tippit, Reba
said, "If Loralyn did this, she must have known the cops
were lookin' for her. She can use this opportunity to go after
Meg and those apples."

Ella Mae nodded while considering another possibility.
"And if Meg pulled the alarm, she probably wanted to create
a diversion so she could get close to one of the remaining
candidates. Savannah or Loralyn."

"What if—" Reba's supposition was cut off by the peals
of a fire engine siren.

Hugh! Ella Mae's heart sang. The thought of seeing
Hugh, of being able to rely on his strength and support in
the middle of this madness, gave her a surge of hope. As
insane as the day was fast becoming, Hugh could help make
it sane again.

"Look! The hotel *is* on fire!" Caroline suddenly cried,
pointing at the eastern end of the resort, where smoke poured
from the shattered windows of a second-story room.

Ella Mae knew exactly which guest was registered to that
room. She'd slipped a sealed envelope containing a fake note
from Julia Eudailey under that same door earlier that morning.

"Loralyn," Ella Mae whispered.

"You think she decided to start this fire right after leavin'
the cabin?" Reba asked. There was a hint of admiration in
her voice. "Maybe dropped by the bar on the way back to

her room to grab a few bottles of vodka? With a little booze, she could really make a major blaze."

"Could be," Ella Mae said. "You heard Opal. Loralyn is completely blinded by her desire. She told us herself that she'd stop at nothing to get those apples. Burning down Lake Havenwood Resort wouldn't bother her in the slightest."

By this time, their group had joined the resort staff, the Camellias, and the rest of the cops on the back lawn. The police were doing their best to keep the women calm, but several were close to hysteria—screeching about murder and wailing as they pointed at the flames licking at the windowsills. Bits of ash began to float out over the treetops and rain down on them like polluted snowflakes.

"I don't see Meg," Ella Mae said, scanning the faces of the Camellias. "Or Loralyn."

"There's Hardy." Reba stood on her tiptoes. "But I can't spot his right-hand man. Hutchins."

"He was supposed to collect Loralyn for questioning." Ella Mae crept to the edge of the crowd. "Good Lord, she must have used her siren's powers on him." Grabbing Reba's arm, Ella Mae said, "I have a terrible feeling that he's been incapacitated—that he's trapped up there in that room."

Reba's expression was grave. "I know. My radar is soundin' louder than the alarm. And the flames are spreadin' fast. Whoever's responsible for this started multiple fires at once. They won't be easy to put out. It's goin' to take a while."

"It has to be Loralyn, then. This fire gives her to time to go after Meg," Ella Mae said, looking around for a way to escape from the cops without being seen. "If she *could* get Meg away from the main building, where would she take her?"

"To the cabins," Reba answered. She pulled her phone out of her back pocket and proffered it to Ella Mae.

"Thank heaven for you, Reba," Ella Mae said. "I left all my things in the kitchen."

Please answer, Ella Mae prayed while dialing Hugh's number. She knew the chances of his hearing his phone were slim and that he was unlikely to answer a call in the middle of an emergency even if he did, but he picked up right away. "Reba? Is Ella Mae okay?"

"It's me! I'm around back, and I'm fine," Ella Mae quickly assured him. "I think there's an unconscious police officer in Room 212. It's Loralyn's room. But Hugh, please send another fireman to rescue him because a second emergency is taking place and I need your help with this one. My mother and Opal Gaynor are involved."

There was a brief pause before Hugh replied, "Just as soon as the water's flowing, I'll find you. Hang tight, Ella Mae. I'm coming."

Ella Mae lifted her gaze to the pair of windows belching yellow-orange flames and black smoke. There were other plumes of smoke rising into the sky from the center of the roof. They twisted upward like reverse tornados as the crackle of the fire chewing through wood grew louder and louder.

"Loralyn might not be a killer, but she's now an arsonist," Ella Mae muttered darkly.

"If she left Hutchins up there"—Reba pointed at the burning eastern wing—"then she left him to die. What would you call that if not murder? Listen to me, Ella Mae. The only way to stop a runaway train is to put a stick of dynamite on the tracks. In this case, Loralyn's the train. And you're standin' next to the dynamite."

At that moment, Ella Mae caught sight of Hugh. He was running down the path skirting the western wing of the resort, his arms pumping furiously as he raced toward the back lawn. The sun glinted on an object in his right hand, and Ella Mae saw that he was carrying an ax.

Shooting a glance at Reba, Ella Mae tensed like a cat preparing to spring. "Are you ready to stop two runaway trains? Meg and Loralyn?"

"Hell, yes. Let's go."

The two women broke into a run.

Chapter 15

Ella Mae heard someone shout, "Stop!"

The voice sounded like Officer Tippit's, but Ella Mae didn't turn around to confirm her theory. She kept running to Hugh. When she reached him, he crushed her against him in a fierce embrace.

"We need to keep moving," she said, reluctantly pulling away. "Loralyn probably set this fire, but do you remember when I showed you that photograph of the Camellia Club's founder? Margaret Woodward?"

Hugh nodded, his brow creased in confusion.

"She's still *alive*, Hugh. Using the magic of the golden apples, she was able to extend her life span and become Meg Edgeworth-Ryan. I don't understand how it works, but I know that she's a murderer. I think she killed Bea. And this morning, Reba and I found the body of her second victim. A woman named Cora Edgeworth. Cora was playing the role of Meg's mother."

Hugh looked utterly lost.

"I know it's hard to take in. I'll explain more on the way to the cabins," Ella Mae said and began to jog. "I have no idea why Margaret committed these heinous crimes, but Loralyn is after those apples and the two women are about to clash. Wait a second!" She abruptly halted, causing Reba to slam into her back.

"This is *not* the time for one of your lightbulb moments, Ella Mae!" Reba chided, rubbing the tip of her nose.

Grabbing Reba by the shoulders, Ella Mae pointed at the smoke plumes rising from the resort's roofline. "Was Savannah on the lawn? I don't remember seeing her."

Reba's eyes lost focus as she recalled the scene they'd just fled. "She wasn't there."

"She could be in grave danger," Ella Mae said, her anxiety mounting. "I never considered the possibility that Loralyn might be *helping* Meg—that everything she's told us has been a lie." Ella Mae swung around, her gaze lifting to the blue hills, to the secret entrance located beyond a boulder wall. "What do we have in Havenwood that cannot be found in Sweet Briar or anywhere nearby?"

Reba followed Ella Mae's glance. "The grove," she whispered in horror.

Hugh looked down at the ax in his hand and frowned. "I don't think I'm prepared to defend you. Not against a woman who's basically immortal."

"Don't worry, hon," Reba assured him. "I had Adelaide stash a few goodies in the woodpile next to their cabin. We won't be goin' into this fight unarmed."

"I just wish we knew exactly who we were fighting," Ella Mae said and started to run again.

Bursting into the same cabin she'd visited that morning, Ella Mae found the living room unoccupied.

"Mom?" she called out, hating the way her voice echoed back to her. Hugh checked the bedroom, but it was also empty.

Reba, who'd gone to the woodpile to retrieve her weapons, entered the cabin and pressed a Colt 1911 pistol into Ella Mae's hand. She then pointed at a note on the coffee table. "Did you see this? It's from Adelaide."

Scooping up the paper, Ella Mae scanned the lines. "She took Henry back to Partridge Hill. He remembered an obscure but incomplete reference to the apples that he thinks may prove crucial in a fight against Margaret. My mom will call as soon as he finds the reference."

Reba stared at the note in disbelief. "Who runs off to read books at a time like this?"

"It must be important." Ella Mae adjusted her grip on the Colt. "Did you give Hugh a weapon?"

"She did," Hugh said, patting his back pocket. "Though I don't feel good about carrying. I try not to shoot women if I can help it."

Reba glared at him. "Feel free to bury your ax in Loralyn's chest, then. We're not picky about how she goes down."

"You need to realize that Hugh's walking into this mess in the middle," Ella Mae scolded her friend. "*We* barely know what's going on and we've been in it since the beginning." She put a hand on Hugh's arm. "Just be on your guard around Margaret and Loralyn. They can't be trusted and they won't hesitate to kill us if we try to take those apples."

Hugh nodded solemnly. "What's our next step?"

"We head for the docks assigned to these cabins," Ella Mae said. "It's the most logical escape route."

Reba moved to the door and did a quick check of the surrounding woods before waving Ella Mae and Hugh outside. "What about Savannah? She could be—" The rest of her thought was interrupted by the ringing of her phone. She answered with a quick, "Talk to me."

Ella Mae watched Reba's face. At first, she listened with intense concentration, but her expression rapidly changed to one of fear. Her white-knuckled grip on the phone terrified Ella Mae. Nothing scared Reba. She'd always been fearless.

"I'll tell her," Reba whispered and lowered the phone. "Henry found the passage he'd been lookin' for. It talks about a time limit on the apples' power. They have to be renewed every century. And the cost is dear. It's exactly one life per apple. A woman's life."

Ella Mae gasped. "This is Margaret's motive? She's recharging the apples by murdering her fellow Camellias?" She felt her stomach turn in disgust. "Bea was the first. Cora was the second. I guess Savannah is the third."

Reba gave the door a furious kick. "We have to stop her before she takes Savannah's life. Henry said that if Meg gets her full vitality back, she won't be like a regular woman. She'll be more like Conan the Barbarian meets Maleficent."

"That doesn't sound good," Hugh mumbled.

"Is she magical?" Ella Mae asked.

Reba shook her head. "No, but if one of our kind *did* get her hands on those apples, her powers would be magnified. Imagine Loralyn bein' able to influence an entire town with her voice. She could convince every man in Havenwood to do whatever she wanted. They'd become her slaves. Or her army."

"Lord help us." Ella Mae was sickened by images of Loralyn wielding such power. Her twisted heart would use the apples to destroy anyone who'd ever hurt her. And when she was through with her revenge, she'd continue causing pain and destruction. Her desire would consume what little remained of the girl Ella Mae had known since preschool.

That's exactly what Loralyn craves—to have everything and everyone that once defined her go up in flames—but I can't let her become this dark phoenix.

Ella Mae was so caught up in her thoughts that she almost didn't notice Reba cock her head to the side. She'd heard something.

"A muffled scream. Someone's scared to death," she said. "This way!"

And then she was running.

Ella Mae and Hugh followed, struggling to keep pace. Though they were in their early thirties and she was in her fifties, Reba was as fleet-footed as a spooked deer.

Reba led them along the banks of the lake and to a resort boathouse. She stopped behind a pine tree and waited for Ella Mae and Hugh to catch up.

"You're not even breathing hard," Hugh panted, his chest heaving.

Ignoring him, Reba pointed at the boathouse. "I think Savannah's in there. I can hear voices, but I can't pick up the whimperin' I heard before, which has me worried." She looked at Hugh. "I want you to approach by the boat entrance. We'll take the side door. Let's go!"

Reba didn't bother with stealth, and Ella Mae knew there was a strong possibility that they were too late to rescue Savannah McGovern. The idea that Savannah might already be dead fueled her anger. It was one thing to possess a lust for life. It was quite another to murder three innocent women to prolong one's lifespan by another century. Ella Mae still couldn't believe that Margaret Woodward was Meg Edgeworth-Ryan. She remembered seeing the photograph of Meg accompanying the online article on the clothing drive the Edgeworths had organized. Ella Mae had looked at Meg's pretty face and assumed that she was a sincere young lady. But there was nothing genuine or charitable about Meg. She was a cold and duplicitous killer.

Having reached the boathouse door, Ella Mae had no more time to reflect on the years Margaret had had to hone her ability to deceive other people. Reba pulled out a trio of throwing stars from the pocket of her cargo pants and glanced at Ella Mae, who raised her pistol to the ready position and gave Reba a quick nod.

Reba yanked open the door and the two women burst into the boathouse.

It took Ella Mae's eyes a second to adjust to the gloom within, but Reba bolted forward. The dimness hadn't affected her vision at all and she raced toward the rear of the building, Ella Mae close on her heels.

Wooden boards creaked and groaned under their feet as they ran, and Ella Mae knew they'd ruined any hope of surprise. Reba seemed unconcerned about this, but when they came upon a stack of canoes obscuring their view of the rest of the space, Reba signaled for Ella Mae to go around the stern end of the pile while she darted around the bow end and melted into the shadows.

The moment Ella Mae stepped out from behind the canoes, she found herself face-to-face with Loralyn, who held a shotgun in her arms. The barrel was aimed directly at Ella Mae's chest.

Loralyn's mouth curved into a triumphant smile. "Hello, pie girl."

Ella Mae darted a glance to Loralyn's right. There, tied to a chair, was Savannah McGovern. Her head hung over her chest and her shoulders were slumped. It looked as though the only thing keeping her upright were the ropes binding her to the chair. Meg stood next to Savannah. She had a small golden apple in one hand and a clear plastic trash bag in the other.

Without even looking in Ella Mae's direction, Meg moved Savannah's limp hand onto her lap. She then pressed the piece of golden fruit, which was the size of a crabapple, into Savannah's palm and paused for a moment. Satisfied that the apple would stay in place, she shook out the bag. The creases and wrinkles disappeared and the bag filled with air. And then, in a swift movement, Meg pulled it over Savannah's head.

"No!" Ella Mae cried. She'd had her Colt pointed at Loralyn so that the two old enemies were at a standoff, but now she aimed her gun at Meg.

Loralyn took two steps closer to Ella Mae. "Shut up, Clover Queen." She spoke the title as though it left a foul taste in her mouth. "I warned you to stay out of this. But I'm glad that you didn't listen to me. Getting rid of you once and for all is going to be the highlight of my day."

Where are you, Reba? Ella Mae wanted to shout, but she kept her gaze locked on Loralyn. She didn't want to indicate that she hadn't come alone.

"Where's runty Reba?" Loralyn asked as though she'd read Ella Mae's mind.

"Going for help," Ella Mae said with as much bluster as she could manage. "You need to stop what you're doing, Meg. Or should I call you Margaret?" Her finger caressed the Colt's trigger. She had to decide quickly if she should shoot Meg before Savannah ran out of oxygen. If only Reba would make her move, Ella Mae would know what to do. Hugh clearly wasn't going to be a factor in this showdown. By the time he entered through the boat ramp, this fight would be over.

"I've had many names. It doesn't matter which one you use," Meg answered in a conversational tone. "You won't be alive long enough to address me by any of them. Now, allow me to finish what I started." She tied the bag around Savannah's neck, leaving no opportunity for air to enter or escape.

"Stop it!" Ella Mae started forward. She couldn't help herself. Savannah was utterly defenseless. She was obviously unconscious and would soon slip into a darkness from which she would never awake.

"Stop!" Ella Mae yelled again.

Loralyn lunged at Ella Mae and gave her a violent shove with the barrel of the shotgun.

A second later, there was a whistle of flying metal and one of Reba's throwing stars severed the plastic bag above Savannah's right ear. The star continued on its path, heading right for Loralyn, but she'd caught the wink of silver as it left Reba's hand and was already reacting. Even as Ella Mae was pulling her trigger, hoping to hit Meg, Loralyn was squeezing hers in an effort to bring down Ella Mae.

Because Loralyn was in motion when she fired, her shot went wide. The shotgun blast punched a hole into the canoe behind Ella Mae's shoulder and splinters of wood exploded in the air.

Ella Mae dove to her left, unable to see if her bullet had hit her target. Fragments of wood rained down, temporarily blinding her, and it was only the sound of Reba's voice that saved her from Loralyn's second blast.

"Move!" Reba bellowed, and Ella Mae obeyed, rolling farther to her left. She could feel the impact of the shotgun pellets tear into the boards where her legs had been just seconds before. Without hesitating, she fired three rounds from her pistol. She didn't expect to hit Loralyn, but she hoped to force her to take cover.

Loralyn jumped to safety behind the canoe stack, which gave Ella Mae time to crawl behind a row of barrels stuffed with oars. She waited there for several seconds, letting the smoke clear and the ringing in her ears ease.

Peering between two oars in search of enemies, Ella Mae

found Reba tearing the plastic bag off Savannah's head. Meg was nowhere in sight.

"She grabbed the apple and disappeared," Reba told Ella Mae as she pressed two fingers against Savannah's neck. There was a line of blood on Savannah's newly shorn scalp from where the throwing star had sliced her skin. Thankfully, it was a shallow cut. If Reba's aim hadn't been so precise, Savannah would be dead by now.

Keeping her eyes on the stack of canoes, Ella Mae got to her feet. She raised the Colt and covered Reba while she continued to examine Savannah.

"She's alive," Reba said. "Looks like they clocked her on the back of the head. She's got a monster-sized bump here, but she'll live."

"Come out, Loralyn!" Ella Mae called. Now that she knew Savannah would be okay, she was ready to deal with Loralyn. "You're outnumbered, so put your gun on the floor and kick it over to me or I *will* shoot you."

While Ella Mae waited for Loralyn to respond, Reba crept around Savannah's chair to where Meg had been standing. She squatted down, clasped an iron ring, and gave it a tug. A trap door opened and Reba squinted down into the opening.

"There's a ladder," she whispered. "And I see footprints in the mud below. We need to get Meg. She'll just take out the next woman she sees. She'll fill that third apple and run." She touched her ear. "I think Loralyn left by the side door. She's followin' Meg."

Ella Mae crept around the canoe stack, but Loralyn wasn't there. "What happened to Hugh?" She pointed at the far end of the building. "He should be inside by now."

"I don't like how this is playin' out," Reba said.

"We're *not* going down that ladder. We'll leave the way we came in. I'm sure both women are headed for the dock."

Reba shot her a worried look. "Where Opal's waiting."

The adrenaline that had surged through Ella Mae's veins during the shootout instantly dissipated. Once again, she felt a cold dread sink into her bones. Outside, the summer heat did nothing to dispel the sensation, and when they reached the boathouse ramp and Ella Mae saw Hugh lying immobile on the ground, she was struck dumb with fear.

She ran to him and dropped to her knees on the rough wood, heedless of the dozens of splinters penetrating her skin. To her horror, she saw a trail of blood running from the back of his head. It seeped into the porous wood and disappeared into the thirsty ground below.

"No, no, no, no," she whispered wildly. "You're okay. You have to be okay." Ella Mae searched for Hugh's carotid pulse. When she couldn't feel any vibration, she stared at her fingertips as though they were to blame. "Come on, baby. You have to be okay."

Behind her, she heard the sound of Reba tearing fabric. It seemed to come from a great distance and barely registered with Ella Mae. The only thing that existed was her need to feel Hugh's pulse beat.

She shifted her fingers a little higher on his neck and let loose a sob of relief when she felt the throb of blood moving through his artery. "There it is. I knew you wouldn't leave me," she said, her words coming out as a half whisper, half sob. "I can't lose you. Not *you*. Not ever."

Reba bent down next to Ella Mae and examined Hugh's wound. "It's not deep, but cuts on the head bleed like crazy, so we've got to stop that flow. Help me roll him on his side."

Ella Mae grabbed Hugh's shoulder while Reba cradled his head. Once he was on his side, Reba pressed one of her socks against the wound. Next, she tied the strip of cloth taken from her shirt around Hugh's head. Knotting it tightly, she looked at Ella Mae. "You can stay with him. I'll go alone."

"No!" Ella Mae's eyes flashed with anger. "Hugh ended up like this because he was manipulated and blindsided. Loralyn probably used her siren voice while Meg snuck up on Hugh from behind." She glanced around. "See that oar? There's blood on it. God, what was I thinking? Now that Hugh no longer has his powers, he can't resist Loralyn's. I deliberately put him in harm's way."

"We'll make them pay," Reba said and then held up a finger. She stood very still, listening. Ella Mae tried to see to the end of the dock that led away from the boathouse. However, there were too many trees in the way.

"They're not on this dock," Reba said, shaking her head. "It's the next one."

Ella Mae kissed Hugh's forehead and whispered, "I'll be right back, honey. I promise."

And then she was running again, following Reba over the moist ground and onto the next dock. They thundered over the uneven boards, not caring how much noise they made. Both women ran with guns drawn, jaws clenched, and eyes glittering with fury.

But they weren't fast enough.

From the far end of the dock they heard Opal cry, *"No!"* just before they heard the deafening report of the shotgun blast. They saw Ruiping's body fly backward over the edge of the dock and slam into the water.

Meg turned and yelled at Loralyn, undoubtedly irate over having lost the opportunity to capture Ruiping's waning life force, but Loralyn simply waved the shotgun at her mother.

Witch! Ella Mae thought savagely. *Loralyn and people like her are why our kind were once burned at the stake. Hunted.*

Tortured. Driven from our homes. Because of the magical
Others *with evil hearts. The minority. The ones like Loralyn.*

"If anyone shoots that woman, it's going to be me!" Ella
Mae yelled, but Reba responded by raising her hand, indicating they should slow down.

"Easy," Reba cautioned. "Loralyn has Opal in a hostage
position. I guess she and Meg feel like havin' a chat."

Ella Mae lowered her Colt. The gun felt incredibly heavy
and her hand trembled. "What about Ruiping? She'll die if
we don't get her out of the water!"

"She's already gone, hon," Reba said very softly. "She was
shot at point-blank range."

A searing rage coursed through Ella Mae and she fought
to master it. She couldn't allow her emotions to cloud her
judgment. Not if Opal's plan had any chance of succeeding.
Earlier that morning, when they'd spoken at the cabin, Opal
had predicted that Loralyn would try to seize the apples and
make her escape from one of the resort's more remote docks.
Seeing the flat-bottom Jon boat tied to the cleats behind
Loralyn, Ella Mae realized that her nemesis had been several steps ahead of her all along.

But were Loralyn and Meg truly working together?
Because Ella Mae saw no advantage in the arrangement for
Meg, and she decided to point out this fact to the murderer
in hopes of eliciting useful information.

"I don't know what Loralyn promised you, but you can't
trust her," Ella Mae said to Meg when they were less than
ten feet apart. She avoided looking down at the water, for
she knew that seeing Ruiping's body would shatter her veneer
of bravado. And if Opal could be the picture of courage and
composure in this moment, which she was, then Ella Mae
could too.

"She promised me her mother's life," Meg answered

tonelessly. "Which is a good thing, considering she just wasted a perfectly good one." She threw Loralyn a look of annoyance and then focused her attention on Ella Mae again. "A shot to the knee would have sufficed. I need the life to ebb out slowly, you see. I only require a little essence—that last bit of vitality—to enter my apple. What chance do I have of capturing that when a woman has a gaping hole in her chest *and* is blasted backward into a lake?"

"I assume this isn't your first time," Ella Mae said icily. "Committing murder in order to live longer, that is."

Meg shook her head. "This is the third century in which I've had to 'spark' the apples. I've never used a Camellia to provide me with essence, however. A few have served other purposes in the past, mostly in regards to my acquiring a new identity. One does what is necessary, and this time, using a Camellia was necessary."

"Why?"

Meg flicked a wrist in Loralyn's direction. "Because the grove is here. It wasn't Bea's idea to hold our annual retreat in Havenwood. Let's just say that I helped her come up with the proposal through the power of suggestion. I had the resort mail a brochure to Atalanta House, and during our biggest fund-raiser, I asked some influential people to mention how much they enjoyed their visit to Lake Havenwood Resort in Bea's presence."

"And right after Bea booked the resort and hired the chefs, you killed her," Ella Mae said. "Why did you murder her in Havenwood?"

"No one would suspect me here," Meg said. "That morning, after I played golf with my husband in Sweet Briar, the two of us went home to shower and change. Being the sweet wife that I am, I brought him a refreshing drink, which just happened to be drugged. That boy woke up eighteen hours later with no memory of the previous day. During that time, I drove to Havenwood, called up to Bea's room from a house phone when I knew she'd be getting dressed for dinner, and told her to meet me at the boathouse. There were a few people around that night, but there's something very predictable about a fireworks show. When they're going off, people look up. No one saw me moving around the grounds. And no one was watching the docks at the moment when Bea was climbing into a rowboat, so I brought an oar down on her head. I then rowed out to deeper waters and dumped her overboard. I held her hand while she drowned, and my first apple was filled with her spark."

That's why I never saw Bea that night, Ella Mae thought. *She took the path through the woods toward the cabins and the boathouse.*

"Why would she meet you by the water?" Reba asked. "She couldn't swim."

"Really? I didn't know that." Meg seemed delighted to discover this fact. "She came because I told her I'd been given the apples and that I'd learned a secret about them. None of the Camellias knew what the apples were capable of. The women *sensed* the apples were special, but since they were only used for ceremonial purposes and could only be handled by the president until they were returned to me, by whatever name I was using at the time, no one could fathom their power."

Unable to keep quiet, Reba threw out her hands in exasperation. "Why take them out at all? Just to make yourself feel superior? Why not just keep them locked in a safe?"

Meg frowned, and in her eyes, Ella Mae saw the woman who'd witnessed the passage of centuries. There was wisdom in those eyes. Loneliness too. But above all else, there was arrogance. In living so long, Meg had forgotten the value of a human life. Only her own mattered. All other lives were expendable.

"At one point, those apples were a source of inspiration," she said. "Back when I believed the Camellias could make a difference. I tried. *We* tried. In the beginning, we were full of passion and daring! But now?" She let loose a bitter laugh. "I'm surrounded by pampered princesses. They can raise money, but they lack spirit. They're afraid to make noise, to ruffle feathers. They may as well be wearing corsets. They may as well return to their embroidery. I'm done with those feckless fools! I want to establish a new order. I want to rule over women who possess *real* power."

"So *that's* where Loralyn comes in," Ella Mae said, suddenly comprehending Meg's aspirations. "You want to create an order of our kind and Loralyn has promised to help you."

Meg studied her curiously. "I didn't think you were one of them."

"She's not," Loralyn was quick to say. "She's as weak as a newborn kitten."

"That's a shame. You, at least, show gumption." Meg seemed genuinely disappointed. Removing an apple from her pocket, she caressed its golden surface with her fingertips and studied Opal.

Ella Mae felt her panic rise. "Loralyn can't get you inside the grove. Even with the apples in your possession, you cannot enter. Only magical beings can enter. There has never been an exception to this rule."

Meg flicked her gaze to Loralyn. "You said that I'd be able to influence all the magical people of Havenwood once I was inside. Is it true that I won't be able to enter this special place?"

"As I've already explained, you need *me* to enter. I've shown you my abilities. You've seen what I can do," Loralyn said testily. "You can't listen to Ella Mae. She has no abilities. She's an ordinary woman. A simple baker."

Meg paused to consider this. "Yes, you were able to disarm

that policeman, Hutchins, by merely speaking to him. And I heard a little boy's voice the night Liz interrupted our ceremony as well. You have convinced me of your worth. It's a lucky thing, too, because I didn't want to wait this long to refill the apples. I've never taken such risks before."

"Because you've never stood to gain such rewards," Loralyn declared. "I told you when we were still in Sweet Briar that I would prove myself to you. I knew my life was at stake if I let you down, but I haven't. As soon as you fill that apple, we'll go to the grove." She pointed toward the blue hills. "After that, it won't matter what mess we've left behind. No one will be able to touch us."

Opal, who'd been sitting mutely on an overturned canoe this entire time, now raised her head and looked at Loralyn. Her face was moon-white and her hair was damp with sweat. "You can have my life, my girl. I offer it freely. I won't put up any resistance. Let me make up for all those years I failed you. Let me help you find your new beginning."

Ella Mae wondered if Loralyn could actually stand there and accept her mother's offer, but to her ultimate horror, that's exactly what Loralyn did. Showing no emotion whatsoever, she calmly nodded at her mother. She then glanced over at Meg and nodded at her, as though granting her permission to get started.

Smiling, Meg reached into her pocket and pulled out another plastic bag.

Chapter 16

Meg's eyes gleamed with delight as she studied Opal. "Such a noble gesture."

Opal pushed down on the shotgun barrel. "You don't need this anymore," she told Loralyn and then fixed an imperial gaze on Meg. "She's my daughter, and I've wronged her too many times to count. This is my chance to redeem myself."

"Be that as it may, I must insist on tying your hands." Meg knelt by her victim's side. "Instinct will kick in and compel you to fight for your life. It doesn't diminish your gesture. It's just that humans are wired for survival."

"Do what you need to do," Opal said with apparent disinterest.

While Meg bound Opal's wrists, Ella Mae met Opal's eyes. "Are you sure about this?" she asked.

Opal's expression softened. "I am. Good luck, Clover Queen, and thank you." She then turned to Loralyn and smiled.

"I love you, my girl. With my last breath, I will think only of you."

Discomfited, Loralyn looked away.

Meg shook out the plastic garbage bag, pulled it over Opal's head, and tied it tightly around her neck. She stood in front of Opal for a full minute, listening to her suck in the trapped air. Ella Mae winced every time she saw the bag move in and out of Opal's mouth. As the seconds passed, Ella Mae's heart raced faster and faster, and her face and hands grew clammy. She didn't think she could take another instant of this madness without doing something to stop it.

Sensing her agony, Reba put a hand on her arm and whispered, "This is what Opal wanted. We must respect her wishes."

"But it's *so* awful . . ." Ella Mae trailed off and tears spilled down her cheeks. She couldn't understand how Loralyn could just stand there and watch her mother die.

However, as Opal's inhalations became more labored, Loralyn's mask of composure finally slipped. She could no longer hide that she was disturbed by what she was seeing. When Meg pulled the apple from her pocket and placed it in Opal's upturned palm, the barrel of Loralyn's shotgun drooped until it touched the dock. She opened her mouth and Ella Mae thought she might be on the verge of protesting. Her eyes had gone dark with anguish, and she kept glancing between the apple and her mother, as though trying to decide which mattered more.

The apple began to glow, and Ella Mae knew that it was time to play her part. Loralyn had been given her chance, but she had failed to choose her mother's life over the chance to possess an object of power.

"This woman is sick, you know!" Ella Mae pointed at Opal. "She has terminal cancer. Is that the kind of spark you want?" She shouted at Meg. "Loralyn is tricking you, you fool! She's poisoning your apple!"

Meg and Loralyn both fixed their attention on Ella Mae and she felt a glimmer of satisfaction. She'd successfully distracted Meg and she knew what would happen next. The moment Meg turned to look at Ella Mae, Opal leapt to her feet and, after lowering her head and shoulders like a linebacker, rammed into Meg.

Though the action must have taken every ounce of Opal's remaining strength, she managed to shove Meg off the dock and into the lake. Opal was right on top of her when they dropped into the water. The two women sank below the surface and the water immediately began to roil and churn. A maelstrom of bubbles erupted around the dock. The bubbles grew and grew until they formed a swell, and suddenly an enormous wave crested over the dock. It was so powerful that it knocked Ella Mae, Reba, and Loralyn off their feet. The wood beneath them rocked and pitched. Loralyn screamed.

Ella Mae plunged her fingers in the space between two planks and held on as the dock violently swayed. Closing her eyes, she had no trouble imagining the scene in the water below her. After all, she had once come face-to-face with the terrifying creature Opal Gaynor transformed into whenever she submerged deep in the lake water.

At that time, the LeFaye and Gaynor families had still been enemies. Ella Mae's mother had sacrificed her life for the welfare of the magical community by merging with the ash tree in the grove. She'd become the Lady of the Ash, and Ella Mae had feared that she'd lost her forever. However, Suzy had found a way to break the curse of the Lady of the Ash and to restore Adelaide to her family. The only hitch was that Ella Mae had to dive to the deepest part of Lake Havenwood and retrieve the enchanted flower growing on the murky bottom. This object of power would give Havenwood's grove a permanent source of magic, but a terrifying beast described in several ancient tomes as part crocodile, part shark guarded it.

When Ella Mae caught her first glimpse of that guardian in the lightless depths of the lake, her blood nearly froze. She'd been so petrified that she'd been unable to swim for the surface. After seeing the creature's long snout, its dagger-sized teeth, black scales, and powerful tail, Ella Mae thought she would surely die alone in the blackness.

The beast had circled her, staring at her, assessing her, with a green eye that was at once alien and familiar. That had been the worst moment. Because right then, Ella Mae had recognized the creature as the mother of her nemesis. She'd expected to be devoured in the dark, icy water, by none other than Opal Gaynor.

However, Ella Mae had survived that encounter, and over time, Opal had become an ally and an Elder. She had now transformed into that beast for the last time. It had been her choice—her wish—to leave this world on her own terms.

"Find a way to lure the killer to the docks," she'd told Ella Mae that morning. "I'll do the rest. I have just enough strength to become a guardian once more. I will drag this woman under and pin her to the bottom. Last spring, you showed the entire world that you would risk everything to keep the people of Havenwood safe. But you have sacrificed enough, Ella Mae LeFaye. This is a fight I can win. A battle of my own choosing. Do not deny me a dignified ending."

"What if Loralyn sides with Margaret?" Adelaide had asked very quietly. "What will you do if your daughter follows this woman's lead?"

Opal had responded with a grave nod. "If Loralyn commits murder in order to acquire the apples, there's no telling what she'll do once she has them in her possession. She must be dealt with, and I trust the rest of you to bring her to justice. Loralyn is my daughter. I cannot hurt her. This other woman, however? I can easily take her out. Her immortality will mean nothing if her ending is entwined with mine. When I'm finished, there will be nothing left of her but fish food."

Hating the idea of Opal sacrificing her life, Ella Mae had argued that there was now a large police presence at the resort and that Officer Hardy was a shrewd investigator who wouldn't rest until he'd brought the murderer to justice. Opal had dismissed Ella Mae's protests with a flick of her wrist. "There is no time to adhere to standard police procedure. We're talking about an immortal serial killer possessing an object of power."

"She has a point," Reba had murmured.

Opal had continued as though Reba hadn't spoken. "Ruiping will scout out the main resort at regular intervals to see if either Margaret or Loralyn have set their own plans into action. If Ruiping sees a clear sign, she'll escort me to the docks. She's already reported that someone has a boat tied up down there. Considering these cabins are supposed to be vacant, I assume the boat belongs to our murderer. Sooner or later, she'll make a run for her getaway vehicle. And when she does, she'll find me."

And even though it was Loralyn who'd arranged for the boat, Meg had ended up on that dock with Opal. The woman who'd been known as Margaret, Maisie, Meg, and many other names believed she'd found her third victim in Opal. She thought she'd stumbled upon a helpless victim who could fill her third apple. Instead, a ruthless killer encountered a brave and selfless Elder. A leader of Havenwood's magical community. In lieu of obtaining another century of life, Meg had been pulled underwater to come face-to-face with her mortality. And it had come in the form of dagger-like teeth and sickle-sharp claws.

Gradually, the dock stopped rocking under Ella Mae.

When it finally leveled out, she opened her eyes. Her knuckles were white from having gripped the boards so desperately, and her forearms trembled.

"It's done," she whispered to Reba. Her voice was hoarse with grief.

Ella Mae glanced over to where Loralyn had fallen. She was already on her knees, staring blankly out at the water. It was flat and calm, as though nothing unusual had happened.

"Mom?" Loralyn called in a faint voice. She'd dropped the shotgun when she'd lost her balance, and now, as her leg brushed the barrel, she sneered and gave the gun a savage kick, sending it skittering across the wood planks and into the water. Crawling to the edge of the dock, Loralyn put both hands in the lake. Spreading her fingers like two starfish, she swirled them slowly around and called to her mother again.

Ella Mae moved next to Loralyn and gazed down into the water. She didn't expect to see anything. She just wanted Loralyn to know that she wasn't alone.

"She's not coming back, is she?" Loralyn asked without looking up.

Fighting back tears, Ella Mae whispered, "No. She said the change would take whatever strength she had left."

Loralyn withdrew her hands from the water and hugged her knees. "Meg's bones will be nothing but dust in the current. She's so old that she would have disintegrated the second she died. She was gone in a flash, taking the third apple with her." A single tear slipped down her cheek. "Taking my mother with her."

"Your mom wanted you to remember her as being strong and brave," Ella Mae said gently. "In sacrificing herself, she also hoped to save you. She was trying to keep you from becoming so corrupted that you'd be unrecognizable. She was trying to stop you from turning into a monster."

Loralyn released a long, world-weary sigh. "She succeeded in stopping me, all right. The third apple is gone, and I have no idea where the other two are. Meg probably locked them in the safe in her hotel room."

"Which may or may not be on fire," Reba murmured.

"You're not getting the apples," Ella Mae said, unable to keep anger from creeping into her voice. "You killed Ruiping. That action has sealed your fate. If only you hadn't pulled the trigger, you could have had a different future. You could have lived out your mother's dream and run Gaynor Farms, but you crossed a line, Loralyn. Even for the sake of your mother's memory, I can't ignore that."

Surprisingly, Loralyn didn't argue. She took off her shoes and her socks and dipped her feet into the water. "I'm not as far gone as you think, but I'll wait here. You can tell the cops where I am."

Ella Mae didn't know what Loralyn meant by her cryptic remark, but she had no time to question her. That was for Hardy to do. She needed to get back to Hugh. Turning away from Loralyn, she nodded at Reba, who responded by taking her phone out of her pocket.

"This won't make a lick of sense to the cops," Reba said, her finger hovering over the screen. "They'll be faced with a missin' woman. Meg. And they'll find a dead woman in the water. Ruiping." Ella Mae shuddered at the thought of Ruiping's body floating on the other side of the dock. As much as she wanted to pull her out of the lake, she knew she couldn't. She had to leave her for the police to find. But she hated it. She hated that she hadn't even looked at her. It was a disgraceful way to treat someone who'd shown Opal such devotion.

"As if those two things weren't bad enough," Reba continued, "there are a thousand questions we can't answer. How do we explain why we bolted from the resort and ended up on this dock? Or where Opal is. And when Savannah comes to, who knows what she'll tell them."

"She'll say that Meg tried to kill her," Ella Mae replied. "And after listening to her statement, Hardy will come to the conclusion that Meg is also a suspect in Cora's murder. When he can't find her, she'll become his main suspect. He'll focus all his energy on hunting her down."

Reba frowned. "Yeah, but what about the fact that this one was Meg's accomplice?" She gestured at Loralyn's back. "How will *she* explain Meg's motive—or her own—without endin' up in a loony bin?"

"Loralyn can tell Hardy that she and Meg were competing to become the next Camellia Club president. She can't mention the apples at all." Ella Mae touched Loralyn on the shoulder. "Are you listening? Because Reba's right. You have to convince Hardy that you did what you did to win that election. If you start talking about magic apples and a woman who lived for centuries, you'll be sent to a psych ward."

"He won't believe that four women are dead because of a club election," Loralyn said softly. "But he'll arrest me and close the case because that's what he needs to do to restore order. Clean up and move on. That'll be the theme after today."

She spoke without a trace of her usual acerbity, and despite the crimes she'd committed, Ella Mae felt pity for Loralyn. They'd never gotten along, but Loralyn was as much a part of Ella Mae's past as was Reba, her mother, her aunts, or Hugh.

"Call the men in blue, Reba," Loralyn said, her eyes never leaving the water. "I know exactly what to say."

In a rare show of deference, Reba walked halfway up the dock before dialing.

"How did it work?" Ella Mae asked Loralyn once they were alone. "How did Meg manage to be Cora's daughter?"

"She handpicked Cora, based on her looks, when Cora was still in college. Arranged her marriage to a wealthy man and made her Maisie's surrogate so she could become a Camellia. Cora and her husband never had a child of their own. When the time was right, a 'distant relation' of Maisie's came to live with Cora. This was Meg, of course. Cora named Meg her surrogate; Meg became a Camellia and married a wealthy man named Andy Ryan shortly afterward. The rest is history."

Ella Mae tried to absorb this astonishing tale. "So Maisie was playing the parts of two women at the same time?"

"Yes, but Maisie required too much work," Loralyn said. "Maisie needed a wig and fake wrinkles created using liquid latex. Meg couldn't wait for her to pass away."

"What about Cora's husband? Was he aware of Meg's true identity?"

Loralyn shook her head as though the man bore no relevance. "Cora's husband was already ill when they were married. Some terminal disease. He died long before Meg appeared," Loralyn said. "And Andy travels all the time on business. He has no idea what his wife is up to. Theirs is one of those marriages in name only."

Ella Mae stared out across the lake toward Partridge Hill. Her home. Her safety and her sanctuary. Her mother was there. Chewy too. She thought of all the summer nights she'd shared meals with her aunts, Jenny and Calvin, Suzy, and the Book Nerds, and of how lucky she was to know the companionship of such smart, loving, and giving people.

"Why did Cora agree to all of this?" she asked.

"For money." Loralyn looked at Ella Mae as though she understood nothing. "Cora was working two jobs to cover her tuition and would still have a huge student loan to pay off as her graduation present. Her parents had died unexpectedly, leaving her a mountain of debt, so when Meg came along and offered her entry to a life of country clubs and housekeepers, Cora leapt at the chance."

Ella Mae thought of Cora, facedown in the bowl of the chocolate fountain. "She paid a high price for that life of luxury. So did other Camellias, I'd imagine. Others Meg had to kill over the years in order to take their place—to become surrogates in their stead. It's why the surrogate rule exists in the first place. It's easy to write the rules when you're the club founder. Did the Edgeworths help convince Bea to take you as her surrogate?"

"Yes," Loralyn said tiredly.

At the mention of Bea's name, both women stared out across the lake toward Partridge Hill. Ella Mae believed that Loralyn had grown fond of Bea. Within a short time, her old nemesis had lost her adopted mother and her biological mother. It was no wonder that Loralyn seemed completely deflated. And while Ella Mae was tempted to leave her sitting there without a word of comfort, to punish her for all the wrongs she'd done, she was unable to be so callous.

"I'm sorry for your loss, Loralyn," Ella Mae said, getting to her feet. "Your mother was a remarkable woman who loved you very much. I'm going to check on Hugh now, but if you need help in the future, you can call on me. I make this offer in your mother's name, and because I want her sacrifice to mean something."

When Loralyn didn't respond, Ella Mae walked up the dock to where Reba was waiting for the police.

"I told the cops to send the paramedics to Hugh. He won't like bein' fussed over. Most men don't, but I want them to look at that cut." Reba pointed at Loralyn. "I'll keep an eye on her. If she tries to get on that boat, I'll stop her. I still have two throwing stars left."

Glancing back to where Loralyn sat, Ella Mae shook her head. "I think she's done running. I believe Opal gave her what she's been waiting for her whole life."

Reba furrowed her brows. "What's that?"

"Proof that she was loved. By sacrificing herself to keep Loralyn from being tainted by those apples, Opal proved just how much she loved her," Ella Mae said. "And that experience has left Loralyn feeling both full *and* empty inside. She's simultaneously grateful *and* grief-stricken. I can't begin to fathom the tumult of emotions that must be churning inside her heart right now. She's too mixed up to do anything but sit there. In a few hours, it'll really hit her."

"Everything that happened today?" Reba asked.

Ella Mae saw a troupe of uniformed policemen heading their way. "Yes. The derailment of her plans. The end of her freedom. The loss of her mom. All of it. And she'll have to face it alone, which is no good. Her loneliness is part of the reason she chose such a dark path in the first place. Loneliness certainly won't help heal or reform her. I doubt it helps anyone."

Reba put her hands on her hips. "I suppose you plan on gettin' involved in her redemption."

"I owe it to Opal Gaynor to try," Ella Mae replied before hurrying off to be with Hugh.

On her knees beside him, she was relieved to discover that the laceration on the back of his head was no longer bleeding. His pulse was strong, and though the skin on his face was warm and flushed from being exposed to the August sun, he didn't feel febrile. And when she brushed his cheek with her fingertips, Hugh opened his eyes.

"What happened?" he croaked, blinking at her. He shifted his shoulders before she could stop him and abruptly winced. "Damn. My head is killing me." Tentatively, he reached up to explore the fabric wrapped around his head. "What's this?"

"Someone hit you with an oar. Pretty hard too," Ella Mae said. Hearing the sound of multiple voices, she glanced up to see two paramedics heading their way. A man and a woman jogged alongside a pair of policemen. "Good. The cavalry's coming."

Hugh struggled to sit up. "I can't let them find me like this. I'll never hear the end of it at the station." He grasped Ella Mae's hand. "Please."

She hesitated. "Okay, but take it slow."

Hugh's arms slid around her back while her arms crossed under his wide shoulders. Carefully, she raised his torso off the ground and then held him steady for several long seconds. "How are you doing?" she whispered worriedly after he remained silent.

"I'm dizzy," he confessed. "And I'm going to be sick. Let go, Ella Mae."

Hugh's fellow volunteers arrived just as he was retching in the mud. They exchanged amused grins and waited for him to empty his stomach before kneeling beside him.

"How'd you end up here, Dylan? Don't you know the fire is at the resort?" a woman teased, putting a steadying hand on Hugh's back. "How many fingers am I holding up?"

Hugh responded by showing her a particular finger of his own. The woman laughed good-naturedly before her tone became brisk and businesslike. "Seriously, Dylan. You're probably concussed. We need to go through all the motions."

While she ministered to Hugh, the male EMT, who introduced himself as Chuck, asked Ella Mae what had happened. Avoiding specifics, Ella Mae pointed at the oar. "Someone hit him with that."

Chuck placed two fingers in his mouth and whistled. One of the cops heading toward the next dock paused and turned. Chuck waved him over and showed him the oar.

"This day just keeps getting crazier and crazier," the cop said.

Under her breath, Ella Mae muttered, "You have no idea."

The next day, despite the fact that Ella Mae had given Officer Hardy a detailed statement and reviewed it with him several times the previous afternoon, he called her back to the station.

Ella Mae passed several Camellias in the hall, but none of them acknowledged her. Even the Eudaileys, who'd been kind to Ella Mae, ignored her and continued speaking to a man in a tailored business suit. There were dozens of similar-looking men milling about the station. Assuming they were attorneys, Ella Mae could only imagine the list of demands being made on the Havenwood Police Department.

"For the most part, the ladies want to leave," Hardy said when Ella Mae asked what the Camellias were after. "And as much as I want to see them go, there are too many inconsistencies in yesterday's statements. I don't like inconsistencies. They prevent me from closing cases."

Ella Mae responded with a vague nod. "How can I help?"

"I'm faced with two major problems. The first is that Meg Edgeworth-Ryan is missing. I've put out an APB on her, but I need you to be perfectly clear on one point: Is the last time you saw her when she and Opal Gaynor plunged into the lake together?"

"That's right," Ella Mae said. "And neither woman surfaced."

Hardy rubbed the stubble on his chin. "We recovered

Mrs. Gaynor's body yesterday evening. Though her hands were not bound, the ME found evidence of rope marks on her wrists."

Ella Mae looked down at her own wrists and bit her lip. She did not want to grieve for Opal in front of Hardy. "When this is over, may I bury her? In my mind, she's a hero. Even though Meg is still missing, Opal's act prevented anyone else from being hurt yesterday." Ella Mae struggled to keep her voice steady. "She doesn't deserve to be put on a metal slab—to be poked and prodded. I know it has to be that way, but as soon as she can be laid to rest, will you allow me to make the arrangements if no other family members come forward?"

Hardy mumbled something that sounded like a yes and then tapped his case file, which was bulging with loose papers. "The second problem I have relates to the death of Ruiping Chen. Loralyn Gaynor claims that Meg Edgeworth-Ryan shot Ms. Chen. In your statement, however, you said that Ms. Gaynor fired the gun." Hardy laced his fingers together and gazed intently at Ella Mae. "Did you see Ms. Gaynor shoot Ms. Chen?"

For a moment, Ella Mae was too shocked to reply. "Well . . . no. Reba and I were too far away. We only heard the shot. I assumed Loralyn was the shooter because she'd fired at me in the boathouse and because she'd been holding the gun when Reba and I reached the end of the dock."

"Divers recovered the weapon this morning. It's encrusted with mud and the likelihood of drawing a clear set of prints is slim to none. Ms. Gaynor insists that the shots she took at you in the boathouse were never meant to hit you. She merely needed to convince Meg that she was on her side."

Ella Mae gasped. "Are you kidding me? Loralyn practically shot my leg off! And she didn't lift a finger to save

Savannah. Letting a woman die would have made Loralyn an accomplice. How does she explain her complicity?"

"According to Ms. Gaynor's statement, she was forced to behave this way in order to protect her mother. Meg threatened to kill her mother if Loralyn didn't follow her instructions to the letter," Hardy said. "Ms. Gaynor admits to disabling Officer Hutchins and starting the fire in the resort. However, she insists that it was Meg, and Meg alone, who was responsible for the deaths of Bea Burbank, Cora Edgeworth, Ruiping Chen, and Opal Gaynor, as well as the attempted murder of Savannah McGovern."

"But Loralyn *helped* her," Ella Mae protested heatedly. "She stood guard, with that shotgun pointed at my chest, and deliberately prevented me from freeing Savannah. If Reba hadn't used her throwing star, Savannah would be dead, and then Loralyn would be an accessory to murder."

Hardy shuffled his papers. "Ms. Gaynor has pled guilty to multiple criminal charges and has been very cooperative. Because of her assistance, we recovered two golden apples from the safe in Meg's hotel room. Apparently, these items were a large part of what motivated Ms. Edgeworth-Ryan to kill her fellow club members. She wanted to become president in order to possess these apples. The whereabouts of the third apple is unknown, and Ms. Gaynor believes Meg has it on her person. Do you agree with that statement?"

Ella Mae pictured the apple sinking to the bottom of Lake Havenwood. She saw it come to rest in a patch of silt and stones. For now, the shiny orb would attract scores of fish. But soon, the mud and muck would cover it. Then its light would wink out like a dying star.

"Yes," Ella Mae said firmly. "I saw Meg put it in her pocket before she went over the edge of the dock. If you find Meg, you'll find the apple too."

Satisfied by her answer, Hardy took a sip from the coffee cup on his desk and grimaced. "Cold," he grumbled. "All right, Ms. LeFaye, I think I have everything I need now. I appreciate your time and—"

"Wait a minute," Ella Mae interjected. "What will happen to Loralyn?"

"Her lawyer and the District Attorney's Office are negotiating her sentence as we speak," Hardy said. "Ms. Gaynor will be going to jail, but as far as which facility and for how long, I can't say. That's not my job. What I need to do now is get these Camellias out of my station and have a conversation with the Chinese Consulate in Atlanta. Dr. Kang has expressed his desire to take Ms. Ruiping home, and I would like to grant his wish as quickly as possible."

With all that had occurred, Ella Mae had forgotten about Dr. Kang. Her cheeks flushed with heat as she felt a rush of shame and sorrow. The healer would have to return to China without his assistant. "That poor man."

"Yes," Hardy said somberly. "Four deaths over a vainglorious title and a trio of little golden apples that can't be worth more than fifty grand—it's sickening. What is this world coming to?" He glanced at a photograph on his desk. It showed Hardy's beloved boxers sitting on a sofa next to a woman Ella Mae assumed was Hardy's wife. "I've been toying with the idea of retiring. After this case, the idea has really taken hold. I believe I've seen enough." Looking a little abashed, he cleared his throat. "Thank you again, Ms. LeFaye. I hope the next time we meet, it'll be in your pie shop."

"I hope so too," Ella Mae said, standing and taking Hardy's outstretched hand. "And I understand what you mean about seeing enough. There does come a time when we need to close certain doors so that others can open. I'm ready to do that as well."

Hardy smiled at her. "Are you? And does this other door have anything to do with a handsome fireman?"

"How did you know?" Ella Mae pretended to be amazed. "Are you sure you're ready to give up policing? You're awfully good at it."

Hardy grinned, and then his grin vanished and he cupped his free hand around hers. "Yes, I do believe it's time you retired too. Not from the pie business—there'd be a riot if you did that—but from sleuthing. I know you're the type of person who tries to set things right. You're no meddling busybody—I'd never accuse you of that. But perhaps it's time, if you don't mind my saying so, that you pursued your own happiness." He gave her hand a paternal squeeze.

Ella Mae was moved by both his speech and the kindness in his eyes. She'd always liked Jon Hardy and she felt guilty that she'd never been able to be completely honest with him about the cases she'd been involved with, but it was better this way. He'd seen enough. He didn't need to know about the existence of magic.

"Perhaps you're right. Perhaps it is time for me to be happy," she said and immediately envisioned the plot of land overlooking Lake Havenwood.

Leaving the station, and its hallways filled with Camellia Club members, behind, Ella Mae got in her pink truck and headed east, toward home. Toward her family, her friends, her dog, and the one person who could grant her the happiness she'd spent her whole life searching for.

She headed for Hugh.

Epilogue

Opal Gaynor's memorial service was attended by hundreds of Havenwood citizens. All of the LeFayes were there, as was Loralyn Gaynor. Verena had exerted her formidable influence on her husband and he'd come through for her again. He'd pulled a dozen strings to ensure that Loralyn had the chance to say farewell to her mother.

Ella Mae expected the townsfolk to treat Loralyn with suspicion or disdain. She was a convicted criminal, and the restoration of Lake Havenwood Resort would take months to complete. However, the editor of the town paper had clearly been swayed into believing Loralyn's claims that she'd been Meg's unwitting pawn. Following a series of articles—written by the editor himself—in which Loralyn exposed the darker side of the Camellia Club by revealing how the teenage girls were pressured into having plastic surgery and how the mothers kept an updated list of the region's most eligible bachelors, Loralyn had become a tragic heroine. She was the woman who'd been forced into committing terrible crimes in order to save her mother—a woman caught up in the greatest women's club scandal in American history. Unlike Ella Mae, the general public didn't know that Loralyn had set fire to the resort and had tried to shoot Ella Mae with a shotgun.

Bombarded by print and television reports of Loralyn's story, most people sympathized with her plight. The governor received thousands of letters from across the state protesting her incarceration. And thanks to a social media campaign run by the staff of her nail salon, her celebrity status continued to grow. She'd become so popular that the Havenwood Police had had to hire extra security for Opal's service. When Loralyn alighted from the sheriff's cruiser outside the church, a crowd of well-wishers instantly surrounded her. They tried to press cards or bouquets of flowers into her hands or snapped photos of her with their cell phones.

The press was there too. In force. They shouted at Loralyn and begged her for sound bytes, but she only responded with a demure smile.

Unable to witness another second of the spectacle, Ella Mae took Aunt Verena's elbow and entered the church.

"I need to know if Loralyn shot Ruiping or if she was telling Hardy the truth when she said that Meg was responsible for all the killing," Ella Mae whispered as the two women made their way up the center aisle to one of the polished pews. "I need to know because it will forever change how I see her. How I treat her. I offered her my friendship, and I won't go back on my word, but can I truly be her friend if she's a killer?"

Verena settled into a pew. It creaked in protest and she rearranged her black-and-white floral dress around her knees. "I don't know. Can you?" she asked Ella Mae. "If not for our brave firemen, Officer Hutchins could have died. Loralyn left him in her hotel room without a backward glance. His life meant nothing to her. She used her voice to enchant him. She took his own handcuffs and secured him to the bed. Then, she gagged him and started multiple fires. The poor man probably lost consciousness believing he was going to die in that room. And what explanation do you think he gave his superiors as to how he ended up in such a compromising position? I doubt he remembers a thing after knocking on Loralyn's door." Verena reached for her hymnal. "My point is that Loralyn *is* a killer. I don't know if she shot Ruiping, but she left that officer to be burned in a fire that *she* started." Putting a hand over her chest, Verena said, "She's a murderer in here."

Ella Mae nodded. Her aunt's thought echoed her own, but she wanted to believe that Loralyn could change—that Opal's sacrifice hadn't been for nothing. She wanted to believe that the love Opal had shown her daughter had thawed the ice in Loralyn's heart. Following her sentencing hearing, she'd been the picture of humility and remorse. Ella Mae could only hope that it wasn't all an act.

Ella Mae glanced toward the altar, where a large portrait of Opal was surrounded by enormous arrangements of white roses, hydrangeas, gladiolas, and most of all, chrysanthemums. Ella Mae didn't see the Opal she'd come to know in the glamorous, haughty-looking woman captured in the portrait. The Opal she'd grown close to had become strongest in heart and spirit when her body was at its weakest. In admitting her faults and seeking her daughter's forgiveness, she'd become the loving mother Loralyn had yearned for. And despite her frailty, her thinness, and the sallow hue of her skin, she'd been incredibly beautiful on the last day of her life. Her eyes had been filled with fire and she'd spoken in a voice of calm wisdom, as though she already had a foothold in the next world and was only lingering in this one until her final task was complete.

Ella Mae's eyes moved to the circular stained glass window above the choir. She studied the troupe of angels smiling benevolently down upon the robed singers and thought of the monster Opal had to become in order to drag a ruthless killer to the bottom of the lake. It had taken a monster to destroy a monster. Magic had saved them.

Opening her hand, Ella Mae touched the spot on her palm where her clover-shaped burn scar had once been. She thought of all the times she'd cursed magic and had wanted nothing more to do with it.

This was not one of them.

At that moment, Hugh entered the church. Ella Mae could feel his presence before she actually saw him. She turned just as he was scanning the crowd, searching for her, and when their gazes met and the corners of his mouth twitched and his bright blue eyes sparked at the sight of her, she forgot about her missing scar.

A minute later, he slid into the pew and took her hand. "Opal would have been thrilled by all the attention Loralyn's getting," he whispered. "Especially from the trustees of Gaynor Farms. And she'd have loved to learn that the Camellia Club will never hold another meeting. The scholarship money will be distributed, but Atalanta House will soon belong to the State." He watched Loralyn shake hands with two elegant men in dark suits. "She's made serious mistakes, Ella Mae. She's done terrible things. But it's good that she could come today. Everyone should have the chance to say good-bye to the people they love." Hugh nodded deferentially at Verena. "I imagine you had something to do with this."

Verena shrugged and turned the pages of her hymnal. "I have no idea what you're talking about."

Hugh smiled at her. "Sure you don't."

"*I'm* not the one recovering from a concussion." Verena tapped her temple. "You're probably as scrambled as a pan of eggs up here."

Hugh groaned. "Not you too. For the past two weeks, I've gotten so much grief from the volunteer crew. They keep putting this Halloween skull in my locker or in the truck. The skull's head is wrapped with bandages made of girls' socks, and the socks change every day. They started out pretty tame. Pink with purple kittens, rainbow unicorns—that kind of thing. But they've evolved. Now it's thigh-high tights with racy patterns and fishnet stockings."

"You should give those to Reba," Verena said. "Fernando is heading back this way next week, and I bet she'd love to add those fishnets to her lingerie drawer before he gets here."

Ella Mae held out her hands. "Please. We're in church. I do *not* want to think about Reba's underwear drawer at the moment."

Suppressing a laugh, Verena turned to greet a friend in the next pew.

"Have you had a chance to talk to her yet?" Hugh asked, indicating Loralyn with a slight jerk of the chin.

"Honestly, I haven't tried," Ella Mae said. "This has too much of a circus atmosphere for a memorial service if you ask me. Between the organ music, the chitchat, the crush of people surrounding Loralyn, and the media presence in the back row, this isn't quite the intimate ceremony I had in mind."

Hugh nodded. "That's because Loralyn's celebratory status keeps growing. If only the masses knew the truth."

"If they did, dozens of people in this building would be

exposed," Ella Mae said, and Hugh knew that she was referring to all the magical people sitting among them. "At least
Loralyn is still involved with Gaynor Farms, which was
Opal's most fervent wish. If Loralyn can behave herself
while she's doing her time and also maintain her current
status with the community, she may serve a shorter sentence
than the one she was given. Someday, the future of a very
valuable and influential company will be in her hands."

"When that day comes, I hope that will be enough for her,"
Hugh said. "I hope she won't set out on another quest like the
one that brought Margaret Woodward to Havenwood."

Ella Mae shook her head. "It won't be enough. Loralyn
is a woman with intense desires, Hugh. She may even feel
them more deeply than the average human. Over the last
year, those desires have caused Loralyn to side with Nimue,
a woman who almost destroyed Havenwood. After that came
Margaret Woodward. It was through Nimue that Loralyn
first learned of the golden apples, and it makes me nervous
to think what other knowledge Nimue may have shared with
Loralyn." Ella Mae was silent for a moment before she continued. "Do you know what Loralyn needs?"

When Hugh shook his head, Ella Mae went on. "To fall
in love. She hasn't experienced enough love. If she had,
maybe she wouldn't be headed back to prison after burying
her mother."

"Maybe." Hugh sounded unconvinced. "Then again, she
was born a siren. Maybe her only hope of finding real love
is a life without magic."

Ella Mae considered this while watching Loralyn make
her way to her seat. As she moved under a stained glass
window portraying Moses parting the Red Sea, a sunbeam
highlighted the glass, coloring Loralyn's face and pale hair

the dark blue of deep ocean water. Her pale blue eyes turned dark and fathomless, and in that moment, she looked every bit the siren.

"I see your point," Ella Mae whispered as the organ music ceased and a hush fell over the sanctuary. "But there's no grove in prison. Her powers will wane to almost nothing. She'll be as close to a human as she can ever be upon her release. She stands a chance of having a genuine relationship then. Not one based on manipulation and enchantment."

"Yeah, but who's going to convince her to do that?" Hugh asked.

Ella Mae squeezed his hand. "We are. Despite what she's done to us and what she's done to others, we're going to be her friends. Opal died hoping Loralyn might come around. I have to carry on that hope. Will you help me?"

"I'll do what I can," Hugh promised.

As she joined the rest of the congregation in bowing her head for the opening prayer, Ella Mae detected the faint perfume of chrysanthemums filling the air. She smiled and whispered a soft farewell to her friend.

August already felt spent by the time the full moon arrived. To Ella Mae, it was the largest, most beautiful, and most terrifying moon she'd ever seen.

"Many Native American tribes call this the Sturgeon Moon," Hugh had said when he'd met Ella Mae outside her front door. He'd pointed at the sky. "Apparently, it's easy to catch that particular fish this month. We should test the theory before September comes. Take a drive to the Great Lakes. What do you think?"

"How can you be so calm?" Ella Mae had demanded, hating the tremble in her voice.

Hugh had responded by taking both of her hands in his. "Because I *know* that rose is going to light up like a torch. Like fireworks. It's going to light up the way *I* do whenever I think of you."

"So why I am so scared? *I'm* the one who wanted to trust in us—to march forward the way most people do—without knowing for certain what our future holds. But here I am, shivering like a wet cat, because we're about to shake a *real* Magic 8 Ball, and the only answer I want that enchanted rose to reveal is, 'It is decidedly so.'" Ella Mae had clung to Hugh until she'd grown calm.

"*I'm* certain, so don't worry about the magic bush," Hugh had said. "And if the petals are printed with the words 'Reply hazy, try again,' I can always set fire to the damned thing."

Ella Mae had laughed then, and the tension bubbling up inside her had spilled out and dissipated like water soaking into parched earth. Hugh had held her and laughed with her until Ella Mae had pulled away and expelled a long, slow breath. "Okay. I'm ready."

Hand in hand, Ella Mae now led Hugh to the entrance of her mother's garden. Partridge Hill had been Ella Mae's home. She'd grown up here. She'd spent endless summer afternoons meandering its winding paths, following the flights of hummingbirds and dragonflies, and picking flowers to turn into crowns and necklaces. But the garden had never been hers. It had always been her mother's domain. Even before Ella Mae had become aware of the existence of magic, she knew there was something unique about her mother's connection to the plants she tended in her gardens and greenhouse.

Tonight, the garden was more enchanting than ever. It was as though the plants were putting on a special display for Adelaide and her daughter. Touched by moonlight, the dewdrops on every leaf took on a diamond sparkle, the spiderwebs glinted like spun silver, and every flower, regardless of what color it had been during the daytime, had turned a shimmering, iridescent white. The closer Ella Mae and Hugh got to the Luna rosebush, the more the flowers pulsed and glowed until it looked like the entire garden had been strung with fallen stars.

Ella Mae's mother was waiting for them near a stone bench engraved with cherubim. She wore a swan-white robe with a deep hood and a belt of silver leaves, and when she pushed the hood back to reveal her face and hair, Ella Mae could hardly believe she was staring at her mother. This tall, slender woman with the silver hair and the ageless face was as cold and distant as the moonlight.

Adelaide raised her arms to the night, silently beckoning to the sky, and a cluster of stars seemed to detach from the center of the Cassiopeia constellation. Ella Mae recognized the shape from the rare nights when her mother would take her to the end of the dock and point out patterns in the indigo canvas that was the August sky.

"There's Cygnus, the swan," she'd whisper. Using Ella Mae's small finger, Adelaide would draw invisible lines in the celestial map above them. "Can you see how those stars form the wings? And there's Lyra, the harp. I can almost hear it strumming. Can you?"

Ella Mae would strain to hear the high, haunting notes, but she never could.

"This one's my favorite. Queen Cassiopeia." Adelaide would direct Ella Mae's hand, tracing the W shape of the stars. "In Greek mythology, Cassiopeia boasted that she was more beautiful than the sea nymphs, so Poseidon punished her by tying her to a chair and placing her in the sky for all eternity. History remembers her for her vanity, but there's usually more to a person's story than one element. Especially when it comes to women."

"What's the rest of her story?" Ella Mae had asked.

Adelaide had smiled. "The constellation is known by other names in other languages, but that gathering of stars has always been a woman. She has always been a ruler. She's always been powerful. However, she was only punished in the Greek tale. In the other versions, which are far older than the Greek one, she was magical. She was a mother of gods. She carried a half-moon scepter and no one would ever dare tie her to a chair."

"I like that story better."

"Of course you do," Adelaide had said. "Remember this when you're older. Don't let anyone else write your story. Not any man. Nor any woman. Write your own."

As Ella Mae watched the lights approach the Luna rosebush, she thought of how unbelievable her story would have sounded to her younger self. If she could go back in time to when she was married and living in Manhattan, what would she tell that naïve version of herself? Would she say that her husband was an adulterer? Would she try to explain that the entire world was populated by a small group of people with magical abilities? Would she tell her that all those books on Arthurian legend she'd read by Mary Stewart, T. H. White, Marion Zimmer Bradley, and Tennyson were based on reality? Would she hint at the existence of objects of power? Enchanted swords, flowers, fruit, and so on?

No, Ella Mae thought, glancing over at Hugh. *I wouldn't change a thing. Because if I changed something, I might not be standing here. And I've been waiting for this moment since a boy named Hugh climbed to the top of a tree to retrieve my kite.*

The stars grew closer and separated, revealing themselves

as fireflies. Slowly, almost lazily, the radiant insects descended upon the rosebush, covering it completely. Adelaide held her palms over the glowing, throbbing mass, and whispered something to them.

"It is done," she declared softly. She made a gentle shooing motion and the fireflies rose into the air and dispersed. What they left behind was a single rose. It shone with their incandescent light, turning every petal into a half-moon against a backdrop of dark leaves. The rose hummed and a shiver of silver light ran across its surface, like a whisper of wind over water.

Adelaide looked at Ella Mae and nodded. It was time.

Ella Mae, who hadn't let go of Hugh's hand since they'd entered the garden, now turned to him. He smiled down at her, but she saw the fear in his eyes. She felt the same fear, but she returned his smile and reached for his other hand.

"No matter what happens next," she whispered to him, "I love you. I have loved you since I knew what it means to love. Nothing can ever change that. Nothing *has* ever changed that. Not time. Not distance. Not finding magic or losing magic."

Hugh's grip on her hands tightened. "We could just walk away. You were right. We don't have to use this rose to know for sure. We can be like everyone else."

Extracting her right hand, she placed it on his cheek. "We will never be like everyone else. And if we don't belong together, then nothing in this world makes sense. Come on, we'll pretend we're kids again. We'll close our eyes and count to three."

"And then we'll go."

Ella Mae closed her eyes and whispered, "One."

She felt a stirring in the air.

"Two," Hugh whispered.

The movement got closer. It was so subtle that Ella Mae thought she was imagining it, but the strands of her hair shifted and she could feel featherlight touches on her shoulders, her arms, and the crown of her head.

"Three," she said in a confident voice, for suddenly, she knew what the tickling sensation was.

She opened her eyes and saw butterflies.

Hundreds of butterflies.

They perched on her and Hugh. They hovered in the moonlight. They fluttered around the Luna Rose—a rainbow of patterned, striped, and spotted wings. Ella Mae's totem creatures. At least that's what they'd been when she was magical.

Is Suzy right? And Opal? Do I still have magic left in me? Ella Mae wondered. *Somewhere deep inside?*

As though in answer, the place on her palm where a clover-shaped burn scar had once marked her skin began to tingle. It was a strange pins-and-needles feeling, but Ella Mae didn't have time to dwell on it because Hugh was reaching out, with her other hand wrapped in his, for the Luna Rose.

She didn't try to stop him. Her body felt electric. Her heart beat in time with the pulsing of the single flower, and she was sure that if she pressed her ear to Hugh's chest, his heart's rhythm would match her own.

And then, her fingertips made contact with the rose's petals. The silken, moonlit petals. The butterflies landed on the rose too. They danced over its surface with quivering wings, and their movement coaxed fresh ripples of white light to flow from the center of the flower to its outer edges. Hugh's hand was also on the rose and it still glowed. It had not winked out like a snuffed candle.

"You are meant to be," Adelaide said with a delighted smile. "No power in this world can sever your bond. Your love will be a beacon. Let it guide you in all things. It will grow stronger through the years, shining through the darkness like the light of this flower. Because you will face difficulties as all couples do, you should carry the memory of this night within your hearts like a lantern. Reach for it during times of trouble. The memory will remind you that what you have found in each other is greater than any form of magic. You have found true love. Respect this gift and live a long and happy life together."

Adelaide whispered a few more words and the rose folded inward. The light slowly seeped away, like water draining from a sink, until it was completely gone.

The butterflies left too, melting into the shadows of the nearby bushes as though they were never there.

"Congratulations," Adelaide said, coming forward to kiss Ella Mae and Hugh. "Go now. Go celebrate."

"Thank you." Ella Mae hugged her mother tightly and then watched her walk away.

When they were alone, Hugh looked at Ella Mae. "I know it's late, but are you up for a short boat ride?"

Ella Mae smiled up at him. "Hugh Dylan, I'd go anywhere with you."

Hugh led her to the end of the dock, where a motorized life raft was tied to the dock cleats.

"Doesn't this belong to the fire station?" Ella Mae asked.

"Sure does," Hugh replied. "I just borrowed it for the evening."

He took Ella Mae's hand as she boarded the wobbly vessel. Hugh hopped into the raft, untied the lines, and brought the motor to life. They were soon zipping over the lake and the wind noise made speech impossible.

Ella Mae didn't care. She was content to sit next to Hugh,

her hair whipping around her face like a whiskey-colored tornado, while he kept one hand on the wheel and the other on the throttle.

She was wrapped in a cocoon of warmth, as though the light from the Luna Rose still glowed within her. But it was more than that. The sensation she'd felt when the butterflies had touched her was still there. Something was stirring within her. Awakening. The feeling was subtle, but it was lovely all the same. It felt like stumbling across a patch of sunshine after a long rain. There was a champagne bubble anticipation to it. Ella Mae didn't know if it was her magic returning or the feeling of pure happiness, but she decided to simply enjoy the sensation without questioning it too deeply.

Hugh approached a dock on the opposite side of the lake from Partridge Hill. It wasn't difficult to spot, seeing as someone had lined its entire length with battery-powered lanterns. The dock stretched out into the dark water like a runway, beckoning them to land.

"Who lit these?" Ella Mae asked after Hugh had cut the motor.

"Me." Hugh flashed her a smile. "Come on, I have something to show you."

He helped her step from the boat onto the dock and then led her to a pair of teal Adirondack chairs positioned at the end of the dock. A fishing pole leaned against the back of each chair and a table tucked between the chairs held a picnic basket and a tackle box.

"Are we fishing for sturgeon tonight?" Ella Mae teased.

Hugh shrugged. "It's good luck to catch a fish during a full moon. Besides, I really wanted to show you the view from here."

Ella Mae swept her arm around the dock. "But—"

Hugh stopped her words with a kiss. "I told you that I believed in us," he whispered into her ear a minute later. "I believed that rose would light up like the summer sun. I believed that we'd be standing here tonight and that I'd have the chance to give you this."

Reaching into the picnic basket, he pulled out a folder.

Ella Mae looked at the glossy cover and, for just a moment, felt a twinge of disappointment. She hadn't been expecting anything, so she had no reason to be disappointed, but she couldn't see how the contents of the folder would complement what had so far been the most romantic night of her life.

Hugh quickly proved her wrong.

"Open it," he said.

Complying, she discovered a packet of legal documents. She shot Hugh a questioning glance, but he merely grinned and whispered, "Read."

It only took a few lines for Ella Mae to understand. Clutching the folder to her chest, she gazed up the hill to a patch of empty land. "You bought it?"

Hugh nodded and his smile grew wider. "It's ours, Ella Mae. We're going to build that dream house. We're going to have the life we talked about."

Ella Mae threw her arms around Hugh. He spun her in circles on the dock as she alternated between laughing and kissing him, the glimmer of lantern light blurring as tears of joy pooled in her eyes.

"I love you," she whispered.

"I love you," he whispered back.

Hugh slowed his spinning until their movement was more like a dance. Ella Mae put her head on his shoulder and the two of them swayed back and forth while the boards creaked under their feet and the stars winked over their heads.

In the distance, Ella Mae heard a gentle splash.

Hugh must have caught the sound too, for he gestured at

the chairs and said, "Are you ready to reel in that good luck fish now?"

"As long as that doesn't require my baiting a hook with a worm," Ella Mae said. "I'm not squeamish. It's just that using live bait doesn't seem to fit with the rest of our evening. The fireflies. The butterflies. I don't know . . ."

"Don't worry," Hugh assured her. "I have a special spinnerbait for you in the tackle box. It's pink, yellow, and purple. But be careful, there's a hook hiding under its colorful skirt."

Ella Mae took a seat in the chair closest to the edge of the dock and opened the tackle box. She saw dozens of different lures, but only one with the colors Hugh had described. Picking it up by its metal head, she dropped the spinnerbait into her palm. Something glinted from within the strands of the silicone skirt, and Ella Mae gently parted the strands, expecting to reveal a sharp hook.

Instead, she found a diamond ring. A beautiful platinum ring with white round-cut diamonds encircling a yellow diamond. It looked contemporary and yet felt very, very old.

Ella Mae gasped in surprise and her fingers began trembling so violently that she nearly dropped it, but Hugh was already kneeling in front of her. He put his palm under her hand to steady her.

"You don't have to keep this ring. I'll buy you a new one tomorrow if you want, but I promised your mother that I'd offer you this one first. You see, your dad gave it to her when he proposed. This ring has been passed down for generations. The setting has been changed, but the stone is really old. Your mom wore it until her wedding day. After that, she put it away for you. When I asked her for her blessing, she took it out and asked me to give it to you. That is, if you'll agree to be my wife. Will you, Ella Mae? Will you marry me?"

Ella Mae could feel the tears shining in her eyes. "Yes. A million times over. Yes!"

When Hugh slid the ring on her finger, Ella Mae felt something like the butterflies' touch. It only lasted for a second, and this time, it was a strong, masculine presence. It belonged to a man with an earthy smell. Ella Mae's father. A man she'd never known.

And then, the presence was gone. However, the ring created a circle of warmth around her finger, and Ella Mae believed that both of her parents were with her in spirit because she wore it. Feeling that her heart might burst if she experienced another dose of happiness, she told Hugh that no ring could ever suit her better.

At the end of the lantern-lit dock, Ella Mae and Hugh celebrated their engagement. Hugh pulled a bottle of sparkling wine out of the picnic basket, and the couple drank from plastic cups as they spoke in low, joyful tones about the future.

Their voices floated out over the moonlit lake.

Tonight, the dark water did not make Ella Mae think of Beatrice Burbank. Nor did it remind her of Ruiping, Meg, or even Opal.

On this night, Ella Mae did not dwell on what had been lost. She was completely focused on what had been found. And that was a chance at happily ever after. Not the storybook kind—Ella Mae knew there was no such thing as a perfect union—but the kind where two people finish each other's sentences. When they dance without music. When laughter is contagious. When fights are resolved before the covers are turned down at night. When wrinkles don't diminish, but enhance beauty. When eternity will still not be enough time together.

Ella Mae had found that in Hugh. She'd found it as a little girl whose kite had gotten caught on a high branch. She'd found her happily ever after that day but was too young to recognize it for what it was. And after she'd become an adult, it had taken her years to find her way back to Havenwood. And to Hugh.

"You found me," she whispered to him now.

"Yes." Hugh bent over and kissed her ring finger. "And I'll never let you go."

They sat there for a long time, holding hands and listening to the lake whisper. Keeping its secrets close.

Recipes

Charmed Black Bottom Peanut Butter Pie

VANILLA WAFER PIECRUST

40 vanilla wafers, crushed
1/3 cup butter, melted
2 tablespoons sugar
1 teaspoon pure vanilla extract

CHOCOLATE LAYER

1 cup semisweet chocolate chips
2 tablespoons light corn syrup
2/3 cup heavy whipping cream
1 teaspoon pure vanilla extract

PEANUT BUTTER MOUSSE LAYER

1 cup cold heavy whipping cream, whipped to soft peaks
1 cup creamy peanut butter
½ cup plus 3 tablespoons confectioners' sugar
Optional: 1 cup extra whipping cream for top and chocolate
    sauce for drizzling

Preheat the oven to 350 degrees. Prepare the crust by crushing the wafers in a bowl or using the pulse button on your food processor. Add the melted butter, sugar, and vanilla. Stir until combined. Press the crumb mixture into the bottom and sides of a 9-inch pie pan and bake in the preheated oven for 12 to 15 minutes, or until the edges are lightly brown. Cool completely before filling.

Combine all the ingredients required for the chocolate layer in a microwave-safe bowl and cook for 2 to 3 minutes, stopping every 30 seconds to stir together. When the chocolate is completely melted, stir the mixture until smooth and pour over the cooled crust. (You can reserve 2 to 3 tablespoons of the chocolate mixture for drizzling over the top of the pie.) Cover and freeze for 30 minutes. Place a large bowl and the metal beaters of an electric mixer in the freezer for a few minutes as well. You'll use these to make your whipped cream.

In the chilled metal bowl, use the electric mixer to beat 1 cup heavy whipping cream into soft peaks. Set aside. In another bowl, mix the peanut butter and confectioners' sugar together. Add ⅓ of the whipped cream to lighten the mixture. Once it is nicely blended, gently fold in the remaining whipped cream. Pour the peanut butter mousse over the chocolate layer. If desired, whip another cup of heavy cream into soft peaks for the top and drizzle with chocolate sauce.

Chill at least 1 hour and up to 1 day before serving.

Charmed Blueberry Icebox Box

SHORTBREAD PIECRUST

1 cup salted butter, softened
½ cup confectioner's sugar
2 cups all-purpose flour

FILLING

1 cup fresh blueberries
¼ cup water
3 tablespoons sugar
1 tablespoon light corn syrup
¾ teaspoon cornstarch
Pinch salt
½ teaspoon lemon juice
1 (8-ounce) package cream cheese, at room temperature
¾ cup confectioners' sugar
1½ cups heavy whipping cream
1 teaspoon pure vanilla extract

Preheat the oven to 350 degrees. In a large bowl, cream the butter and confectioners' sugar. Blend the flour into the butter mixture. Press the mixture into the bottom and sides of 9-inch pie plate. Bake for 12 to 15 minutes, or until the edges are lightly brown. Cool completely before filling.

In a saucepan, stir together the blueberries, water, sugar, corn syrup, cornstarch, and salt. Bring to a boil over medium heat. Reduce the heat to medium-low; cook until the mixture begins to thicken and the berries begin to burst, approximately 5 minutes, stirring occasionally. Remove from the heat; stir in the lemon juice. Transfer the mixture to a small bowl, and let cool. When cooled, cover and refrigerate until chilled (1 to 2 hours).

In a large bowl, add the cream cheese and confectioners' sugar. Beat at medium speed with an electric mixer until smooth. Add the cream and vanilla; beat at high speed until stiff peaks form. Gently fold in the blueberry mixture. Spoon the filling into the prepared crust. Lightly cover, and freeze until firm. Garnish with fresh whipped cream, sprigs of mint, or fresh blueberries.

*You can easily substitute other berries for the blueberries in this pie. For example, 1 cup of strawberries with a chocolate cookie crust is a delicious twist on this recipe. A triple berry pie with a graham cracker crust is another winner. Use Ella Mae's recipe as your base and have fun experimenting!

Charmed Lactose-Free Key Lime Pie

VANILLA WAFER PIECRUST

40 vanilla wafers, crushed
⅓ cup unsalted butter, melted
2 tablespoons sugar
1 teaspoon pure vanilla extract

FILLING

3 egg yolks (keep the whites for the meringue)
1 cup sugar
1 teaspoon pure vanilla extract
2 tablespoons all-purpose flour
3 tablespoons cornstarch
¼ teaspoon kosher salt
1¼ cups water

1 tablespoon unsalted butter
½ cup fresh or bottled key lime juice
1 teaspoon lime zest

MERINGUE TOPPING

3 egg whites (saved from the filling)
¼ teaspoon cream of tartar
8 tablespoons sugar

Preheat the oven to 375 degrees. Prepare the vanilla wafer crust by crushing the cookies in a bowl or using the pulse button on your food processor. Add the melted butter, sugar, and vanilla extract. Stir until combined. Press the crumb mixture into the bottom and sides of a 9-inch pie pan, and bake for 6 to 8 minutes. Cool completely before filling.

Reset the oven temperature to 425 degrees.

Separate the eggs, setting the whites aside in a mixing bowl for later. In a medium bowl, beat the yolks.

In a saucepan, add the sugar, vanilla extract, flour, cornstarch, and salt. Over medium heat, gradually add the water. Cook, stirring constantly, until thickened (approximately 5 minutes). Reduce the heat and add the beaten egg yolks. Cook another 2 minutes. Add the butter, lime juice, and lime zest. When the mixture is smooth, remove the pan from the heat.

Beat the egg whites you set aside earlier until frothy. Add the cream of tartar and continue beating. Gradually add the sugar and continue beating until stiff peaks form. Your mixture should look shiny.

Pour the key lime filling into your vanilla wafer crust and top with meringue. Make sure to spread the meringue all the way to the edges. Use a spatula or the back of a spoon to create peaks once the meringue has been spread.

Bake for 5 minutes or until the meringue is golden brown. To check, use your oven light. Do not open your oven door. When the desired look is achieved, remove the pie from the oven and cool on a wire rack for at least 1 hour. Chill for at least 4 hours before serving. Occasionally, key lime pies can "weep." If this happens, carefully pour off the excess liquid and put in the freezer for an hour.

*To make this a dairy-free pie, use a butter substitute wherever the recipe calls for butter.

Charmed Tomato Pie
with Cheddar Crust

WHITE CHEDDAR PIECRUST

2½ cups all-purpose flour, plus extra for rolling

1 teaspoon salt

1 teaspoon sugar

1 cup (2 sticks) unsalted butter, very cold, cut into ½-inch cubes (place in the freezer for 15 minutes before use)

6 to 8 tablespoons very cold water

1 cup grated sharp white Cheddar cheese

FILLING

6 to 8 Roma tomatoes, peeled, sliced, salted, and drained

½ cup chopped fresh basil

3 scallions, thinly sliced

8 slices cooked bacon, chopped

½ teaspoon minced garlic

1 teaspoon dried oregano
2 cups shredded mozzarella cheese
¼ cup sour cream

Combine the flour, salt, and sugar in a food processor; pulse to mix. Add the butter and pulse until the mixture resembles coarse meal and you have pea-sized pieces of butter. Add the water 1 tablespoon at a time, pulsing until the mixture begins to clump together. Add the cheese and pulse again until it is worked into the mixture. Put some dough between your fingers. If it holds together, it's ready. If it falls apart, you need a little more water. You'll see bits of butter in the dough. This is a good thing, as it will give you a nice, flaky crust.

Mound the dough and place it on a clean surface. Gently shape it into 2 disks of equal size. Do not overknead. Sprinkle a little flour around the disks. Wrap each disk in plastic wrap. Refrigerate one disk for at least 1 hour. (Put the other disk in a plastic bag in the freezer for up to 3 months. Or double the filling recipe and make two pies at once.) Remove the first disk from the refrigerator. Let it sit at room temperature for 5 minutes or until soft enough to roll. Roll it out with a rolling pin on a lightly floured surface to a 12-inch circle. (Ella Mae uses a pie mat to help with measurements.) Gently transfer it into a 9-inch pie plate. Carefully press the pie dough down so that it lines the bottom and sides of the pie plate. Use kitchen scissors to trim the dough to within ½ inch of the edge of the pie dish.

Preheat the oven to 375 degrees. Prick the crust with a fork or use pie weights. Place the pie dish on a parchment-lined baking tray and bake the crust for 10 minutes. Remove from the oven and let cool.

When the crust is cool, add alternating layers of tomatoes, basil, scallions, and bacon. Set aside 5 or 6 tomatoes and enough basil to garnish the surface of the pie. Top with garlic and oregano. In a small bowl, blend the mozzarella and sour cream. Spread the mixture over the top of the pie. Add the remaining tomatoes and basil. Cover loosely with aluminum foil.

Bake for 30 minutes. Remove the foil. Bake another 30 minutes. May be served warm or cold.

Keep reading for a special preview of
Ellery Adams's next Book Retreat Mystery . . .

Murder in the Secret Garden

Coming soon from Berkley Prime Crime!

"I don't like killing things," Hemingway "Hem" Steward told his mother as she handed him a garden trowel.

Jane Steward—single mother of twin boys and manager of Storyton Hall—gave her firstborn a skeptical look.

"I don't," Hem insisted. "Except for mosquitos and flies. And everybody hates them. I should get paid to kill them."

"What about spiders?" Hem's lookalike, Fitzgerald Steward, otherwise known as Fitz, poked his brother with the tines of the hand rake Jane had given him. "You squish them because you're scared of them."

Hem glared at Fitz. "Am *not*."

"Are *too*."

Jane stepped between her sons before their argument turned physical. "You shouldn't hurt spiders, Hem," she said. "Many species eat the mosquitoes and flies we dislike so much. And since Fitz is so comfortable with spiders, ask *him* to relocate them outside from now on."

Fitz paled slightly over this suggestion, but with both his mother and brother watching him, he adopted a display of bravado. "Fine," he said, puffing out his chest. "I'm not afraid."

"Good." Jane picked up the first of three plastic buckets lined up in the maintenance shed and beckoned for her sons to follow suit. "Let's get going. I'd like to finish this chore while we still have some cloud cover. It's supposed to be really hot today."

As they walked, the twins grumbled over having to work on a Saturday, especially since school had only let out for the summer yesterday. However, their complaints weren't very impassioned and Jane knew that they looked forward to digging in the dirt. Her boys loved being outdoors, and though they occasionally griped about their chores, they usually settled into a given task by turning their work into a game. Jane noticed that even the most mundane job could become the equivalent of swabbing the deck of a pirate ship or sweeping out a dungeon prison cell. She put her sons' vivid imaginations down to their constant exposure to books and book lovers. Even at the tender age of seven, they were reading, and understanding, books meant for a much older audience.

The three Stewards lapsed into silence as they walked to their cottage, which was formerly the estate's hunting lodge. Like the behemoth manor house it faced, the lodge had been dismantled in the 1830s and transported from its original seat in the English countryside to a remote valley in western Virginia. These days, the house served a dual purpose. The front half was occupied by Sterling, the head chauffeur, and the back, by Jane's little family.

One of the things Jane loved about her home was its walled garden. Because she and her sons lived on the grounds of a resort where the majority of the guests enjoyed long strolls, it was difficult to secure much privacy. Luckily, both an evergreen hedge and a low wrought iron fence protected their small yard from nosey parkers. The only way to gain entry was to pass through their gate, and as Jane now unlatched it and pushed against it with her right hip, it squeaked in protest.

She winced. "I need to oil those hinges."

Fitz patted the gate as though it were an obedient dog. "Isn't it kind of like a burglar alarm? When it squeaks, we know someone's coming in."

"Yeah, and then we can show them our moves!" Hem dropped his bucket to better demonstrate a series of air punches. Jane and the boys had been taking tae kwon do lessons from Sinclair, the head librarian, and the twins were always looking for an excuse to show off their latest punch, kick, or defensive maneuver.

"Save your energy for the weeds," Jane advised. "I've let them go for too long, and with all the rain we've had, they're threatening to overtake the entire vegetable patch." She pointed at a dandelion growing next to a potato plant. "Just look at the size of this one! Its roots probably go all the way to China!"

Hem and Fitz exchanged glances of amazement, but then Hem frowned. "No, Mom, it couldn't do that. Fitz and I read a book about dinosaurs and it had a picture of what the middle of the earth looks like."

"A giant fireball. It would burn roots like that!" Fitz snapped his fingers.

Jane smiled. Over the past winter, the twins had devoured every book they could find about dinosaurs, but by the end of the school year, their interest in the resplendent reptiles had waned. These days, only magic and wizardry captivated them. Their nightstands were stacked with books they'd purchased with their allowance, and they were listening to the Harry Potter series on CD. These were a birthday gift from Aunt Octavia. Jane liked to play them while she was cleaning up after supper. This way, the boys could spend an hour with Harry with the lights on and their mother moving about in the kitchen. There were some frightening scenes in those stories, and though the twins adored being scared by fantastical tales, Jane deemed it best that they listen to Mr. Potter's adventures in her presence.

"You're right, the roots don't go to China, but they do go surprisingly deep. You can't just yank the plant out by its top or the whole weed will just regrow."

"Like a lizard's tail," Hem said, studying the dandelion with admiration.

After casting a brief glare at the offending plant, Fitz lunged at it. "I bet I can get it out."

Before Jane could protest, he gathered the weed in his fist and pulled. The dandelion snapped at the base, leaving a white eye of root staring up at them.

Seeing the dismayed look on her son's face, Jane squeezed his shoulder. "Don't worry, it happens to the very best of gardeners. What you need is the proper tool."

Fitz took the item she proffered. "It looks like a stick for s'mores."

"It does," Jane agreed and showed her sons how to push the divided head of the weeder into the ground. Grasping the remains of the root with one hand, she worked the tool under the root until it finally released its hold of the soil and slid free. She placed it in the bucket with a triumphant flourish and then, with the boys on their knees beside her, pointed out which plants should be removed.

"All this grass has to go, but it's tricky stuff so leave it to me," she said. "You two focus on the dandelions and chickweed. See which ones I mean?" She pointed at multiple examples. "Bad, bad, bad. Got it?"

"*Bad?* That's not true," said an unfamiliar voice in a critical tone.

Jane glanced up to see a woman standing at the edge of the garden bed. She wore a black dress, black boots, and a black sun hat with a large brim. With the sun behind her, her face was completely cast in shadow. The hair that framed her face was dark and wiry. The stranger had come upon them without having made a sound and now loomed over them, as though she had every right to be there.

"Take the dandelion, for example. You can eat the young leaves, make wine out of the flower, and roast the root to produce coffee," she said in a deep, authoritative voice. She pivoted her head slightly, addressing the boys. "The root can also be turned into very useful medicine. It can help people with kidney or liver problems. Those are organs, which are located right around here and here." She indicated the areas on her torso. "Pretty handy for a *bad* plant, wouldn't you say?"

Jane, who'd been momentarily entranced by the dandelion trivia, looked over at her sons and saw that they were staring at the woman with a mixture of fascination and alarm. Their expressions put Jane's maternal protective instincts into high alert, and she swiftly got to her feet, weeder in hand, and took a step toward the intruder.

"May I help you?" she asked. There was something innately sinister about the woman's black garb and the manner in which she'd noiselessly appeared. "This is a private residence," Jane continued. She struggled to maintain a cordial tone. After all, she was the manager of Storyton Hall. She couldn't allow a stranger—and possible guest—to note her discomfort. "But maybe you didn't notice the sign on the gate."

"Oh, I saw it," the woman replied breezily.

The twins exchanged anxious glances.

Hem pulled on Fitz's sleeve and muttered, "The gate didn't squeak. How did she get in without it squeaking?"

And before Jane could ask another question, Fitz squinted up at the lady in black and whispered, "Are you a witch?"

Jane's eyes widened in horror. Despite the fact that the same word had also crossed her mind, alibiet briefly, she glowered at her son and intoned, "Hemingway Steward! Apologize this instant!"

The woman startled them all by tossing back her head and laughing heartily. The movement caused her sun hat to slip, revealing brown hair threaded with filaments of gray and a freckled forehead. "Young sir, you wouldn't be the first person to call a lady with a keen knowledge of plants a witch. Personally, I prefer the term 'cunning woman.' Such women used herbs to heal people during the Middle Ages. I'm better at healing gardens." She smiled at Jane. "That's why I'm here. To help with your garden."

"I'm sorry?" Jane was totally confused.

The women held out her hand. "I'm Vivian Cole, a member of The Medieval Herbalists. I came a day early for our gathering because I wanted to read, explore the area, and spend a little time with Mrs. Hubbard before the scheduled activities begin."

Jane relaxed a little. "You're a friend of Mrs. Hubbard's?"

"A new friend, yes," Vivian replied. "After our president, Claude, booked this event, he told me that our celebratory feast was being combined with a wedding reception. The bride-to-be needed assistance coming up with a medieval menu, so I volunteered to handle it. Mrs. Hubbard and I have been pen pals ever since."

Vivian shifted position. Sunshine fell on her dress, and

Jane realized that it wasn't solid black at all. The cotton fabric was actually dotted with tiny white flowers. The light also washed over Vivian's face, revealing a woman in her late fifties with sun-speckled skin and a generous number of laugh lines.

Something clicked in Jane's memory. She suddenly recognized the woman standing before her.

"Of course!" she exclaimed, reddening. "Vivian Cole! You restore historic gardens. I can't believe it took me so long to realize that. I'm so sorry." To hide her embarrassment, Jane hastily introduced herself and the boys. "Weren't you in charge of the restoration of the magnificent gardens at The Mount, Edith Wharton's home?"

"It was one of my favorite projects," Vivian said with a nostalgic sigh. "I particularly loved the walled garden. There's nothing like being inside a walled garden at night. You employ all of your senses in the dark, and even the most ordinary plants are transformed by moonlight. Their scents, their shapes, the shadows they cast—the plants can either turn into complete mysteries, or they can reveal their secret selves."

Jane didn't quite know how to respond to this unusual remark. Judging from the way her sons were gaping at Vivian, they still believed she was a witch.

With a rather forced laugh, Jane gestured at her modest vegetable patch and said, "This is hardly comparable to a garden bed at The Mount. I'm sure you have better things to do than—"

"Examine your spinach?" Vivian smiled. "I love diagnosing sick plants. It's a hobby of mine. May I?" She pointed at the row of spinach.

Jane nodded in assent.

Vivian knelt in the dirt and cradled a spinach leaf in her

hand. She peered at it intently before gingerly folding it inward and peering at it some more.

"Infected," she murmured gravely and then waved for the boys to come closer. She tapped the leaf. "Do you see how the veins have turned yellow?"

"Yeah," said Fitz. Jane nudged his rump with the toe of her shoe and he quickly amended his answer to, "Yes, ma'am."

"This is caused by a disease spread by leafhoppers," Vivian explained.

Hem cocked his head quizzically. "Is that like a grasshopper?"

"More like a cicada." Victoria touched the leaf's paler underside with the tip of her index finger. "When the leafhopper feeds, they inject toxic saliva—their drool—into the plant. They also carry teeny tiny virus bugs around with them that they spread from plant to plant."

"Gross," Fitz grimaced, but leaned closer, his eyes gleaming with interest.

Jane, on the other hand, was genuinely repulsed by the idea of insects spreading disease among her vegetables. "What can I do?"

"We'll start by removing the infected plants. It's time to harvest the healthy ones before they bolt. You can plant another lettuce variety in its place." Vivian looked at the boys. "The leafhoppers can't jump all around the garden like it's a big hopscotch board if we make life tougher for them. To do that, we need to get rid of all the weeds. Are you up for the challenge?"

The twins responded with a unified cry of, "Yes, ma'am!"

She smiled widely at them before fixing her attention on Jane again. "Once we're done with the harvesting and weeding, you can plant marigolds around the perimeter and in the center of the vegetable patch. Marigolds deter a host of garden pests. How does that sound?"

"Wonderful. Thank you so much." And before Jane could offer Vivian a cold glass of water or escort her to the gate, the expert gardener had helped herself to one of the hand trowels and was already digging up one of the diseased spinach plants. "Please," Jane said, feeling uncomfortable. "You're a guest of Storyton Hall. You shouldn't be working in my garden."

"But this is where I'm most content," Vivian said. "Let me stay, won't you? I'll sit on the other end and be very quiet. You won't even know I'm here."

Having no choice but to acquiesce, Jane offered to get Vivian a set of tools and a pair of gloves. When she returned from the maintenance shed, Vivian and the twins were chattering away like old pals. Clearly, if the boys still considered her a witch, they'd come to the conclusion that she performed white magic, not dark.

"What about mosquitos and flies?" Hem was asking her. "There were a billion last summer!"

"You could plant basil," Vivian said. "Those bugs hate basil. Your mom could also use the leaves to make a salad with fresh tomatoes and mozzarella cheese."

Jane handed Vivian her tools. "Sounds delicious."

Fitz pointed at the small pile of dandelions in his bucket. "Can we use these, Ms. Vivian? Didn't you say they weren't bad?"

"They're not bad, Fitz. No plants are, but we have to make choices about which plants we want in our gardens. We've chosen not to have dandelions in this garden." Vivian pursed her lips in thought. "You could feed them to a goat. Or a pig."

Fitz and Hem grinned at each other. "Pig Newton!"

By the time they finished telling Vivian about the most

famous pet in Storyton Village, the spinach plants had been pulled and the twins were making excellent progress with the chickweeds. Jane, who'd given herself the job of rooting out the dandelions and invasive grasses, made a silent vow to weed the garden on a more regular basis in the future.

Much later, four hot, sweaty, and dirt-encrusted workers crossed the back lawn leading to the manor house and paused by the kitchen door. "Are you sure you won't come in for a drink?" Jane asked Vivian. "Mrs. Hubbard always keeps a supply of sun tea and lemonade on hand."

"What I want most is a shower," Vivian said. "Between my morning hike and the lovely hours spent in your garden, I probably smell worse than Pig Newton. I'll take a rain check on the sun tea." With a wave, she headed for the guest entrance.

"Pig Newton doesn't smell," Hem said, instantly coming to the pig's defense.

Fitz looked at Jane. "It's true. Mr. Hogg put a baby pool under the tree behind the Pickled Pig Market. Mr. Hogg tosses some Cheerios in the water, and while Pig Newton's busy eating, Mr. Hogg gives him a good scrubbing."

"We could all use a good scrubbing," Jane said. "Wash up to your elbows, both of you, or Mrs. Hubbard will have a fit."

As though the mention of her name had conjured her from thin air, Mrs. Hubbard appeared from inside the closest pantry. "Hello, my darlings! You're just in time for lunch." Her apple-cheeked face was more flushed than usual. She exhaled loudly and put a hand over her ample chest. "I've been running around like a madwoman making sure we have everything we need for the Billingsley-Earle wedding." Sliding a notepad into her apron pocket, she smiled at Jane and the boys. "As for you three, you can be my official taste testers. I want to add new sandwiches to the Rudyard Kipling

Café's summer menu. Take a seat at the counter and I'll be right back with the first candidate."

She paused to issue orders to the kitchen staff and then returned carrying three plates. "Turkey club with herb mayonnaise. I mixed fresh parsley, thyme, and basil in with the mayo. There's locally grown lettuce and tomatoes and crunchy bacon too. I know how much you boys like your bacon."

"Is this spinach?" Fitz lifted off his top slice of bread and pointed at a few pieces of mayo-smeared lettuce. Jane caught the apprehension in her son's voice and knew that he was picturing the diseased leaves from their vegetable garden.

"No, honey. That's romaine." Mrs. Hubbard put her hands on her hips. "Now put your sandwich back together, take a bite, and tell me what you think."

Hem hurriedly yanked the tomato slice out of his sandwich before taking an enormous bite. His right cheek inflated like a balloon, and he grinned at Mrs. Hubbard and gave her a thumbs-up.

Though Jane took a more conservative sample of her sandwich, she was immediately impressed by how many flavors and textures Mrs. Hubbard had managed to squeeze between two slices of bread. The fresh tomato and lettuce slices lightened the heaviness of the crispy bacon and salt-and-pepper-seasoned turkey, and the aromatic creaminess of the herb mayo provided the perfect finish.

"This is a keeper," she told Mrs. Hubbard.

With a nod of satisfaction, Storyton's head cook walked to the prep station and returned with three small bowls. "Watermelon salad with fresh mint to round off your meal."

"Ms. Vivian says that mint helps you digest," Hem informed her.

Mrs. Hubbard looked pleased. "She found you, then? Good!"

"She knows *everything* about plants," Fitz said. "She's like Professor Sprout in the Harry Potter books. Ms. Vivian could teach Herbology at Hogwarts."

"I believe she would take that as a high compliment." Mrs. Hubbard gestured at their empty plates. "Vivian encouraged me to experiment with different herb combinations based on recipes from the Middle Ages. You should see my kitchen garden, Jane. Vivian mailed me dozens of seed packets when we first started writing each other. With her help, I'm now growing a medieval herb garden. I have the more exotic plants at home because they require more care. I even have licorice!"

"Can you make candy?" the boys asked in unison.

Too caught up in her narrative to be misdirected, Mrs. Hubbard winked at them and chattered on. "I'm growing ginger too. Can you believe it? I hope to harvest my first crop of baby ginger in October. To me, these herbs are as precious and wonderful as one of those illuminated manuscripts would be to you, Jane, my dear."

At the mention of illuminated manuscripts, Mrs. Hubbard's voice faded as Jane's mind turned to thoughts of Edwin Alcott. The last communication she'd had from the man she'd been falling in love with had been in the form of a mysterious package. Inside the package, Jane had discovered a missing page belonging to the Gutenburg Bible hidden in Storyton's secret library. Edwin had recovered it from some untold place in the Middle East and sent it to Jane in an attempt to prove to her that he was not a book thief—not in the pure sense of the word anyway. He had promised to explain himself when he returned to Storyton, but that had been months ago, and Jane's doubts about his character had grown more and more with each passing day.

I should just forget about him, Jane chided herself for

the hundredth time. *He must be a thief and a rogue. Why else would he stay away? Why else would he make his sister worry? Or make me promises he never meant to keep?*

"Mom?" Fitz waved his hand in front of Jane's face and she blinked.

"Sorry," she said. "I drifted off for a second there."

Mrs. Hubbard studied her closely. "You should stick your nose in my rosemary plant and take a deep breath. That'll clear your head. If you're not growing any in your own garden, take some of mine. You could whip up a lovely rosemary lemon chicken for supper—it'll help focus all of your minds."

"We don't need to focus," Hem countered. "It's summer!"

Smiling at him indulgently, Mrs. Hubbard said, "So it is. But there's a saying about idle hands and the devil." She shot a conspiratorial glance at Jane. "If it's all right with your mother, I'd like to hire you boys to weed and water my kitchen garden. The groundskeeping staff is too busy to deal with it. And in all honesty, I think you two would take better care of my plants. Not because the groundskeepers aren't hard workers," she hurriedly added, "but I believe you boys will come to love the garden as I do. You'd have to tend the plants for an hour every day except for Sundays. I'll pay you on Friday. In cash. Are you interested in the job?"

The twins laced their fingers together and made begging motions. "Can we, Mom? *Please?*"

"Only if Mrs. Hubbard and I can come to an agreement about your wages," Jane said. "Thank her for the delicious lunch and then go play while we talk."

Hem and Fitz hugged Mrs. Hubbard before racing out of the kitchen. As soon as they were gone, the two women settled in for a good-natured haggling session.

"They should be doing the job for free," Jane began.

"Stewards have been maintaining Storyton Hall for centuries. Even my great-aunt and great-uncle have chores, though their tasks are far less physical."

"But Master Hem and Master Fitz are children," Mrs. Hubbard countered. "Let them see what's it's like to earn money for a job well done—a job not assigned by a teacher or a parent. It'll do them good. Give them a sense of pride."

Eventually, Jane capitulated. It was nearly impossible to say no to Mrs. Hubbard.

"Time to bake the scones," Mrs. Hubbard said, rising to her feet and smoothing her apron, which was embroidered with tiny pink and white teapots. "And since several of our herbalists have checked in early, I've added cheddar and chive biscuits to the tea menu, so I'll have to make those as well."

It never failed to amaze Jane that Mrs. Hubbard, who rarely left the kitchen, was able to keep tabs on the goings-on at Storyton Hall. It didn't hurt that the majority of the employees fed her the choicest tidbits of gossip in exchange for a piece of shortbread or a slice of Victoria sponge.

"Maybe I shouldn't have taken the day off," Jane mused aloud. "I wonder who else has arrived early."

"Vivian told me that she'd seen their group's president getting out of one of our cars just as she was heading out on her hike this morning. She didn't want to delay her walk, so she didn't stop to say hello." Mrs. Hubbard's jovial face suddenly clouded over. "And the *third* early arrival showed up just before you and the boys came into the kitchen. Billy carried her bags to her room and declared that her luggage had a nasty odor."

There was an unmistakable note of disapproval in Mrs. Hubbard's voice.

"Do you know this guest?" Jane asked the cook.

Mrs. Hubbard snorted. "It's Constance Meredith."

Jane frowned. The name was familiar, but she'd reviewed so many names recently in reference to both the upcoming wedding and The Medieval Herbalists booking that they'd all begun to blend together.

"You'd probably recognize her by her *stage name*. Does the Poison Princess ring a bell?" Mrs. Hubbard asked. The note of disapproval had morphed into outright disdain.

"Ah, the Poison Princess!" Jane smiled. "Ms. Meredith's talk is supposed to be one of the highlights of the upcoming week. According to Mr. Mason, the group president, she's their most famous member. She's served as an expert witness for dozens of murder trials, advised physicians, toured the world giving lectures on poisonous plants, and appeared on several television shows dealing with illusive medical diagnoses." Jane's smile faded as she examined Mrs. Hubbard's troubled expression. "You're worried. Why?"

Mrs. Hubbard twisted the corner of her apron and pulled a face. "At first, I was thrilled to discover that the Poison Princess was staying at Storyton Hall. As you know, I hardly ever use the computer, but I went into Mr. Sinclair's office and asked him to pull up her website. The more I read, the more I disliked the woman. I watched some video clips and they made my skin crawl. Constance Meredith is as cold as the White Witch of Narnia. And you should listen to how she describes the terrible effects these poisonous plants have on people—she *admires* the power of the plants. I could tell that she didn't give a fig about any of the victims. She bears watching, Jane. Trust me."

Jane reached out and took Mrs. Hubbard's hand. "After what happened during the Romancing the Reader convention, I wouldn't dream of ignoring your hunch. I'll keep a close eye on her. I promise."

"There's something else."

"Yes?" Jane asked, feeling an inexplicable sense of dread.

Mrs. Hubbard squeezed Jane's hand for emphasis. "Don't let that witch within a mile of these kitchens. Or near any food, for that matter. She knows a hundred different ways to kill someone using plants. And several of those plants are growing right outside our back door."